THIRSTY

A NOVEL

PRAISE FOR *THIRSTY*

"A revelation. In this stunning, messy-hearted, soul-soothing novel, Hammonds gives readers a means to examine, confront, and be curious about what alcohol can mask and destroy within us. This book will save lives, I have no doubt."

—**MARIAMA J. LOCKINGTON,** STONEWALL HONOR AUTHOR
OF *IN THE KEY OF US* AND *FOREVER IS NOW*

"Jas Hammonds remains one of literature's most electric voices. Breathtaking and courageous, *Thirsty* challenges our social norms, perception of addiction, and expectations for all kinds of love. I was dazzled and devastated by every page."

—**JEN ST. JUDE,** AUTHOR OF *IF TOMORROW DOESN'T COME*

"A vibrant, affirming look at addiction, resilience, and what it means to take charge of your own life."

—**REBECCA BARROW,** AUTHOR OF *AND DON'T
LOOK BACK* AND *THIS IS WHAT IT FEELS LIKE*

"Vulnerable, tender, heartbreaking, and so full of hope. *Thirsty* is a compelling exploration of interiority that feels universal by a profound and incredible author."

—**SARA FARIZAN,** AWARD-WINNING AUTHOR
OF *IF YOU COULD BE MINE* AND *DEAD FLIP*

"*Thirsty* is an undeniable force. A knockout with nuance. This stunningly crafted story tugs at the reader with breathless pace and sharp insights that ultimately delivers the hope of recovery."

—CORY McCARTHY, BESTSELLING AUTHOR
OF THE STONEWALL HONOR WINNER *MAN O' WAR*

"Utterly consuming and tenderly poignant, *Thirsty* is a fearless exploration of toxicity, addiction, rage, and healing. A transformative novel that readers will cling to long after the final page."

—JULIAN WINTERS, AWARD-WINNING AUTHOR
OF *RIGHT WHERE I LEFT YOU*

"Poignant and gutsy. *Thirsty* is a brilliant exploration of girlhood and desire and what it means when we haven't been taught to love ourselves. With the promise of hope and hard-fought insight, Blake's journey is both compelling and confronting. A must read."

—STEPHANIE KUEHN, AWARD-WINNING AUTHOR
OF *WE WEREN'T LOOKING TO BE FOUND*

"Visceral and engrossing, *Thirsty* by Jas Hammonds plunges readers into the glittering world of country clubs and luxury boats—a world Blake is desperate to be part of as she battles crippling anxiety and self-doubt with one more round. This book is astounding in its searing authenticity and tenderness."

—ALEXANDRA VILLASANTE, AWARD-WINNING AUTHOR
OF *THE GRIEF KEEPER*

ALSO BY JAS HAMMONDS

WE DESERVE MONUMENTS

THIRSTY

A NOVEL

JAS HAMMONDS

ROARING BROOK PRESS

NEW YORK

Published by Roaring Brook Press

Roaring Brook Press is a division of Holtzbrinck Publishing
Holdings Limited Partnership

120 Broadway, New York, NY 10271 • fiercereads.com

Our books may be purchased in bulk for promotional, educational, or
business use. Please contact your local bookseller or the Macmillan Corporate
and Premium Sales Department at (800) 221-7945 ext. 5442 or by email at
MacmillanSpecialMarkets@macmillan.com.

Library of Congress Control Number: 2023040530

First edition, 2024

Book design by Julia Bianchi

Printed in the United States of America

ISBN 978-1-250-81659-7

1   3   5   7   9   10   8   6   4   2

for the drunk girl in the mirror

CONTENT WARNING

Thirsty includes depictions of alcohol addiction, self-hatred, suicidal ideation, racial microaggressions, transphobic rhetoric, and nonconsensual outing. For a full list of content warnings, please visit jashammonds.com.

Please read this story with care. And, perhaps, a cup of tea.

HOW TO BE THE LIFE OF THE PARTY

ARRIVE LOOKING FINE AS hell. But not *too* fine. You should be a disheveled, *I just put this together* fine. An effortless fine.

Everything should always appear effortless.

Keep up with the heaviest drinker in the room. It's important to impress her. You don't want people to think you're boring. Plus, you're funnier when you're drunk. And what good is being the life of the party if people can't laugh at you?

Make out with your girlfriend because she smells like sweet honey, because her lips taste like sea salt and sugar, because she's redwood tree tall. You want to climb her, crawl inside her, live like this forever. Tell her she looks beautiful under an arc of neon light. Silence the little girl in your throat who wants to plead, *Tell me you love me*, because, confession? Even after four years together, you still aren't sure sometimes.

Drink something strong and smoke something sweet and light up the room like a firecracker. Compliment people's outfits and mean it. Scream *I love this song* and prove it by singing every word.

Don't worry. Have a drink, and another. Be chill. Tuck your anxieties in your bra so no one besides you will notice them poking you like warped underwire. Ignore the voice in your head that believes everyone secretly hates you.

Dance. Dance. *Dance!*

(Your insecurities can't catch you if you keep moving.)

Glimpse traces of That Feeling whenever you notice yourself in mirrors and coffee table reflections. That *Feeling* of swollen lips, invincibility, sexiness, power. *Belonging.* That Feeling is a song, and you are the maestro. You never want this crescendo to end.

You are not a loser. Not anymore. You have made it. You are one of Them.

Or . . . you will be.

Soon.

Drink.

That's right, keep going.

You have an audience to please.

JUNE

CHAPTER 1

I LOVED THE SOUND of my own name.

"Dance with me, Blake."

It wasn't vanity. Not entirely . . .

"Blaaaaaake."

Hearing my name reminded me I was <u>here</u>. I existed. I had a witness. And it felt good to be seen.

"I love you, Bee."

My girlfriend's breath was hot in my ear. We were dancing. I loved dancing with Ella Spencer. This gorgeous statue of a girl who only had eyes for *me*. She was electric, and so was I. We were Blake and Ella, Ella & Blake, the couple Landstown High voted Most Likely to Still Be Together in Ten Years for yearbook senior superlatives. Only ten years? A decade sounded insulting when the honor was first bestowed.

We were going to last forever, I just knew it.

We were on Josiah Winters's yacht, *Byte Me*. I didn't know what time it was. The string lights looked pretty and so did my girlfriend, my beautiful, beautiful girlfriend. Someone handed me a drink and I downed it without asking what was in it. It was pink and it was pretty, what more did I need to know? I was here and everything was good.

Someone shouted over the music, "*You aren't going to fucking believe this!*" Josiah. Loud-ass Josiah. Ella and I swayed toward the knot of our coworkers clustered around the bar, and there was Roxanne Garcia, glowing under a crystal chandelier. She grinned at me over a martini glass like the Cheshire Cat. She was so pretty she made my teeth hurt.

"Mr. Peterson hosted a costume party on his boat last weekend and he showed up in blackface," Josiah said, and declarations of "Shut up!" and "I *know* you fucking lying!" exploded from the group like confetti. Ella snaked an arm around my waist, and I sank into her.

(My beautiful girlfriend—who chose *me*!)

Josiah had evidence. He airdropped it to the entire party so we could see. When Ella opened it, she laughed and called him an asshole, but when I saw the photo, my anger was scarlet and slingshot fast. I hated the Petersons. I served Mr. Peterson and his miserable, entitled family all the time at the Snack Attack Shack. More than once he'd snapped his fingers to get my attention because he didn't know my name.

"I hate him," I spewed, tossing my phone onto the bar with a clatter. "He's such a racist piece of shit! Someone . . . someone"—the room swayed—"someone should teach him a *lesson*."

"Uh-oh," Ella said. "Big Bad Bee's coming out."

(You know what's even better than the sound of your own name? A *nickname* someone created just. For. You.)

"I love it when Big Bad Bee comes out!" Josiah cheered, his pale cheeks ruddied from wine.

"Who's Big Bad Bee?" someone asked.

How could they not know?

I sashayed around the bar and plucked the cotton candy vape out of my best friend Annetta's hand. She muttered, "Not like *I* was using that," when I took a giant hit. I looked so cool.

"*I* am Big Bad Bee," I declared through a cloud of sweet smoke. The crowd cheered, "Bee! Bee! Bee!" but all I heard was, *Me*—

Me.

ME!

I was in the bathroom. Swirling like I was going down a drain. I grabbed the sink for balance and my eyes snagged on the girl in the mirror. She looked so good. Wild black curls, straight white teeth, smoky eye makeup that hadn't budged all night. No more Little Blake. This was Big Bad Bee.

"I'm so sexy," I purred, grabbing my chest and shimmying my shoulders. Someone giggled. A toilet flushed and Ella—*my* beautiful girlfriend—joined me at the mirror. She'd been here the whole time?

"Yeah, you are," she said, running her tongue along her bottom lip. Her mouth was grenadine red.

Inside the golf cart bay. It was hot. Summers in Virginia were always so damn hot, even at two in the morning. Was time *was* it? Who knew. Who cared. Not me, Big Bad Bee.

I was drinking something fruity. Watermelon? No, grapefruit.

"You should chill," Annetta said. She was always popping up like some overbearing Whac-a-Mole just when the party was getting good.

Ella came over with a frosty bottle of rum and topped me off. "She's *fine*, Nettie. My Bumblebee needs her nectar."

I sipped and winked at Annetta.

Buzz, buzz, bitch.

Someone mentioned Frank Peterson again, and I got riled up again and told everyone how much I hated him again. When I turned around, Roxanne Garcia was there. Somehow she was always there.

"You know, Blake . . ." My name fell from her pink-painted lips like scribbled cursive, impressive for just one syllable. "The Serena Society fiercely condemns racism and anti-Blackness in all its forms."

I knew. Of course I knew. I wanted to be a Serena Society girl so bad it took everything in me to not throw myself at her feet right then and there. I nodded like a hungry disciple.

Roxanne's mouth slid into a pout. "So what are you going to do about it?"

This is where things got hazy.

Outside, the parking lot. It was so hot. Asphalt sizzled beneath my feet. Why was I barefoot?

Tunnel vision. I was searching for something. I had a feeling I'd know what it was when I found it. Alcohol surged through my body, propelled me forward.

At my back, a chorus line: "*Big Bad Bee! Big Bad Bee!*"

A heavy paint can. Hot tin, liquid gold. It was in my hands and the lid was off. It was in my hands and my palm was bleeding, but I didn't care. I was Big Bad Bee.

A desperate hunt. The wooden dock groaning beneath my feet. So much laughter. I was the reason.

"Who wants to see me fuck up this white man's boat?!"

Their cheers lit me up from the inside. There it was: That Feeling! I was glitter and whiskey and audacity, I was THAT BITCH! A symphony of encouragement. Only one dissenter—

"This isn't a good idea! Blake, stop—"

Roxanne's laughter drowned everything. She was the president of the Serena Society and she was happy. Whatever she wanted, I'd do. I lifted the paint can over my head.

My target? Frank Peterson's yacht, *La Dolce Vita*. I flung the can with *everything*. Yellow paint. A neon swirl, lighting up the night. Spraying and splattering across pristine white.

"Yoooooo!"

"Blake's fucking wild, bruh!"

"Big Bad Bee! Big Bad Bee!"

I loved the sound of my own name.

CHAPTER 2

I WOKE UP IN ELLA'S BED, the only mementos from the night a throbbing headache and yellow paint caked beneath my fingernails.

Ella stirred awake. "Morning, Bee." She yawned and said, "Last night was unbelievable. You should've seen Roxanne's face. No one thought you were gonna do it."

I rotated my left hand and winced at a large red gash that sliced my palm in half. I looked at Ella in confusion.

"The paint can," she explained, propping her head up. Her long waves, recently dyed fiery red, splayed across her silk pillowcases. "You cut yourself on the lid."

My fingers curled over the cut, palm pulsing, raw and tender. Ella snuggled against my neck and kissed the underside of my jaw. I ran my tongue over my teeth, still not used to how slick they felt without braces.

"You are so *wild*," she murmured. She sounded pleased, thank goodness.

I sat up, head pounding, and squinted against the honey morning light spilling through Ella's sheer ivory curtains. Her chubby tabby cat, Nina, yawned at the end of the bed. A clock bounced around the snoozing computer monitor across the room. Nine thirty. We were about to be late for work. Ella sat up, too.

"You okay, Bee?"

I looked at her. She wore no trace of last night on her face. Her pink lips were moisturized, soft brown eyes bag-free.

"You're not worried about Mr. Peterson, are you?" Even her breath smelled fresh. "Because you shouldn't be. He's the worst, remember? He totally deserves it."

"What did I do?" I asked, and she laughed.

"You threw paint all over Frank Peterson's yacht because he's a racist piece of shit."

I froze. The night was foggy, but the paint under my fingernails was real and flaking all over Ella's lilac duvet.

"Shit," I said. "Did someone see? What if—" The thought was too terrifying to finish. I didn't know how much yacht detailing cost, but it sure as hell was more than I made at my crappy minimum-wage job. I couldn't afford the repair. Would Mr. Peterson go after my parents? They didn't have money, either. But—

"Hey." Ella shook my shoulders. "Don't freak out."

"I'm not freaking out," I lied.

Outside, the humidity amplified my anxieties. Even stopping by our favorite coffee shop, Perk-U-Later, for large iced mochas didn't help. Thoughts of being fired once my boss discovered I'd ruined the yacht of one of the club's wealthiest members ran through my mind incessantly. I'd be out of a job, no paycheck, no longer able to hang out with Annetta and Ella during the day. And I was 99 percent sure the Serena Society wouldn't accept someone who couldn't keep a simple summer job.

But by the time Ella and I pulled into the employee parking lot of the Crystal Grove Golf and Yacht Club, she'd convinced me everything would be okay. Mr. Peterson *had* gotten what was coming to him. He was by far the most pompous member of the club, the most annoying. He was the kind of man who rattled his empty glasses at waiters and let the ice cubes ask for another round. He was constantly bragging about his luxury yacht, *La Dolce Vita*, boasting about it so often that it became a running joke between me, Ella, and Annetta. Whenever Mr. Peterson passed us at the pool, we'd place our hands on our hips, jut our chests out, and mock him.

It cost 3.9 mil, you know? Before I poured another mil in for renovations, of course.

She's 108 feet. Could've got something longer, but the wife said no!

The name just came to me. I spent some time in Italy, you know? Let me tell you all about this beautiful Italian gal I met . . .

I'd been accompanying Ella and her family to the club for four years and working there for the past two, and not once had I ever heard him utter a thank-you to any staff member. His wife was also a nightmare, his son was a brat. He'd been known to drop a racial slur in passing conversation, even though it was widely known he liked to cheat on his wife with Black women. He was also running for mayor of Virginia Beach in the fall, and his ugly face had been plastered on campaign flyers and television ads for months now.

"He deserved it," Ella repeated as she backed her Range Rover into a tight space. "Besides, he's so rich he could just buy another boat if he wanted to."

She was right. Ella was always right. I relaxed against the leather seat and took another sip of iced mocha. My palm was still throbbing, even after Ella wrapped it in gauze.

"You're fine," Ella said, flipping her visor mirror down to check her reflection. "You impressed Roxanne. At the end of the day, that's all that matters." She applied a careful coat of kohl to her lashes, taking the time to flick the wand up at the ends. We were already fifteen minutes late, but Ella Spencer rushed for no one.

The Crystal Grove Golf and Yacht Club was in its usual Saturday morning frenzy as we began the long walk to the pool. Ella got on her phone to wish her fifteen thousand followers good morning. I usually loved being shown off in her videos, but today I stayed out of the frame. Instead, I listened to the birdsong drifting from the towering trees that lined the club's main road, hoping it would ease my headache. The sun was blazing hot, and it felt awful after leaving the Range Rover's glorious A/C. Golf carts whizzed by on rolling hills of emerald, a parade of old white men. Many of the drivers called out to Ella, undoubtedly proud of themselves for remembering her name, not that it was hard. Ella and Annetta were the only Black kids of Crystal Grove members, so they had a fifty-fifty shot on getting it right.

"Morning, Miss Spencer!"

"Love the new hair!"

"See you at the pool later!"

Ella laughed a tinkling laugh and hollered responses. She had charisma for days, inherited it from her parents. She remembered people's birthdays and little facts about their lives, asked you how that doctor's appointment went last week. When she talked to you, she could make you feel like the only person alive. And she'd always been like that, like Jupiter, the biggest planet in the solar system, the prettiest. I trailed behind like one of her rocky moons with a name no one could remember. These white men didn't care about me. My parents didn't shell out the club's five-figure annual membership fee. I just worked here.

When we entered the pool gates, Ella blew me a kiss and strode to her lifeguard chair to lord above everyone. I sighed as I took in the crowded deck full of sunning housewives and bratty preteens. I was late and bound to hear about it, so I slapped on my Good CGGYC Staff Member smile and headed for the Snack Attack Shack.

Inside, Annetta was cleaning the blender. Our boss, Todd, hovered over her shoulder like an unhelpful gnat, scolding her on proper sanitation techniques.

"Good morning," I trilled. I snatched my name tag off the counter and pinned it to my lime-green polo. "Todd, the pleats on your shorts look *impeccable* today."

Annetta bit back a grin. Todd's face pinched.

"What time is it, Blake?" he asked.

I zeroed in on his splash-proof G-Shock watch. "Why don't you tell me, Todd?"

"It's 10:20. As in, twenty minutes after your shift began."

I flashed him my most dazzling smile. "Isn't time merely an illusion?"

"Don't start with me," Todd said with a sigh, and Annetta laughed, grateful to no longer be the focus of his constant scrutinizing. "You girls think this is a joke? Mr. Donohue is on edge this morning. I'm sure he'd have no problem firing you if I marched you over to his office."

"Awww, what's wrong with Daddy Donohue?" I was pushing it, but the comment made Annetta laugh again, so it was worth it.

"There was an act of vandalism last night," Todd said, resting a hand on the slushie machine, bracing himself. "Someone defiled Frank Peterson's yacht."

Annetta averted her gaze, and my stomach churned. I shoved my hands in my pockets. I thought I'd scrubbed away all the evidence, but my palm throbbed in protest.

"What happened?" I asked, desperate to find out how much the club knew. Were there cameras around? Was Mr. Peterson about to burst into the Snack Attack Shack and fire me himself?

"That's none of your business," Todd said with a smug little grin. "*Your* business is to be on time, Ms. Brenner."

I nodded at his pleated shorts. "I'll try to be on time, Todd."

"CGGYC staff members do not *try*," Todd said, enunciating every syllable. "CGGYC staff members *do*. Can you *do* for me, Ms. Brenner?"

"Yes, Todd."

He straightened his visor, satisfied. "I'll be back before the lunch rush. Blake, you're on register."

I groaned. Todd knew I hated working the register. "We'll discuss putting you on expo when you show up on time," he said. He pulled the dreaded Snack Attack hat off the back of the door and placed it on top of my head. It was an embarrassing thing, shaped like a shark with a tail pointing skyward. Its jaws clamped over my curls.

"Why doesn't Annetta have to wear this when she's on register?" I protested.

"Annetta is never twenty minutes late," Todd said. When he was halfway out the door, he added, "And don't forget to use the official Snack Attack Shack greeting!"

"Welcome to the Snack Attack, what are you munchin' on?"

Someone cleared their throat, and I looked up from the register to see Frank Peterson. My stomach somersaulted—less than ten minutes at work and I was already face-to-face with the man whose yacht I'd thrown paint all over twelve hours earlier.

"You should really look at people when you're serving them," Mr. Peterson said. His eyes were hidden behind douchey Oakley shades, but I still felt myself withering beneath his glare.

I swallowed. "Sorry about that, Mr. Peterson," I said. "What can I get for you?"

"An order of fries. And a chocolate milkshake."

"Member number?" I asked, even though I really should've had it memorized. Club members hated being asked mundane questions.

"This one's on the club," Mr. Peterson said, now distracted by his phone. "After what happened to *La Dolce Vita* last night, it's the least they can do."

"Right," I said. I glanced at the cook, Tristan, and he dropped a fryer into sizzling grease. The blender whirred to life as Annetta started on the shake. "It'll be right up, sir."

Mr. Peterson grunted and picked up a call. I quickly looked at my hands, making sure there wasn't any paint left under my fingernails. My heart pounded, sure he was going to see guilt written all over my face. But he was rambling on the phone, making plans for an afternoon round of golf.

Past his shoulder, I had a perfect shot of Ella perched in her lifeguard chair. She was scanning the water carefully, red hair cascading down her back. She'd always taken her job seriously, even though she'd never needed the money. She claimed having a job would look good on her application to Jameswell University, the most elite college in the Southern Ivy League. *I need to convince the admissions department I wasn't raised with a silver spoon*, she'd told me and Annetta when she convinced us all to apply for jobs when we were sixteen. She'd lucked out with the cool lifeguard position while Annetta and I got stuck with the Snack Attack Shack. While we'd sweated in a grease pit for two summers, Ella chilled under a large umbrella and soaked up attention. Annetta and I always joked that Ella still ended up with a silver spoon while we'd been handed sporks. Nevertheless, she was right about hard work paying off—the three of us were bound for Jameswell in the fall.

"Order up!" Tristan called as Annetta slid the milkshake down the counter. I handed Mr. Peterson the striped paper basket of fries and his shake. He walked away without saying thank you.

"Well, he's got my vote," Annetta joked. "Seriously, he's going to be the worst politician. He can't even *pretend* to be nice."

"Someone should teach him a lesson," I replied. "Oh, wait." I giggled as I met Ella's gaze across the pool. She held her hand up in a backward C, and when I mimicked her, we formed an entire heart.

"How's your hand?" Annetta asked, concern etched on her dark brown face.

I lowered my hand. The gash throbbed beneath the gauze.

"It's fine," I lied.

"Fine," she repeated dully. Her raised bushy eyebrow sent a hazy snippet from last night bubbling to the surface—a smear of blood and Annetta using her own T-shirt to apply pressure.

"It hurts a little," I admitted with a sigh. "But it was worth it, right?"

She drummed her fingers over her pocket, itching to pull out her vape. She always did that when she was uneasy. Annetta Jones and I had been friends for nearly four years, and working side by side for two, so I knew her every tell. Ever since her parents' divorce, her anxiety had been through the roof. Ella and I jokingly called her Nervous Nettie. Now it seemed like the only thing that truly calmed her down was her colorful assortment of vapes.

"I just worry about you," Annetta said, and I laughed at how genuinely afraid she sounded. Like I was about to go to war or some shit. I flicked a dishrag her way.

"Okay, Nervous Nettie, I get it," I said. "I'm a clumsy bitch."

"Clumsy bitch or not, you need to watch it around Todd. He's looking for any excuse to let you go."

"Do you promise?" I asked, and Tristan laughed without looking up from his phone.

Annetta shrugged. "Just trying to look out for you."

I swiveled on my stool just in time to see the pool gates open. Roxanne Garcia strutted in, her curves barely contained in a rainbow string bikini. She was surrounded by her usual gaggle of college friends, and Ella waved and blew them all kisses. I tried to swallow my jealousy.

Stop, I told my anxious brain. Ella loved me. Sure, Roxanne was beautiful, older, Serena Society president *and* Jameswell University's self-proclaimed Big Lesbian on Campus. But Ella took *me* home last night. We'd been together four years. I didn't have anything to worry about.

While her friends set up camp near the diving board, Roxanne headed for the snack shack, her flip-flops thwacking the concrete. I straightened on the stool as I took in her tall Coke-bottle figure and honey-brown skin. She was drop-dead gorgeous, and she knew it. As a member of the wealthy Garcia family, Roxanne had been a fixture at Crystal Grove for as long as I'd known Ella, but our age gap had kept her at a distance. That was all changing this summer.

A few weeks ago, Mrs. Spencer threw me, Ella, and Annetta a huge graduation party at Crystal Grove and formally introduced us to Roxanne. Roxanne was immediately smitten with us, especially when she found out we were all queer, too. *Lesbians are taking over the Serena Society*, Roxanne had joked before inviting us to a party on her family's yacht, the *Bewitched*. Thus began our unofficial induction as Serena Society hopefuls. We'd been anxiously waiting for the official pledge process to start ever since.

"Hi, Blake," Roxanne said silkily. Her gaze skipped to Annetta. "Hi, Annetta."

"Hi," I said breathlessly. Annetta muttered a hello and drifted over to the sink to wash dishes. Roxanne looked amused.

"Someone must still be hungover from last night," she said, pushing her oversized sunglasses up into her brown hair. "How are *you* feeling, my little wild one?"

Honestly, I felt like shit. The caffeine from my mocha was fighting a losing battle with my hangover. But I knew Roxanne didn't like light-weights, so I shrugged.

"Great. Ready for the next one."

"That's my girl," Roxanne said, and I melted under her proud smile.

The next two hours passed in a blur of hamburger and veggie wrap orders. When there was finally a break, Annetta made us strawberry smoothies. She added a dash of Oreos in mine, just the way I liked it. We cheers'd and sipped, savored the chill in the steam of the fryers.

"Is Roxanne still here?" Annetta asked.

I surveyed the pool but didn't spot her. "Nope. Why?"

"She gives me the creeps," Annetta said. "Whenever she looks at me, I feel like she wants to eat me."

"Maybe she likes you," I said, brightening. If Roxanne liked Annetta, maybe that meant she had no interest in Ella.

Annetta made a face. "She's too old."

"She's twenty-one!"

"Exactly. She's a senior. Too old to be looking at freshmen like that. And you know she's not my type."

"Actually I *don't* know." I nudged her elbow. "Care to elaborate?"

"Oh, look, you have a customer," she said breezily, and I laughed and resumed my place at the register. As open as Ella and I were about our love life, that's how closed off Annetta was about hers. I'd seen her in shambles after her parents' divorce, she'd cleaned vomit out of my hair, and I'd helped her insert a menstrual cup for the first time. But whenever the topic of romantic relationships came up, Annetta was an icy fortress. Impenetrable to even those closest to her.

Another hour passed. More entitled assholes were served. Annetta and I exhausted our usual games of Guess How Much That Woman's Bathing Suit Cost and Who's Had Plastic Surgery Since Last Summer? She coaxed my puffy curls into two neat boxer braids and we played tic-tac-toe on the back of an inventory sheet. I got Tristan to make me a grilled cheese with extra cheese, and even though I ate slowly, there were still three hours left on our shift when I finished.

"*Please* let me take the first break," I begged Annetta. "If I don't get out of this shack, my eyeballs are going to pop out of their sockets and slide into my undies and come out of these cargo shorts. Do you want to see that? Do you?"

"You disgust me," Annetta said without looking up from her phone. "Please leave."

I grabbed two Styrofoam cups, filled them with crushed ice and lemonade, making sure to leave room at the top. "Be back in fifteen!" I said, throwing off the shark hat.

Once outside, I held the cups up, knowing Ella would get the hint that it was time for our ritual. Two minutes later, we were strolling through the pool gates together.

"I'm so *bored*," Ella whined. "Can we trade places so I can hang out with Nettie?"

"You'll have to wear the hat," I replied.

She wrapped an arm around my waist and kissed my shoulder. "Done. You make that hat look sexy."

"You're a horrible liar."

"Seduce me, Shark Bae."

"Let's go then, Princess Ariel." I tugged on a lock of her red hair, and she laughed and shoved me and we kissed our way to the parking lot.

"I overheard Mr. Peterson on the phone," she said against my lips. "Ripping club security a new asshole."

I pulled away. "What did he say?"

She lowered her voice into an annoying drawl. "'How can there not be any security footage? What am I paying you people for?' Blah blah blah."

I felt sick. "You think he's going to find out?"

Ella scoffed. "Nah. The cameras near the dock have been down all summer. That's why he was pissed. Relaaaax, Bee."

I took a deep breath. We reached the Range Rover and climbed in. Ella grabbed two rum minis hidden beneath a pile of clothes in her back seat. We dumped them into our lemonades and enjoyed them with the windows down.

"It's almost time, Bee," she said.

"For what?" The cup was cold in my hands. It seeped through my bandage, chilled my palm and my worries.

"Serena," she said. "The process will start any day now. My mom's been hinting." She wiggled her eyebrows. "And Roxanne texted me after she left the pool. Saying you *really* impress her."

My anxieties about the yacht and getting fired softened at once. I took another sip, then another, thinking of Roxanne Garcia's delighted laughter when I threw the paint can. It felt good to prove I belonged in her inner circle. Even better to know I could still impress Ella after all these years.

"This is it, Bee," Ella said, tapping the steering wheel with a manicured fingernail. "In the fall, we'll be at Jameswell. We'll be in Serena. It's going to be so perfect." She got this faraway look in her eyes, and I could tell that she was envisioning us on the porch of the Serena Society house in the fall, wearing sapphire-blue sweaters with the swirling gold calla lily emblem. It was one of the reasons she dyed her hair, insisting Vampire Red would go well with Serena's official color. I tipped my cup back, and by the time I finished, I was soft and giddy, not a care in the world.

"Love you till we're playing shuffleboard at the retirement home?" she asked. It was our favorite game, *Love You Till*. We were always filling in the blanks.

"Love you till we're flinging mushy peas at each other," I replied. Ella leaned over the center console and kissed me. The feeling of her mouth on mine always felt like the crest of a roller coaster. Four years later, and I still felt the rush. I clenched my empty cup and held on.

CHAPTER 3

AFTER WORK, ELLA DROVE us back to her house, snaking through the Crystal Grove neighborhood ten miles over the speed limit. She chattered on and on about the Serena Society and the impending pledge process.

"Did I tell you how my mom looked when I mentioned it yesterday afternoon?"

She had. Multiple times. She told me again anyway, and my stomach dropped like it did every time I thought about the Serena Society. The possibility of joining their ranks was becoming more real every day, and I couldn't imagine what would happen if I somehow failed the pledge process. I didn't want to picture Ella's disappointed face. Didn't want to think about her meeting some other girl who was worthy of the society's sapphire bracelet and breaking up with me. I didn't want to let Mrs. Spencer down. While Ella rambled, I closed my eyes and rested my head against the window.

The Spencers lived on the outskirts of the neighborhood, in a cul-de-sac with a driveway so deep you couldn't see the house from the road. Ella pressed a button on her sun visor, and the sleek entry gate slid open. I never understood what the Spencers were trying to keep out in a neighborhood like Crystal Grove. Their neighbors owned gigantic yachts and Jet Skis for every member of the family. They had garages full of fancy camping gear and sent their children to schools that required crisp uniforms and entrance exams. Ella steered the Range Rover down the driveway, and the gate slid closed, sheltering us from the world.

Mrs. Spencer was in the kitchen wearing a bubble-gum-pink apron, haloed in the glow of multiple ring lights. She was decorating cupcakes with little yellow suns and chatting animatedly to her phone, which was cradled in a tripod. Her dewy face lit up when she noticed us.

"Come say hi, girls!" she said, waving us over. Ella and I obliged, waving to the thousands of people watching live. Mrs. Spencer awarded us with freshly frosted cupcakes.

"These two are my favorite taste-testers," she told the camera with a cheeky grin. "No one will humble you like teenage girls." The comment section was a flurry of emojis and comments that flew by too fast to read.

We bit into the cupcakes, and my groan of approval was genuine—they were lemon and cream cheese, my favorite. Mrs. Spencer's creations never failed to delight.

"It's delicious," I said, my mouth full. Mrs. Spencer beamed.

Ella kissed her mother's cheek, leaving a dab of cream cheese behind. "Mahal kita, Mommy," she said. The hearts on Mrs. Spencer's screen were nonstop, a steady red stream of approval. Her followers loved it when family made special appearances in her videos.

Ella and I took our cupcakes upstairs so Mrs. Spencer could finish filming in peace, polishing them off before we made it to the air-conditioned sanctuary of Ella's bedroom. Once inside, Ella started pulling at my lime-green Snack Attack polo, our lips meeting in a frenzy of kisses.

"With your mom downstairs?" I asked when she yanked my shirt over my head. We'd done it countless times when her parents were home, but I always felt nervous at the prospect of getting caught.

"She's gonna be live for at least another hour," Ella said. She kissed her way down my neck, fingers effortlessly unhooking my bra.

I was still stinky and sweaty from work. When I pointed that out, Ella pulled me into the bathroom so we could take a shower together. She stripped out of her bathing suit, her soft brown curves inviting me closer. I was reaching for her when my gaze caught my sliced palm, and my anxieties came back in a crushing wave.

"You really think they won't find out?" I asked.

She rolled her eyes. "God, Bee, you're starting to sound like Nettie. You're *fine*."

I didn't feel fine. Even as Ella beckoned me into her marble shower. Even as we kissed under the waterfall showerhead. It wasn't until Ella began massaging my shoulders that I finally started to relax.

Maybe she was right. I'd lasted a full day without being pulled into the management office to explain myself. And in Crystal Grove, a day equaled lifetimes because club members waited for nothing. Drinks magically appeared in their hands seconds after the request, no matter the ingredients. Any maintenance was dealt with swiftly, often overnight, affirming the belief that money could buy time. If someone knew it was me who threw the paint across Mr. Peterson's yacht, I probably would've been fired by now. Plus, the cameras were down.

Ella was right. Everything was going to be fine.

We were toweling off when I noticed my phone buzzing beneath my discarded clothes. I unearthed it, and my heart sank when I was greeted with my older brother's photo.

"Let me guess," Leon said when I picked up. "You forgot."

I covered my face with my hand. "I'm sorry."

"You can't answer your texts? I've been out here waiting for you."

Guilt flickered as I pictured him parked outside the country club, still in his uniform, straight out of work.

"I'm at Ella's," I said. "Sorry, I forgot."

"These dinners were *your* idea in the first place," Leon grumbled, always quick to remind me. He hung up without saying goodbye.

"It's Brenner family din din night?" Ella asked from inside her closet.

"Yep," I said with a sigh. Of course I'd forgotten about my family's weekly dinner. It was an idea I'd concocted in middle school after I'd grown sick of eating alone. But—between my parents' chaotic work schedules, Leon living on the nearby military base, and me spending most of my time with Ella—getting together for Quality Time was a near impossible task these days. Sometimes I didn't know why we still bothered. My family had always felt like four tires on a car moving at wildly different speeds.

Ella let me borrow a long purple silk dress that was so light I still felt naked when I slipped it on.

"Pick me up after?" I asked when Leon texted that he was outside.

"Of course," she said, and we kissed goodbye.

On my way out, I waved to Mrs. Spencer. True to Ella's word, she was still filming.

"Wait!" she called. She hurried over with a glass container full of lemon cupcakes, their yellow suns cheery and bright. She kissed me on the cheek. "For your family," she said, and a tiny, ridiculous part of me wanted to correct her and tell her she and the Spencers *were* my family. Instead, I just thanked her.

Outside, Leon's Toyota idled, a wail of electric guitars thrashing from the speakers.

"A little fancy for pizza," Leon muttered, glancing at my dress when I slid into the passenger seat. His freshly shaven jaw flexed as he threw the gearshift into reverse. He shot the Spencers' house a dirty look before peeling off.

"Sorry I take pride in my appearance," I snapped. Once upon a time, he would've laughed. Instead, his eyes flicked to the gauze wrapped around my palm.

"What happened to your hand?"

"I cut it at work."

"We've got two months, Blake." Leon turned the music down. "Two months."

"I *know.*"

"Mom and Dad need all the help they can get."

I kneaded my hands on my thighs, wishing I could fast-forward to the part of the night where I'd have Ella in my arms and a drink in my hand.

"Mom and Dad are about to move over a thousand miles away. You can't just *forget* when we have plans with them," he said as we wound through Crystal Grove. I smirked when we bypassed a FRANKLY? I'M WITH PETERSON! campaign sign in someone's lawn.

"Sorry I have a job," I said.

"Like I don't?" He paused at a stop sign and bit his bottom lip in frustration, a habit we inherited from our mom. We looked so alike people used to think we were twins.

"Sorry I have a job *and* a life," I said. "Unlike you."

"Jesus, Blake," he muttered. "You've always been so fucking dramatic."

TAP WATER

Leon was wrong. I hadn't *always* been dramatic. In fact, I used to be shy. Really shy.

On paper, it wasn't hard to see why. I was still in elementary school when my boobs and my feet started a race to see which could grow bigger. Throw in constellations of acne and a storm of frizzy curls? I was the perfect punching bag. When my classmates started making fun of my crooked teeth in sixth grade, I stopped talking. But that only made me a more appealing target.

Awww look at widdle Buck-Tooth Blake wif her widdle books.

Watch out, everyone! Bigfoot Brenner coming through.

Guys, quit making fun of her. It's not her fault she's poor! She probably can't afford braces.

They'd pinch me, snap my bra, trip me just to elicit a response. I tried to bury myself in books, drown my body in baggy clothes. Nothing worked. In seventh grade, someone started a rumor that I had no tongue.

You could literally punch Blake Brenner in the face and she still won't say anything.

My mom was a timid, quiet woman who couldn't teach me anything about being bold. Instead, she filled my anxious, shaking hands with books with corny titles like *Unlock Your GURL Power* and *Junior High Blues: How to Make School Suck Less!* Whenever I was particularly sad, she'd let me tag along during her late-night shifts at 7-Eleven and we'd see who could build the most ridiculous pile of nachos.

My dad, however, tried an assortment of distractions. Girl Scouts, hoping I'd find grounding in the great outdoors. Tae Kwon Do, praying I would kick my way to confidence. Once, he took me and Leon up in his friend's Cessna to show me there was a whole world out there beyond school bullies. And while Leon fell in love with flying the moment we left the runway, I squeezed my eyes shut and cried and cried and cried.

Leon and Dad tried to get me to look, just *look*, at how the Chesapeake Bay Bridge dipped and vanished, spat cars out of its underwater tunnel. *Stop being dramatic*, Leon yelled. But all I could see was us crashing into the ocean far below, our watery grave an expanse of black wrinkled wrapping paper. I imagined my funeral and saw empty rows of pews—no one from my school would miss me enough to attend. When we finally landed, the disappointment in Dad's eyes made me feel like I was wearing one of those lead aprons you use at the dentist to keep you safe from X-rays. Except I didn't feel safe. I felt smothered with panic. I was a withering, sobbing mess.

So maybe I was a little dramatic. But I didn't necessarily see that as a bad thing, especially in a family like mine. I was raised by simple, practical people who lived simple, practical lives. My mom had worked the night shift at the same 7-Eleven for over ten years because she'd always hated mornings. My pilot father handled engine failures and cracked windshields with calm, practiced skill. Witnessing the mounting student loan crisis, Leon enlisted in the Navy the day after he graduated high school. In fact, my family was so rational that they often failed at showing *any* big emotions—especially during the times I needed it the most.

For example: When I was fourteen, I came out as a lesbian. Ella and I had been dating for nearly three months, and she had grown tired of feeling like my secret.

"But I'm afraid," I'd told her when she pressed me to come out for the millionth time.

"What's the worst that could happen?" she asked.

"What if they don't accept me?" I'd hoped that wouldn't be the case. After all, my parents always voted Democrat. I remembered Mom smiling at the television the day gay marriage was legalized and saying, *Well, what wonderful news!* before flipping the channel. But still. The anxious, ever-worrying part of my brain had spent countless nights conjuring nightmares of my dad pushing me out of a plane after I told him.

"You're so dramatic," Ella said, rolling her eyes. "Just tell them." So freshman year, on a gloomy day before winter break, she rode the bus home with me so we could share the big news. We role-played the conversation, Ella pretending to be my dad, giggling when she inexplicably adopted a posh English accent. She held my chapped hand the entire bus ride to my apartment complex.

Dad wasn't home from work yet when we trudged through the front door and kicked off our wet boots. Mom, still in her pajamas after working the night shift, muted the television.

"Well, if it isn't Thelma and Louise!" Mom said, giving Ella a warm hug. They'd met when my mom had dropped me off at the Spencers' for Ella's Halloween slumber party. At the time, I think she was in awe of Ella's massive house and just thrilled that I'd finally made a friend that she didn't register Ella's lingering kiss on my cheek as anything other than platonic. But now we were about to announce that we were An Item, and I hoped that smile would still be on her face after the conversation.

Mom asked if we wanted some water. We followed her into the kitchen, and shame rose in my throat as Ella took in our chipped linoleum floors and small wooden dining table from Goodwill and white refrigerator that hummed sporadic songs. It smelled faintly of burnt popcorn. It was the first time Ella had ever been in my home, and I was about to make myself sick wondering what she was thinking. I'd always known she was a rich girl, but it wasn't until she was standing in my apartment in her thousand-dollar Fendi boots that I truly realized how deep the class chasm stretched between us.

Mom filled two plastic cups with tap water, and it tasted metallic. Nothing compared to the fancy filtered water speckled with cucumbers and strawberries Mrs. Spencer always offered when I went over to Ella's. Mom muttered something about needing to go grocery shopping as she hunted through the pantry. She unearthed a Pop-Tart wrapped in silver foil and handed it to Ella. I wanted to die.

"Sorry it's not much," Mom said, her cheeks flushed. I wondered if she was also thinking about Ella's big house across town. If she was as embarrassed as I was. "I've been meaning to go to the store."

"I love strawberry Pop-Tarts, Mrs. Brenner," Ella said, graciously accepting it like a treasure. "They're my absolute favorite." Mom's shoulders relaxed, melted by Ella's easy charm.

We watched a *Maury* rerun while we waited for Dad, munching on the Pop-Tart even though it tasted like chalk. Mom asked the usual questions about school, and Ella answered with gusto. She was the kind of girl who was easy to love off the bat—straight As and a cheerleader with a smile that wowed a crowd every Friday night. And I kept wanting to point to her, show her off as proof that my middle school torment days were behind me. This beautiful girl had chosen *me*, and I was no longer lonely.

When Dad arrived, he tossed his suitcase and lunch bag in a pile near the door, grumbling about weather delays in Philly. He was a pilot for a small regional airline that shuttled people up and down the East Coast, and he was always complaining about mechanical problems and long taxis at major hubs. Mom cleared her throat, and Dad's warm brown face lit up when he noticed me and Ella sitting on the couch.

"Ella! What a nice surprise. Are you staying for dinner?" He said it as if something other than our microwave would be doing the cooking. Like the typical dinner at the Brenner household wasn't fast food or a pizza that sat in the freezer under a fine layer of frost.

"No, thank you, Mr. Brenner," Ella said. "My mom should be picking us up around six."

"We're having dinner at the country club," I said, impatience flaring.

I'd asked their permission two weeks ago and had reminded them at least twice since then.

"Ah, yes," Dad said. "The Christmas party at the fancy country club. How could we forget?"

When the silence became too loud to ignore, Ella looked at me, brown eyes filled with excitement. Before I could lose my nerve, I wrapped my hand in hers, but my parents didn't notice over the yelling on the television. Mom clucked her tongue at a twelve-year-old girl on-screen whose favorite hobby was apparently slapping her mother. The title in the corner declared, *My Teen Is Totally Out of Control!*

"Should I tell them?" Ella whispered. I nodded, desperate for her to take control as she often did. She cleared her throat, flipped her silky hair over her shoulder and announced, "Blake and I are dating."

The most groundbreaking, earth-shattering, dramatic secret I'd ever had entered my living room the same time as a girl on *Maury* was flipping a table.

"Is this true, Blake?" Dad asked, his brow furrowed.

I nodded, watching their expressions morph from shock to hesitant confusion.

"Do your parents know, Ella?" Mom asked.

"They already know I'm a lesbian," Ella said, beaming proudly. "We're telling them tonight that Blake and I are a couple!"

"Oh," Mom said. She grimaced at the distraught yelling on-screen and turned the volume down. She set the remote control on the coffee table and looked at me, almost nervously. "So . . . you're a lesbian, too?"

I sucked in a breath. "Yes."

"Are you sure? You're so young," Dad said.

Annoyance licked my heels—*of course I was sure!*—but Ella swooped in to save me.

"How young were you when you realized you were straight, Mr. Brenner?" she asked with a light chime of laughter.

Dad hesitated, then tilted his head in a *touché* gesture. "Well," he said. He tried to smile, but it came out like a grimace. Disappointment flickered in his eyes. It was so similar to how he looked at me after my plane-ride-induced panic attack. As if any hope he had of relating to me had officially vanished.

"We're happy for you," Mom said after a few awkward beats of silence.

"Yep. We are . . . happy," Dad said, but he didn't sound happy at all. In fact, he was more excited when Leon went to homecoming with some random girl even though they never made it past a second date. Here I was in an entire relationship—my very first one!—but based on their reactions, I might as well have just announced the seven-day forecast. A seed of resentment nestled in the pit of my stomach, ready to bloom slowly over the next four years.

Mom returned her attention to *Maury* and Dad left to change out of his uniform. The world moved on. I kept waiting for the celebration, but as the seconds ticked by, I realized one wasn't coming. I should've been grateful that they were accepting, that there was no screaming, but I wasn't. All I wanted was to be whisked away from their insignificant responses and my insignificant life.

So was I dramatic?

Maybe. But I'd never admit that to Leon.

I'd lived in the Winward Commons apartment complex my entire life, but when Leon pulled into the parking lot, it didn't feel like home. That sense amplified when we walked into our unit and were greeted with a sea of gaping boxes. My parents' impending move should've been a cause for celebration, but as I looked around, I just felt empty.

Dad had recently been hired by a legacy airline. He was finally going to be flying wide-body planes and have layovers in Paris and Shanghai instead of Roanoke and Albany. The only catch was that his new base was in Dallas. And with Leon in the military and college on my horizon, there was apparently no better time for my parents to pack up and head west.

Now Dad lounged in his worn recliner, flipping through sports channels. "Our children have arrived!" he announced, stopping on highlights from a Nationals game. Mom bustled out of the kitchen, her wispy brown hair in a messy ponytail. She hugged me and Leon tight. She smelled like pizza.

"I was getting worried," she said. "Pizza got cold."

Leon eyed me but said nothing. He shrugged his jacket off and draped it over the armchair. Mom smiled, green eyes searching me.

"I miss you," she said. "I feel like I barely see you anymore."

"This smile isn't paying for itself," I said, flashing my recently straightened teeth. When I was in tenth grade, my parents finally found an orthodontist with a gracious payment-plan system. But with our rent rising every year, the extra expense wasn't something my family could spare. So, in addition to being a college résumé booster, my job at the Snack Attack Shack became a way for me to help. The two years of painful tightenings and sore gums had finally paid off, but the same couldn't be said for the outstanding bill they'd created.

"I know, I know." She touched the end of my braids gently. "Your hair is pretty. Ella did it?"

"Nettie."

"I wish I'd had someone like Nettie when you were growing up," she said. "Maybe you wouldn't have looked like you'd just been struck by lightning in so many of your baby pictures." Our attention shifted to the family photos on the wall, a portrait of me and Leon with frizzy, wild curls smack in the middle.

Or you could've just learned how to do our hair, I thought, but I didn't want to hurt her feelings. We used to joke all the time about how my hair didn't hold a proper curl until I figured out which products worked for me on my own in high school. But now I couldn't help but hear Ella's voice echoing: *Your mom is so hopelessly white.*

And she was. It was always jarring hearing Mom's passive-aggressive comments after spending time at Ella's house. Mrs. Spencer would *never* say something like that. Unlike my mom, Mrs. Spencer actually learned how to style Black hair before Ella's older sisters were born. Even though Ella mostly wore her hair straight or wavy now, her tight natural curls had been laid from the very beginning, as evidenced in her adorable baby pictures.

I handed her the cupcakes. "They're lemon. Mrs. Spencer made them."

"That's nice of her," Mom said. She took the cupcakes into the kitchen and returned with two boxes of pizza. "Let's eat."

The dining table had boxes strewn all over it, so we ate in the living room. Dad in his recliner, Leon on the floor with his plate on his lap, me and Mom snug on the couch. Dad and Leon dominated the conversation as usual, talking about one of Dad's recent aborted landings. Because Leon was an air traffic controller, he and Dad spoke a language Mom and I didn't understand. We half listened and munched on our slices while they talked aviation. But when the topic shifted to Leon's love life, Leon coyly admitted he'd recently started dating some girl.

"Oh yeah?" Dad asked. "Tell me about her!" And he looked so proud.

In my four years of being with Ella, Dad never looked at me like that or even *asked* about her. It used to piss me off, but I'd learned to tune them out and mentally go elsewhere. And "elsewhere" was always the Spencers' bright, sunny house, where I felt loved and celebrated and always included.

I was envisioning me and Ella in our own house someday when Dad muted the television. "So," he said, slapping his hands on his knees. "Let's talk about the move. The next two months are going to be pretty hectic. I've got training and apartment hunting in Dallas to deal with."

"And one of our managers just quit at our Suffolk location," Mom said. "So I'll be over there more than usual."

"They're always working you ragged, Mom," Leon said. "You can't get a break? It's 7-Eleven, not the Navy Seals."

Mom waved a hand. "Someone's gotta do it," she said, and I felt suddenly sad, remembering our fluorescent-lit nights behind the counter, quietly reading together between customers.

"Obviously we're gonna need some help around here," Dad continued. "We expect you both to pack up your rooms yourself. We don't have money for movers."

Leon nodded, and I rolled my eyes. Of course it'd be easy for him to pack up his room. When he shipped off to basic training four years ago, he left behind nothing more than a few dusty trophies from his wrestling days. My room, on the other hand, would need the entire summer to pick apart. I got a headache whenever I went in there, assaulted by mounds of books and relics from hobbies long forgotten. Artifacts of my eighteen years filled every corner of my bedroom, while Ella's was wiped clean twice a week by a housekeeper. Reason number five hundred and sixty-eight I loved the Spencers' house.

"But we also carved out time for fun," Mom said now, and her words rushed together at the end of the sentence, so I knew she was excited. "Ta-da!" she cheered, brandishing something from behind her back. "Four tickets to Busch Gardens!"

Leon and I looked at each other, surprised. A rare moment of sibling solidarity. Family outings were not common occurrences in the Brenner household. If my parents weren't working, we simply didn't have the money.

"It's supposed to be fun," Mom said, smile fading from her pale freckled face. "There's roller coasters, those carnival games . . ."

"We'd love to go," Leon said at the same time I insisted, "It sounds great!"

"Good," Dad said. "Because we're going." His face softened when he looked at my mother. "We just wanted one last outing with you guys."

"You're getting so grown," Mom said. She looked at me. "You're always at Ella's."

"And you'll be at Jameswell this fall," Dad added, then he looked to Leon. "Who knows where your next duty station will be? Let's have a little bit of fun before life happens too much, huh?"

The ceiling fan whirred overhead. Leon picked up one of the tickets. "This is great," he said. "Right?" He zeroed in on me. His gaze said everything his lips couldn't.

Put on a happy face for our parents. We've only got two months.

"Right." I forced a smile. "Just say when."

CHAPTER 4

THE TEXT MESSAGE CAME a week later in the middle of our shifts. When our lunch break rolled around, Ella frantically waved me and Annetta out of the Snack Attack Shack. The three of us walked to the parking lot, reading the message over and over. It was from an unknown number.

> Bewitched. Tonight. Midnight.
> SS

Ella squealed as we climbed into the Range Rover. "I knew it. I *knew* it."

"About fucking time," Annetta said. But she was pulling out her shiny purple vape, so I knew she was anxious, too.

The message was obviously from Roxanne—the *Bewitched* was her family's yacht—but I still had butterflies. It had been easy to believe that everything I knew about the Serena Society was a fantasy, a tale Ella and Annetta had spun to fascinate me on hot summer nights. Or a way for Mrs. Spencer and Mrs. Jones to keep us motivated throughout high school. But now the proof was hot in my hands, and I had to set my phone on the dashboard before I dropped it.

"What are we going to wear?" Ella mused, running a hand through her hair. "Oh my God, we have so much to prepare. I have to tell my mom!" She connected her phone to the Range Rover's Bluetooth, and we eagerly waited for her mom to pick up.

"Yes, love?" Mrs. Spencer's tone was teasing.

"We got it!" Ella cried. "Me, Nettie, and Blake got the message just now! We start tonight!"

Mrs. Spencer gasped in delight, but it was all for show. Of course she knew tonight was the night. She was the Serena Society undergrad advisor. "How wonderful, anak!" she said. "Tell me everything."

While Ella somehow managed to spin a three-word text message into a five-minute story, I turned to the back seat to grab a rum mini from the secret stash. Annetta watched me, eyebrows raised, and I mouthed, *What? We're celebrating!* I poured it into my bottle of Coke and offered her some, but she shook her head and held up her vape.

Whatever. More for me.

"I'm so proud of you girls," Mrs. Spencer said through the speaker. I took a sip of my rum and Coke, hands buzzing with excitement. "This summer is going to change your lives."

SPIKED HOT CHOCOLATE

If there was one thing Maricar Spencer was committed to more than her family or the Serena Society, it was social media.

She was known to her two million followers as @MamaMaricar, and she was a woman who seemingly had it all. A doting husband, three gorgeous daughters, a big house overlooking the bay. She had impeccable fashion sense and a whip-smart eye for interior design. She could make you laugh, drop a tidbit of motherly advice, and bake a delicious apple strudel in the span of a carefully curated sixty-second video.

But her true love was organization, and she had the sponsorship deals and affiliate links to prove it. Her followers often joked that she should've had a label maker permanently welded to her hand. She poured milk from plastic jugs into glass carafes, filled her fridge with clear bins that showcased her organic fruits and veggies. Her bathroom counters had cotton balls and Q-tips nestled in jars that descended in size like nesting dolls. Basking in her meticulous presence for longer than five minutes would leave you feeling like maybe *your* life could drastically improve, too, if only you made a trip to the Container Store. At least that's how she made me feel four years ago on that December day I came out to my parents. When her sleek silver Audi pulled into my driveway mere moments after Ella and I announced we were dating, the world instantly felt neater.

"Hello, Blake," she said as I slid into her buttery, heated back seat. I flushed, loving the way she said my name, like I was a grown woman. Her equal. "It's lovely to see you."

"Hi, Mrs. Spencer," I replied with relief, and she glanced at me in the rearview, her signature red lips curving into a smile.

While she steered carefully out of my apartment complex, Ella chatted animatedly about how excited she was for winter break. The Spencers were spending the holidays in Key West, and I had flashes of hot jealousy whenever she brought it up. I didn't know what was worse—having to spend two weeks without her or the fact that her family could afford tropical vacations and mine couldn't.

Before dinner, we stopped by the Spencers' house. Rain had turned to sleet, and as we wound down the driveway, large, drooping trees swayed hard in the winter breeze. When their house came into view, I gasped. I hadn't seen it since they put their Christmas decorations up, and a million twinkling white lights outlined their massive French country home. It looked like something out of a fairy tale.

Initially, I'd been worried about not having anything to wear for my first dinner at the country club, but Ella eased my concerns. "Just borrow something of mine," she'd said, so easily. As if there'd never been a question of whether she'd look out for me. Her closet was bigger than my bedroom, and as I ran my fingers over her racks of designer clothes, I felt safe. Taken care of. She selected a red dress that hugged my every curve, and when she told me I was beautiful, I believed her.

My sole winter coat was a faded puffy parka that didn't exactly scream *elegance*, so Mrs. Spencer let me borrow a gray peacoat that fell past my knees. When we emerged from the house in the swirling snow, I felt like we were princesses, draped in velvet and cashmere. Mr. Spencer showered us in compliments, saying he couldn't believe how lucky he was to be having dinner with three beautiful women. Mrs. Spencer laughed and kissed him, caressing the side of his dark brown face. A delicate silver bracelet encrusted with sapphires sparkled on her wrist.

By the time we pulled up to the sprawling Crystal Grove Golf and Yacht Club, the snow was piling up. A valet briskly greeted us, and I watched in amazement as Mr. Spencer passed off the keys to his Mercedes-Benz to this stranger he didn't even know. That was when I learned confidence and wealth were often two sides of the same coin. The Spencers moved through the world as if they knew everything would work in their favor. It was the complete opposite of the nervous demeanor I'd inherited from my mom, and I felt an ache deep in my throat telling me to stand straighter, hold my head high. Music and laughter tinkled through the club's front doors, and Ella gave me an excited hug before we entered.

The Christmas tree inside was at least twenty feet tall. Servers in tuxedos circled the lobby, offering food I'd never heard of, such as beef tartar and prosciutto-wrapped persimmons. In a space of mostly white people, the Spencers and I stood out. I kept smoothing my frizzy curls and yanking down my dress. Everyone was so *loud*, and I wanted to fade into the wallpaper.

But then I noticed how people were smiling at us. Making room for us, nodding at us. It was then I realized the Spencers were a family that people not only *knew*, but respected and admired. Mr. Spencer was dapper in his fitted gray suit, full beard trimmed short, his voice commanding but not obnoxious. Mrs. Spencer looked like Filipino royalty in a slimming black dress that showed off her sharp shoulders. Ella, a perfect combination of both of them, trailed behind and pointed out every nook and cranny of the club.

We sat down for dinner in the restaurant that overlooked Linkhorn Bay, where course after course magically appeared. I would take one sip out of my water glass and someone would reach over my shoulder to fill it back up to the brim. Mr. and Mrs. Spencer split an expensive bottle of red wine, and we dined on shrimp cocktail, Chilean sea bass, and squid ink linguine. I'd never seen such a spectacle; a fancy night out for my family was Olive Garden, where Leon and I could gorge on endless breadsticks.

When mini gingerbread cheesecakes were presented for dessert, Ella announced the good news. "Blake and I," she said, lacing our fingers together, "are a couple."

"That's what I'm talking about!" Mr. Spencer said, and when a waiter floated by, he ordered cocktails for him and Mrs. Spencer and hot chocolates for me and Ella. When they appeared moments later, Mr. Spencer dashed our hot chocolates with some of his whiskey.

Mrs. Spencer scoffed, still smiling. "Really, Isaac?"

"Oh, it's just a taste. It's not every day our baby girl announces a new relationship," Mr. Spencer said. "This deserves to be celebrated!"

"You two make a beautiful couple," Mrs. Spencer agreed, toasting us with her cordial. "We are very excited for you."

I wanted to cry at the polar opposite reaction they had from my parents. I held up my glass, let myself be honored, and drank. I could barely taste the whiskey, but the mere knowledge of its existence in my cup made me feel fuller, older, and sophisticated. I instantly wanted more.

The Crystal Grove club's annual holiday party was in full swing by the time we finished dessert. Mr. Spencer excused himself to chat with work colleagues, and Mrs. Spencer introduced me to a beautiful, elegant Black woman who also wore a sapphire bracelet on her wrist. It was Lorraine Jones, local news anchor and all-around badass. Sitting next to her was her daughter, Annetta.

Mrs. Spencer introduced Mrs. Jones as her close friend and sister. For a moment, I thought she meant sister literally.

"You're Ella's aunt?" I asked, extracting my hand from Mrs. Jones's firm shake.

Mrs. Spencer and Mrs. Jones laughed and explained they weren't blood related, no. But they were Serena sisters, and that was just as important.

Outside of the occasional teacher, I hadn't grown up around women of color. Mom's estranged family was as lily white as her, and Dad was an only child, my Black grandmother dead before I was born. Instantly, I wanted to cling to these women. I was curious and desperate to learn everything about them. I wanted to know what products Mrs. Jones used to get her twist out just right, wanted Mrs. Spencer to teach me how to find my perfect foundation shade. I studied them longingly while Ella pestered them about whatever this Serena thing was. Even Annetta had looked up from her phone, vaguely interested.

"Honestly, Maricar, you haven't caved yet?" Mrs. Jones asked. "I told Annetta years ago."

"*I* respect the tradition of waiting until the sixteenth birthday," Mrs. Spencer countered before sipping her wine. This, of course, only made Ella more curious, but Mrs. Spencer and Mrs. Jones told us to go dance.

"You need to make friends anyway," Mrs. Jones told Annetta as we reluctantly drifted away.

Annetta looked as if she'd rather peel a sack of potatoes with her fingernails than hang out with me and Ella. But her expression morphed from boredom to horror when Ella swiped a half-empty bottle of wine from an abandoned table and tucked it under her arm like a football.

"You're gonna get caught!" Annetta hissed.

"We're fine!" Ella said, but I noticed her hands shaking. She hurried out of the restaurant, and Annetta and I stayed hot on her heels, attempting to block the smuggled bottle from view.

We breathed a sigh of relief when we were in the clear, and Ella led us to an empty, dark library. She flipped on an electric fireplace and the three of us were bathed in a flickering artificial orange glow. Ella took a swig straight from the bottle, then pointed it at Annetta.

"You," she said slowly, "need to tell us everything you know. Now."

Annetta folded her arms across her chest. This was before she started wearing contacts; her eyes squinted behind large black frames. "Why should I tell you anything?"

"Because we've known each other for years! You can trust me!"

"Just because our moms are close doesn't mean you know me,

princess," Annetta shot back. Ella didn't even look offended at the barb. She *was* a princess and, up until that point, Annetta had no desire to get to know the rest of the country club kids. She later told us that she'd spent her entire childhood thinking they were a bunch of boring snobs. Ella was the exception. She was far from boring, and she had something Annetta appreciated—

Persistence.

"How about this?" Ella said. "You tell me what you know and I'll do your homework for a week."

"We don't even go to the same school."

"Doesn't matter," Ella said, batting her eyelashes. "I'm smart. I'm already in an AP class."

"I'm already in two," Annetta said, batting her eyelashes back. Since I was a solid B student in nonadvanced classes, I stayed out of it and watched in amusement as they went back and forth like lightning-fast tennis players.

"Tell me and I'll tell you a secret."

"I don't care about your secrets."

"Tell me and I'll let you have some of this wine."

"I don't want any wine."

"What, are you scared?" Ella challenged.

Annetta pushed her glasses up her nose, eyes darting around the library. "I'm not scared."

"Seems like it to me."

Annetta snatched the wine bottle and took a gulp to prove herself. She made a face. "This tastes *awful.*" Still, she took another sip before passing it to me.

"They're talking about the Serena Society," Annetta said. "You seriously haven't heard of it?"

Ella shook her head slowly. It was the first and only time I'd ever seen her out of the loop. I thought she knew everything, understood all. I took a sip of the bitter wine and then another, waiting in anticipation. Annetta was right. It *was* gross, but I needed something to focus on besides my pounding heart.

"It's a secret society our moms are part of," Annetta explained. "They joined in college. At Jameswell."

Ella's eyes widened. "Secret society? Tell me everything . . ."

That night in the library, a friendship blossomed as Annetta told Ella and me everything she knew. Unlike national societies, the Serena Society only existed at Jameswell, so underground that even the deepest internet searches about it revealed very little. It was only for women of color who showed immense promise in changing the world. Politicians, actors, novelists, and activists were among its ranks. Ella and I listened with rapt attention, passing the wine bottle back and forth until it was empty.

"It's basically a club for powerful, badass women of color," Annetta concluded with a shrug. But the look that had crystallized on Ella's face was one of a girl obsessed.

Eventually, Annetta headed back to the restaurant in search of dessert, leaving Ella and me alone. We were tipsy, our throats heavy with the weight of a new secret.

"Imagine!" Ella said as she twirled down the club's empty, echoing halls. "*We* could be Serena Society girls!"

The night wore on. We discussed the Serena Society and imagined our futures as college girls. We snuck into the musty gym and howled with laughter as I tried and failed to maintain my balance on a bloated exercise ball. I fell to the floor and the room swirled. Ella helped me up and guided us to a weight bench with her lips on my neck.

"You're perfect," she whispered urgently as we twisted together on the bench. "Promise me we'll stay together forever?" Her eyes were low and her cheeks were flushed and hot. I promised, and that night, Ella's fingers slipped between my thighs for the first time and everything shimmered like twinkle lights. Afterward, we couldn't stop giggling as we returned to the party and danced in the middle of it all with Mrs. Spencer and Mrs. Jones and the rest of the adults who were drunk and floating and beautiful.

I woke up the next morning in Ella's king-sized canopy bed, still in my dress, Ella fast asleep beside me. It was the start of many mornings that would look just like that—dry throat, swollen lips. My heart pounded when the memory of what we did in the gym rushed back. I wanted to relive the entire night, an intense yearning for this world of fancy food and warmth and women of color who were exciting and full of life and so different from everything I'd ever known. I could still feel Ella's hot fingers and taste our wine-drunk kisses.

I was thirsty for more.

On the night of our first Serena task, Ella darted around her bedroom, trying on an array of crop tops and flowy dresses and booty shorts. She emerged from her closet and gazed in disappointment in her full-length mirror before disappearing again. Annetta and I perched on the edge of her bed, Nina weaving between our feet with gentle purrs.

To calm my nerves, I focused on the photos pinned on the corkboard above Ella's computer. They were mostly of the two of us over the years—embracing at prom and homecoming, kissing on the beaches of the Outer Banks, Miami, and the Bahamas. There was one of me, Ella, and Annetta posing at a Halloween party when we were fifteen—Ella as an angel in a sexy lace bodysuit and fluffy wings, Annetta as Sherlock Holmes, and me, a devil with horns and a red-hot pitchfork. Sometimes I missed the girls we were at that age. When our friendship was still new and there weren't any cracks yet.

"Ugly, ugly, ugly!" Ella burst from her closet with a leather skirt around her knees. "You guuuuys! I have nothing to wear."

"Careful," Annetta said without looking up from her phone. "Someone might think you're nervous."

"I'm not nervous," Ella said, sounding very nervous. She sank to the floor and scratched Nina between her ears. "First impressions are just . . . everything."

I nudged her with my foot. "You would look beautiful in a trash bag. You know that."

She looked up through her eyelashes. "I just want us to do okay."

"We'll be fine," I said. But my heart fell, knowing her definition of "us" really meant just me. Annetta and Ella were born for this life. *I* was the only one who had to apply for student loans and financial aid because my dad couldn't just write a check for tuition the way their investment banker fathers did. My paychecks went to helping Mom pay off my braces while they spent their money on clothes and coffee runs. My parents used the word *price*; theirs said *investment*. They were daughters of Serena women, legacies destined to carry their mothers' torches. And even though I wanted Serena as much as them, even though I thought I deserved it as much as them, I was the daughter of a woman who worked the night shift at 7-Eleven. Not an influencer like Mrs. Spencer or a national news anchor like Mrs. Jones. I needed Serena to prove that, although I wasn't born into this world of privilege, I belonged here just the same.

And deep, deep, deep down in the pit of my stomach was a future so horrible that it made me nauseous to think about: Ella breaking up with me if I didn't get accepted. I refused to start college as the thirteen-year-old lonely loser I'd desperately spent the last five years trying to outrun.

Ella glanced at the time and groaned. "I know we should probably nap, but I'm too nervous."

"How long will the task take?" I asked.

She shrugged. "Could be a couple of hours. Could be all night."

"Kill me now," Annetta muttered.

Ella narrowed her eyes. "A lot of girls *would* kill you for the chance to be in your shoes, Nettie."

"Tell them to pull up, then!" Annetta yelled. We laughed and the tension melted away. Ella drifted back to her closet, still on the hunt for the perfect outfit. Annetta took a couple hits from her vape, and I assumed the role of the DJ in hopes that music would be a good distraction. The irony of Annetta being dubbed the nervous one when I was ready to throw up at the thought of what the night held.

An hour later, the three of us sat at Ella's vanity, admiring our reflections. Annetta—having the clearest skin out of all of us—chose a more natural look and only wore a coat of clear gloss and refreshed her twist out with some water and styling cream. Ella was as gorgeous as ever, her red hair falling in sleek waves, eyes smoky and striking. She made my eyes pop with gold shimmer and colored my lips a deep purple. They knew I fidgeted with my hair too much when I was nervous, so Annetta styled my curls into two long boxer braids again.

"Ladies," Ella purred, "you are looking at three future members of the Serena Society."

Please, please, please let that be true, I prayed to the universe. Annetta nibbled at a nail.

"You okay, Nettie?" Ella asked. "Don't tell me you're getting nervous now. You've only been blasé about this whole thing for four years."

Annetta sighed. "No, it's . . . I don't know, it's nothing."

There was a knock on Ella's bedroom door, followed by Mrs. Spencer's muffled voice, asking if we were decent.

"Come in," Ella called. Mr. and Mrs. Spencer appeared, bearing three bouquets of calla lilies that'd been dyed an unnatural royal blue. They must've cost my entire paycheck.

"We wanted to see you off," Mr. Spencer said.

"You're all so beautiful!" Mrs. Spencer gushed. Her smile was warm and familiar as she handed me a bouquet. I buried my nose in the petals and inhaled, but they didn't smell like anything.

"I know your mom is so proud of you," Mrs. Spencer said, handing Annetta her flowers. "Have you talked to her yet?"

Annetta mumbled something that wasn't a yes, wasn't a no. Ella imperceptibly shook her head, silently begging her mom to leave the topic alone. It'd been over two years since Mrs. Jones divorced Annetta's dad and left Virginia (and her family) in the dust for a high-profile news anchor job in New York. It was still a sore subject Annetta refused to talk about.

"What time are you off?" Mr. Spencer asked swiftly.

"It starts at midnight," Ella said, "so we should leave soon."

Mrs. Spencer chuckled. "Serena tradition."

I ran my finger along a petal. "Any tips?" I asked, looking up at Mrs. Spencer's bracelet. I couldn't remember a time when she wasn't wearing it. I thought about the night I first noticed it at the Crystal

Grove Christmas party. That night of haze and glitter, wine and sapphires. Belonging.

Mrs. Spencer smiled. "Just remember the pledge process is supposed to be fun," she said. "Just be yourself, and it'll be okay."

I wanted to ask her what version of myself she was referring to. The skittish girl afraid of heights? The girl who felt like an alien in her own family? Surely not the drunk girl who threw buckets of paint across people's three-million-dollar yachts. None of those versions seemed worthy of the Serena Society. As if she could read my mind, Mrs. Spencer gently guided my chin to look at her.

"You got the invitation for a reason," she said. She meant it, and I knew how lucky that made me. Most of the pledges wouldn't be incoming freshmen. And none of them would have the luxury of being the girlfriend of the advisor's daughter. I thought of my future—golden couple status with Ella, surrounded by powerful women of color, connections I couldn't dream of five years ago—and curled my fingers around the lily stems.

After wishing us good luck, her parents left. It was nearly eleven, and every passing second felt like piles of sand accumulating on my chest. I would be buried by midnight. Ella went to her closet to select a purse, and I followed her with a jittery heart.

"Is the bottle still in here?" I asked, leaning against the doorframe.

Her smile was devilish. "Of course." She rummaged around in the pocket of her favorite Versace coat. Out came a half-empty bottle of gold tequila.

"Bring your sexy ass in here, Nettie," Ella called, twisting the cap off. "And bring three shot glasses!"

Annetta joined us in the closet and with two souvenir shot glasses.

She handed Ella an Aspen one, gave me Amsterdam. The glass was cold. Heavy.

"You so nervous you forgot to count?" Ella asked. "There's three of us, boo!"

"I'm good," Annetta said. "I vaped."

Ella ignored her. She ran to her bookshelf and came back with another shot glass—Rome. "Trust me," Ella said. "This night calls for *liquid* courage. Nervous Nettie needs to stay home. We need Normal Nettie tonight."

"Nice Nettie," I added with a giggle. "Ooh, or Noteworthy Nettie!"

"Naked Nettie!" Ella yelled, and Annetta finally cracked a smile and relented. We held out our shot glasses and Ella filled them up to the brims.

"To Serena," she said, holding hers out for a toast.

"To Serena," Annetta and I echoed. We clinked glasses and threw our heads back, the crisp tequila hitting my tongue with a warmth only an old friend could deliver. Annetta made a face and coughed into her armpit.

"God, that shit is strong," she complained. Still, Ella poured us another round—for good luck. The second one went down smoother, and my nerves started to soften like putty. I rested my forehead against Ella's and inhaled her honey-scented hair products.

"Love you till aliens take over the planet," Ella said. "And wipe our memories clean."

I laughed. "Love you till the dinosaurs make a vicious comeback."

"Oh, Blake," she said, dancing out of the closet. "I'd love you even then." She twirled on her plush carpet, hair flying like autumn fire. I watched her in a trance, marveling that I was lucky enough to love her at all. She plucked a lily from her bouquet and slipped it behind my ear. It was too big and felt awkward, but she said I looked beautiful, so I kept it there.

We traipsed down the Spencers' spiral staircase in a parade of nervous giggles. Then out to the garage where the Range Rover awaited us. As I climbed into the passenger seat, the tequila kindled inside me, turned my stomach into a fireplace. I tossed my insecurities inside and let them burn down into ash.

"Y'all ready?" Ella asked.

"Hell. *Yes*," I said, alight. Glowing.

Ella shouldn't have been driving after two shots, but she knew the streets of the Crystal Grove neighborhood like the lines on her palms. We blared music the entire time, laughing and singing along. When I pulled my visor mirror down to check my lipstick, my cheeks were red. I loved how alive I looked. I caught Annetta's eye in the back seat and she stuck her middle finger up, her personal way of saying she cared about me. These were the times I loved the most. The three of us together, looking sexy and full of fire, embodying That Feeling.

We were invincible.

The security guard at the club entrance recognized the Range Rover and waved Ella through. My heart pounded as we bypassed a row of FRANKLY? I'M WITH PETERSON! campaign signs bordering the dark cresting waves of the golf course.

Ella pulled into the parking lot at the water's edge and cut the ignition. Two girls slipped out of a car next to us and headed for the gently bobbing sailboats and yachts.

"How many girls are there going to be again?" I asked.

She popped a mint and passed the tin to me, then Annetta. "Thirty or so to start," she said. "But they always end with twelve."

I placed the mint under my tongue as the tequila's heat roiled in my stomach. The confidence boost it had given me was fading. "So a majority of these girls won't last until the end of the summer?"

Ella laughed. "They won't last until the end of the night." She checked her reflection one last time and wiped her pinkie over a lipstick smudge. "Ready?"

"As I'll ever be," Annetta mumbled from the back seat.

When I didn't answer, Ella tore her eyes away from the mirror. She saw the hesitation on my face and squeezed my hand. "You have nothing to worry about, Bee. You heard my mom. You deserve to be here. You're my girl." She reached behind my ear and threw the lily on the dashboard. "Don't wear this, though. Ariana told me it's bad form to wear blue during the pledge process."

"Why?" I asked.

"You have to earn it."

The three of us emerged from the car into the muggy night. It was ten till midnight, and a steady stream of girls headed for the docks, just as hungry for this opportunity as we were. Ella grabbed my hand; I grasped Annetta's with my other. Together, we headed toward the sounds of slapping water, toward the *Bewitched*, toward the Serena Society, toward more.

CHAPTER 5

LIVING UP TO ITS NAME, the *Bewitched* had cast a spell on everyone clustered around its main deck. It was surprisingly quiet, nothing like the past few weeks where Ella, Annetta, and I had partied hard with Roxanne and the rest of our friends from Crystal Grove. The Garcias' yacht was among the nicest at the club, but unlike Frank Peterson, they never felt the need to brag about it. With three decks, five cabins, multiple lounges, and a Jacuzzi, the *Bewitched* was a luxury yacht and sang for herself. Ella led me and Annetta to the front of the crowd. I shivered even though the night was heavy with humidity.

"Welcome, welcome!"

Roxanne Garcia strode through the sliding doors that led to the first-floor lounge. Her honey-brown hair was up in a messy bun, and her feet were shoved in a pair of fluffy white bunny slippers. Her supple cheeks were red from the heat or wine, probably both. When she spotted Ella, her eyes lit up.

"El!" she squealed, crushing Ella in a hug. "I'm so glad you could make it!"

"Wouldn't have missed it," Ella giggled.

Roxanne kissed her cheek, then Annetta's, then mine. "You too, my little party animal!" she whispered to me. Then to the crowd: "Come inside! Let's get this night started!"

I flushed at her attention, ignored the jealousy that seemed to radiate off some of the other girls. I swore my palm throbbed in response. It was mostly healed from the paint can incident, but it still felt like a gentle reminder that Roxanne seemed to like me better when I was wild. And if wild was what the society wanted, wild was what I would be.

The main deck lounge twinkled under an array of string lights. Music played through hidden speakers. Roxanne pushed through the crowd, telling people to relax and get comfortable. Some girls leaned against the wall; some took places at the ten-seater dining room table. Ella, Annetta, and I sank into a plush love seat, and I was safe. Grounded. Sandwiched between the two of them, I'd make it through whatever the night brought. Bottles of wine and rum and vodka and tequila and whiskey glittered like diamonds on the glass coffee table.

"Don't judge my plastic cups, y'all!" Roxanne said. She and a short Southeast Asian girl with a black bob and a climbing-rose thigh tattoo took their places in the center of the room. They balanced trays of plastic champagne flutes and started passing them out. "No one has the time to be doing dishes after y'all leave," Roxanne said. "And for the love of God, don't spill shit on my parents' furniture." Laughter broke out, the vibe in the room mellowing even more. My shoulders relaxed when Ella passed me a glass of sparkling wine.

"Does anyone have any music requests?" Roxanne asked.

Someone called out a name and, almost immediately, a fast-paced tempo filled the room. Girls danced in their places, awkwardly gripping their drinks.

Roxanne shook her hips and held her glass up high. "Are y'all ready to have a good time?"

"Yes!" we shouted.

"I can't *heeeeear* you!"

"*YES!*"

"Good!" Roxanne cheered. "Then put your glasses in the air and toast to Serena!"

"To Serena!" we chorused, and I was instantly fourteen again, delighted for the first time by a Serena woman. I tipped my champagne and downed it in two gulps. It was light and crisp, spring in a glass. Heat rushed to my head.

"I'm so glad all thirty-four of you could make it out tonight," Roxanne said. "For those of you that don't know, I'm Roxanne Garcia and I'm the incoming president for the Serena Society undergrad chapter." She nodded at the girl with the thigh tattoo. "And this is my vice president, Alice Bui."

Alice smiled politely, but her eyes were razor-sharp. Combing over the pledges, considering us.

"Alice and I are going to refresh some supplies," Roxanne said. "While we're gone, please introduce yourself to at least three girls you don't already know." She locked in on me, Ella, and Annetta again and gave us a small smile, as if she was telling us to make her proud. Then she and Alice disappeared and the room settled into an awkward quiet.

Ella was the first to make a move. She leaned across the coffee table and stuck her hand out to a tall girl with braces. "Hi! I'm Ella Spencer."

That set everyone else in motion. A Black girl with short curls approached me nervously, tugging at the hem of her royal-blue skirt. We shook hands and introduced ourselves. Her name was Malia.

We chatted about Jameswell and prospective majors before two other girls descended on our conversation, and suddenly, names and faces became a blur. There was Keiko, who was from Atlanta but spending the summer at one of Jameswell's incoming freshmen programs. Khadija was from Norfolk, Prerna was a sophomore biochem major, and Eden had rings dripping from each finger. I repeated my stats in a loop like a news ticker.

Blake Brenner. Born and raised in Virginia Beach. Here with my girlfriend, Ella Spencer. Both incoming freshmen. I'm not sure what I want to major in.

I'd made my way through a large chunk of the living room by the time Roxanne and Alice returned. Roxanne turned down the music and silence fell promptly.

"Hello again, ladies," Roxanne said. "We're just about ready for the night to begin."

Sparks shot off in my stomach, a mixture of nerves, excitement, tequila, and sparkling wine.

"Unfortunately," Roxanne continued, and a tense silence blanketed the room, "not all of you will be joining us." On cue, Alice unfolded a piece of paper and began reciting names.

"Taylor Monty. Kortney Peters. Kennedy Evans—" Someone gasped, and Alice looked up with narrowed eyes before barreling on and slicing more dreams. "Stella Lopez. Khaliah Gregory. And Malia Adams."

I locked eyes with Malia; she was rigid.

"You can go home now," Alice said, tone laced with finality.

No one moved. Roxanne poured another glass of sparkling wine and frowned. It was the same pout she gave me before I threw paint on the Petersons' yacht. When she'd told me that the Serena Society fiercely condemned racism and anti-Blackness.

So what are you going to do about it?

My palm pulsed again.

"Please, ladies," Alice sighed. "We do not have all night."

One by one, the girls left. Malia didn't even look at me as she pushed through the crowd. Kennedy burst into tears. A petite Black girl with a shaved head raised her middle finger as she left. "Fuck y'all," she snarled. "Wannabe AKAs."

"Thank you, Kortney," Alice said, folding her paper. "Drive safe."

"Thanks for coming out!" Roxanne called as the last girl slammed the door behind her. Roxanne sighed, clearly unfazed. "What can you do?"

"Don't wear Serena colors," Ella muttered, and I froze, realizing all the girls who'd been let go were wearing some shade of blue. Was that all it took?

"That's right, Ella," Roxanne said. "It's honestly so simple."

"So simple," Alice echoed.

"We're here to have a good time," Roxanne said. "And honor our legacy. Any true woman of Serena would know to never wear blue on the first night." Her eyes searched the crowd. "Anyone know why?"

"You have to earn it," Keiko replied simply.

"That's right," Roxanne said, pleased. "You have to earn it."

I stared at my bare knees, overcome with gratitude for Ella, who'd knowingly dressed me in all black. Surely I would've been cut from the process already without her. It was so easy to mess up, how was I going to survive the rest of the summer? How was I going to prove no one wanted this more than me?

"Tonight's going to be fun," Roxanne said, leaning against a credenza. "We're gonna have a couple of drinks, get to know each other a bit more. Alice and I will tell you about the society, and we're going to end with an easy game. Sound good?"

Everyone hummed in agreement, and I took two deep breaths, trying to calm myself. I had to chill out. Ella gave my knee a quick, excited squeeze.

"But first things first." Roxanne zeroed in on me. "Blake, would you do the honors of being guest bartender? My right-hand woman?"

My stomach burned as everyone waited for my response. Ella nudged my side, and I flew to my feet.

"Of course," I stammered. God, my voice was so shaky, so unsure. I cleared my throat. "What do I have to do?" I asked, steadier. Good. Better.

"Mix some drinks with me!" Roxanne pulled me behind the bar, where an assortment of mixers, garnishes, and frosty bags of ice greeted us. She handed me a scoop and muttered under her breath, "Just don't throw paint on *my* boat."

I laughed, unsure if she was joking. "Of course not."

Roxanne untwisted a chilled bottle of Grey Goose and poured two shots. "Serena tradition," she said. "Bartenders take first shot."

I didn't tell her it would be my third shot of the night. The burn from the tequila in Ella's closet felt so long ago. With all eyes on us, Roxanne and I entwined our arms like a couple on their wedding day, counted to three, and swallowed. I wanted to vomit. I'd always hated straight vodka, but my disdain was eased by my position as Roxanne's lucky chosen one. The president had selected *me* to be her right-hand woman, even above Ella. Maybe Mrs. Spencer was right. Maybe I was meant for Serena, too.

I belonged here.

I belonged here.

"The *Bewitched* bar is open for business!" Roxanne sang. Girls began lining up and placing vodka cranberry and gin and tonic orders. My anxiety lightened the more drinks I made.

I belonged here . . .

Water. I had to drink water.

"... Society was established in 1951 when eleven girls at Jameswell University ..."

Wait, what did she say? 1951. Okay, yes. Nineteen fifty-one, I knew that. Fuck, why is Annetta looking at me like that?

"... other sororities had started losing their exclusivity ..."

How many drinks did I have? Only four, right? That tequila in Ella's closet should've worn off by now ... Sparkling wine ... Grey Goose shot ... that second Grey Goose ...

"It's important to know—"

"To Serena!"

"*Cheers!*"

"*Cheers!*"

"*Cheers!*"

Ella nudged me. Handed me a dark drink. I sipped. Whiskey and Coke. Deeeelicious!

Annetta sighed. Snatched whispers.

"Chill out. She doesn't need to drink any more."

"She's *fine*, Nettie."

I found myself again. Head spinning, but still smiling, I clutched my glass and tipped it toward Annetta. "I'm *fine*," I repeated after Ella. Some girl with a long blond wig snorted across the living room—*bitch*—and I straightened in my chair, forced my eyes to focus.

"I'm fine," I said again, this time with a shrug.

I'm fine.

We were still docked, but the room was romping. Everyone looked prettier in the chandelier's dim light. Music blasted, a song about twerking, working, something. I was perched like a cat on the couch, watching everything unfold around me. Roxanne, still wearing her ridiculous bunny slippers, danced with a tall girl with long braids, both of them yelling out lyrics. When they dragged Ella up to join them, she tried to pull me along.

"Dance with me, Bee," Ella said, but I felt Annetta shooting daggers. I shook my head, pointed to my drink with a woeful shrug.

I was fine.

Alice's history lesson was finished, taken over by rambunctious laughter and waning attention. Everyone was drunk.

> *See? See? You're fine. This is what you're supposed to be doing.*
> *You fit in, you belong. Just drink a little bit more, but not too much.*
> *That's right . . . nice and easy. You can't look like a punk in front of*
> *Roxanne.*
> *You have to handle your liquor.*
> *You have to keep up.*

I stared at Roxanne's sapphire bracelet and drank. I thought about the thrilled looks on everyone's faces when I threw the paint can and drank. I thought about Mrs. Spencer handing me the bouquet of lilies. Drank. Her saying she was proud of me. Finished the glass. When the image of Ella breaking up with me flashed through my mind, I desperately looked around for a refill.

Annetta gently wiggled my glass away. She set it on the ground, her face pinched.

"What are you doing?" I asked.

She looked at me, shook her head. "Saving you."

You're such a loser.

You don't deserve to be here.

These girls are rich. These girls are funny. These girls are smart.

You are not.

Ella, my beautiful red-haired siren, handed me a bottle of cider.

"It's like grown-up apple juice," she said with a giggle. Her brown eyes were glassy and filled with stars.

I loved her so much. I told her so.

"Hi, I'm Corinne . . ."

". . . are you okay?"

The drinks stopped, and the game began. I didn't know what time it was. The string lights looked pretty.

"Puzzles!" Roxanne cheered.

"Count off by four," Alice instructed.

Ella was a four. I was a two, just like Annetta, who'd wandered to the other side of the room.

She's trying to get away from you.

You're embarrassing, you know that? Completely worthless.

You're a loser, you don't even belong here.

You don't even belong here.

You don't even belong—

Alice led us downstairs—how big *was* this boat?—and divided us by group into four dark cabins. I stumbled in last, and Alice placed a box in my hand. Food? I was looking at it upside down, couldn't read what it said. Annetta sighed and yanked the box out of my hands. She was shaking. She looked mad. *Mad at me?*

"Finish the puzzle," Roxanne said. "Last group out is cut."

"That's not fair. Are you serious?" someone in group three asked.

"It's only 'not fair' if your group doesn't win," Alice snapped. "Time starts when we close the door, and don't even *think* of turning on the lights. You'll be immediately disqualified."

"But it's dark in here," someone said. Me?

Roxanne thrust a strobe light in my hand so hard I nearly dropped it. "Don't tell me Bad Bee is afraid of the dark," she said with a smirk.

"It's *Big* Bad Bee," I corrected.

She slammed the door in my face.

Spinning rooms and strobing lights did not mix. Especially when trying to put together a five-hundred-piece puzzle of a cat playing with a ball of yarn. It was such a cute cat! It was brown and chunky and reminded me of Nina, which reminded me of Ella and—

"Blake, please!" Annetta snapped. "Focus!"

"Just go sit in the corner if you're going to be worthless," Keiko said. "Someone turn that fucking strobe light off!"

"We have to keep it on," the girl with braids said. Khadija?

"They never said that," Keiko said. She switched the light off, bathing us in darkness. The moonlight didn't reach the windows of the lower deck.

"Wait!" I suddenly had an ingenious idea. "I have a flashlight . . . on my phone. Why don't we just use that?"

Keiko growled, "Is this girl serious?"

Annetta guided me to the full-sized bed and sat me down. Her brown eyes looked so tired. *Tired of me?*

"Just sleep, Blake," she said. "We'll handle it."

"I finished the top border!" someone cried.

"Good job," Keiko said, and hot anger flashed through my core. I wanted to be useful, I wanted to help. How dare *she* call me worthless. She didn't even know me! I was Ella's girlfriend. I was Roxanne's right-hand woman. Mrs. Spencer said I belonged here.

"Find the corner pieces," I mumbled, my head hitting the pillow. No one answered, so I repeated myself. "Find the corner pieces! That's always . . . the . . . best . . . help . . ."

"Thank you, Blake," a soothing voice said. I liked that person. "Just go to sleep, love."

"Blake, wake up, wake up, wake up."

I jolted awake. The cool blue light of dawn trickled through the window. I was still in bed, cheek pressed against the mattress. Annetta helped me up, and the minute my feet hit the floor, I swallowed the urge to vomit.

Alice stood in the doorway, admiring the completed puzzle on the floor. Keiko and the other girls had bloodshot, zombie-red eyes. I had no idea how long I'd been asleep.

"Excellent," Alice said, nodding. "You all can go home now." She left and went to check in the next cabin, where another group was screaming they were finished, too.

Keiko whirled around and glared at me.

"You've got some nerve," she hissed. "This is the last time you will ever ride my fucking coattails. I didn't come all the way from Atlanta to not get into the Serena Society over some drunk girl."

"Calm down," Annetta said.

I wanted to throw up. I wanted to hide. How did this happen?

"Keiko, chill out," a girl with a short afro said. Eden? "We finished, that's all that matters."

Keiko looked like she wanted to rip me to shreds but was too tired to do so. She stormed out of the room, and the rest of the girls slowly followed. A sudden, terrifying thought seized me.

"Ella." I looked around. "Where is Ella?"

"Relax," Annetta said. "Her group finished first, about thirty minutes ago."

Of course they did. I swayed a bit and brought my hand to my forehead, trying to steady myself.

"You on the other hand . . . ," Annetta said, and my gut plummeted again.

"What?"

"*You* were a hot mess. You drank too much."

I reeled. "I'm fine—"

"No, you're not," Annetta interrupted. "Honestly? I think you have a fucking drinking problem."

She took off, and I followed her up the stairs in shocked silence, shame and disgust and rage threatening to boil over. I desperately tried to remember everything that happened, but I kept coming up with static. The night was a notebook with missing pages, a frame with no photo.

We made our way through the *Bewitched*'s lounge. All traces of the party had vanished like magic. The air smelled like lemon disinfectant spray and made me want to hurl. Annetta scooped our phones from the coffee table. Apparently, they'd been taken before we started the puzzle.

Ella was waiting in the Range Rover, head resting against the steering wheel. Her sleepy eyes lit up when Annetta and I climbed in. The lily was already wilting on the dashboard.

"You finished," she said, proud.

"Yup," Annetta mumbled.

I was too ashamed to tell Ella I had nothing to do with it. Ella kissed me, and I turned my head when I caught a whiff of stale vodka on her breath.

"I don't feel so good," I whispered.

She chuckled. "Shouldn't have mixed the light and dark liquors?" When I didn't say anything, she started the car. "Let's get you home, baby."

As we drove, Ella yawned and recounted how well her group worked together, how they divided and conquered the puzzle with ease. I leaned against the window and closed my eyes, hoping she would think I was asleep. But my gut was a hard knot, abs straining under my shirt as I struggled to keep the tears from falling as I sat with Annetta's words. I kept waiting for her to tell Ella everything, but she was silent in the back seat as we pulled into her cul-de-sac.

The Jones's house sat prominently on the golf course's ninth hole, a sprawling brick ranch that seemed too big to hold just two people now that Mrs. Jones was gone. Annetta's father was in the driveway, tossing his briefcase into his Lamborghini SUV. Annetta had called it his mid-life crisis / postdivorce gift to himself.

"Morning, girls!" Mr. Jones called as Ella pulled into the driveway. "Late night?"

"We're starting the process for Serena," Ella said. Annetta climbed out the back seat without a word.

She hated me. I'd embarrassed her.

"Ah," Mr. Jones said, staring at Annetta's back. She slammed the front door and he flinched. "I take it things didn't go well?"

Ella waved her hand dismissively. "It went great. She's just got a case of the Netties."

The Netties. That's what Ella had dubbed Annetta's frequent mood swings following her parents' divorce. They weren't as common now but still popped up from time to time. Mr. Jones—*all* of us—had learned to leave her alone whenever she was in a bad mood.

"Maybe she just needs to sleep it off," Mr. Jones said. He looked past Ella and gave me a tired smile. He looked like he'd aged ten years since Mrs. Jones left him. "Good morning, Blake."

"Morning," I croaked. I could barely look at him because he and Annetta shared so many of the same features—thick brows, full lips, warm brown eyes.

Thunder rumbled in the distance and Mr. Jones checked his watch. "The office calls. Gotta pay off this baby somehow." He patted the Lamborghini's hood. "You girls get home safe!"

"We will!" Ella replied.

We backed out of the driveway and I spared a glance at Annetta's bedroom window, hoping to spy her face between the curtains. But her window remained empty. A horrible feeling spread through my body as I remembered her words.

I think you have a fucking drinking problem.

CHAPTER 6

WHOEVER CONTROLLED THE weather must have owed me a favor because the sky cracked open as soon as Ella entered Winward Commons. For a moment we just sat there in the parking lot outside my building, quietly watching the rain pour in sheets and rush down the windshield.

"You sure you don't want to stay over?" Ella asked, entwining her fingers with mine. "I can ask my mom to make your favorite blueberry pancakes."

It was a tempting offer, but a vicious hangover was creeping in my peripheral. I didn't want Mrs. Spencer to see me hunched over her daughter's toilet, vomiting up the night. She believed I was worthy of the Serena Society, and I didn't want anything to taint her vision of me.

"I'm okay," I said, kissing Ella's knuckles. I held my breath when we kissed goodbye, not wanting to catch another whiff of her liquor-soaked mouth.

I ran to my front door through a curtain of rain and let myself inside. The apartment was dark and quiet. Empty. I should've been grateful my parents were working and wouldn't see me like this, but I only felt small. Like Little Blake. I slid against the door, tears welling in my eyes, the alcohol wearing off like a slimy slug trail.

I hit the floor. Brought my knees to my chin. I tried to close my eyes, but that made everything worse. I swallowed and swallowed, trying to force the lump in my throat to go away. I couldn't get Annetta's words out of my head—

I think you have a fucking drinking problem.

The tears arrived all at once. I cried as quietly as I could, even though I was home alone. I prayed for my mind to shut up, for the room to stop spinning. I pulled out my phone to call Ella and tell her to come back so I didn't have to be alone with my thoughts. Instead, I found myself texting Annetta.

> I'm so sorry. I know I messed up majorly.
> Please please please forgive me?

A text bubble appeared. Then disappeared. I stared at the screen for a full minute until it returned.

> We'll talk about this later. Go to sleep.

My heart sank. My hands shook. I wanted to talk *now*. Wanted her approval now, wanted her to tell me everything was okay now.

> Are you mad at me?

> I'm worried about you.

Somehow, that felt worse than anger. I took three deep breaths, willing the hangover to stay away, willing myself to get it together.

All I wanted was to impress Roxanne and get into Serena. I wanted Mrs. Spencer to be proud of me. I wanted Ella to love me. Annetta was wrong. I didn't have a drinking problem. Maybe I overdid it last night, but I didn't have a *problem*.

I tried to stand, but the world tilted. I crawled to the living room instead. There was a half-empty glass of water on the coffee table. I chugged it. Then I settled onto the couch because my bedroom felt impossibly far.

For minutes, I stared at Annetta's words, trying to figure out what to say. I wanted to let her know I was fine. She didn't need to worry about me. But my eyes fluttered closed before I could type a word.

SPOILED CHARDONNAY

I was invited to join the Spencers on their Christmas vacation to Key West freshman year, but I didn't go. The morning after the Crystal Grove holiday party, Ella and I blearily made our way downstairs and joined her parents for breakfast. I was so busy devouring Mrs. Spencer's delicious blueberry pancakes that I thought I misheard Mr. Spencer asking how I felt about Florida in December.

"I'm not sure, sir," I said. "I've never been to Florida."

"Well, how about it? We leave tomorrow. Our family would love to have you." He winked at Mrs. Spencer.

"Um, I would love that," I stuttered. "But I don't have a plane ticket . . . ?"

Mrs. Spencer waved a hand. "Oh, you wouldn't have to worry about that, honey. You say the word and we'll take care of it."

I nearly fell out of my chair.

Ella was so excited to ask my parents that she didn't even finish breakfast. "They have to say yes," she said. "Christmas won't be the same without you."

Returning to my house after the Crystal Grove party felt like trading in a technicolor world for a black-and-white one. One where there was off-brand apple juice in the fridge instead of champagne. Mom was fast asleep after her graveyard shift, and Dad was watching the highlights from an NBA game, decompressing after a long stint of flying.

"How was the party?" he asked.

I sank onto the couch and shrugged. "It was fine."

"How did Ella's parents take the news that you two are dating?"

My skin prickled. "They didn't *take* it. They were thrilled. They celebrated it."

"No need to jump down my throat," Dad said quickly. "You can't blame me for needing some time to digest this information. The world is a whole lot different from when I was a kid."

My phone buzzed. It was Ella, desperately waiting for my answer. Dad flipped the channel to football and dug his hand into a bag of chips. There were crumbs all over the floor, and for the first time in my life, I felt a twinge of embarrassment that he was my dad. I thought back to Mr. Spencer's sleek suit and how he dipped Mrs. Spencer in the middle of the dance floor, drenched in disco ball shimmers. I couldn't remember the last time my parents hugged, much less danced. When Dad wasn't flying, he was watching television. And when Mom wasn't at 7-Eleven, she was asleep.

"We don't have anything planned for Christmas, right?" I asked.

Dad shoveled another handful of chips in his mouth. "Your brother is coming home on leave."

"Besides that."

"What are you getting at, Blake?"

I dug my toe into the worn carpet. "Ella invited me to spend Christmas with her and her family," I said slowly. "It would mean a lot if I could go."

"I don't see why not. Is she having a dinner at her house?"

I hesitated. "Her parents invited me to Key West."

Dad paused with a chip halfway to his mouth. "*Key West?* Are you kidding me? We don't have that kind of money, sweetheart. You don't even like to fly."

But I didn't care about the logistics. "Please, Dad," I begged. "I'll fly for this! You wouldn't have to pay for anything. Ella's parents will take care of it. They have the money."

Dad grew visibly uncomfortable. "It's Christmas," he sputtered. "And you're fourteen. You need to be with your family."

I begged and pleaded, but there weren't enough prayers in the world to make him change his mind. I would be staying in Virginia all winter break while Ella and her family jetted off to Key West first-class. Nothing swayed him, not even a call from Mr. and Mrs. Spencer assuring him I'd be well taken care of.

"My wife and I appreciate the offer," Dad said gruffly into the phone. "But this is so last minute and Blake needs to be home for the holidays. Surely you understand."

The Spencers left for Florida the next day, and I refused to come out of my room. I cried into my pillow when Ella shared beautiful selfies and shots of puffy clouds outside the airplane window with her hundreds of followers (she didn't hit the thousands until tenth grade). I convinced myself I was going to be replaced by another girl whose parents were infinitely cooler than mine. Another girl who would've been sitting beside her on that airplane, holding her hand. Any girl besides me.

Dad ordered takeout for dinner in an attempt to lure me out of my bedroom. "I got Chinese," he said, voice muffled through the door.

"I don't want Chinese!" I cried, snot-nosed and sniveling. "I want my Louise!"

"Your *what*?"

"Ella! My Louise! Me and Ella are Thelma and Louise, and you're keeping us from each other!" I didn't even know who Thelma and Louise were—Mom always referred to us as such, and I'd just assumed they were some iconic lesbian couple.

There was a long pause. Then Dad said, "Thelma and Louise drove themselves off a *cliff*," and that was the last time I used that analogy.

Leon arrived later that evening, and I gritted my teeth when he called me a dramatic baby through the door. I ached with loneliness. It slithered into my veins and made the world pointless and blurry. Surely I'd ruined everything by turning down the vacation; I was going to return to my dull life when Ella inevitably dumped me for someone better. For three months, I'd been the center of her attention. Now we were apart, and I was terrified her focus was going to wander.

It was after midnight when I finally crept into the kitchen to load up on supplies. I piled my arms with fruit snacks and Pop-Tarts, ready to make them stretch as long as possible. But I paused when I noticed a bottle of wine tucked behind a carton of expired milk.

My parents rarely drank, much preferring to get lost in television after a long day of work instead of alcohol. And yet, there was a nearly full bottle of white wine, innocently waiting. I looked over my shoulder to make sure no one was watching and grabbed it. I twisted off the cap and sniffed. It smelled horrible, but wasn't alcohol supposed to be pungent? I thought of Mrs. Spencer swirling wine in goblets, smiling for all her followers. I thought of Ella's fingers between my legs and how weightless the red wine made me feel. I tucked the bottle under my arm, scooped the rest of the snacks up, and hurried to my room.

I video chatted with Ella. She laughed in delight when I tipped the bottle back and let the sour wine slide down my throat.

"You're so wild," Ella cackled, and I was filled with sunlight, knowing I hadn't lost her attention, at least not yet. I inspired her to sneak into her rental condo's minibar and smuggle little bottles of tequila for herself.

We drank together across the miles. The details of her trip— snorkeling in impossibly blue water, zipping around on Jet Skis—didn't fan my jealous flames so much once the wine had reached the bottom of the label. Later, I'd have a hangover so vicious I'd be praying for death, but right then . . . I was weightless. The loneliness retreated. The world was still blurry, but in a better way.

Ella and I drank and talked about how much we loved each other between sips. Blushing furiously, we described in stuttering details what we'd do to each other if we were in the same room.

"I'd . . . put my fingers between your legs. Like you did to me in the gym," I said before burying my face in a pillow. Ella laughed and laughed and laughed.

"You're so cute, Bee," she said. Her words always felt as if they were wrapped in gold.

"Love you till we're Serena Society girls?" I asked.

"I'll love you forever," Ella promised.

By the time I finished the entire wine bottle, Ella was passed out. I quietly admired her pixeled face and made a drunken wish that we'd stay together forever.

I woke up in the early afternoon. The apartment was still quiet, but I had a knitted blanket thrown over me, so Mom was probably home from work. After chugging another glass of water, I made my way to my parents' bedroom.

I knew she'd be asleep, but a tiny part of me hoped she was awake. I felt awful, even worse than this morning. I was queasy and dehydrated with a headache kicking like a drum. As kids, whenever Leon and I were sick, we could always count on Mom to tend our ailments with ice-cold ginger ale and a can of chicken noodle soup. She'd put on *The Price Is Right* or *Unsolved Mysteries* because she said daytime television always made her feel better as a kid.

As I walked down the hallway, Annetta's words roared past my ears like thunder—*I think you have a fucking drinking problem*. I pushed it away, swallowed past the grime. I didn't need her negativity right now. I needed to curl up in a ball, have Mom make me some soup. But when I pressed my parents' bedroom door open, I was met with darkness and soft snores.

So I went to my room and crawled into bed. The rain was tapering off, but everything still felt gray. I was about to fall asleep again when my phone lit up with a call from Ella.

"Bumblebee!" she said when I picked up. How in the world was she so *chipper*? "How are you feeling?"

"Like shit," I mumbled.

"Awww, sounds like you need some hair of the dog. I'm 'bout to come pick you up. Roxanne invited us over for mimosas."

"She did?"

"Yeah, she's having some of the pledges over for happy hour so we can talk about last night. Wasn't it wild? I can't believe they cut thirteen girls off the bat."

Thirteen girls gone. Only twenty-one remaining. Me—impossibly, somehow—still in the running even though I'd only been a burden.

"Yeah," I said, trying to shove the shame away. "They cut those girls over the most trivial shit."

"It wasn't trivial. It's simple. Don't wear blue."

A wave of nausea turned my stomach. "How could they have known that? Not everyone has two older sisters and a mother to guide them through this."

"Less competition." I heard the chime of the Spencers' garage. "Anyway, I'll be there in ten. You need me to pick anything up on the way?"

"Some ginger ale?" I asked, the sweet feeling of relief propelling me upright. "And something greasy."

"Cook Out okay?"

I was debating between a cheeseburger or a spicy chicken sandwich when Annetta's words boomeranged back and sucker punched me in the gut.

I think you have a fucking drinking problem.

"Bee?"

Out of nowhere, I started crying.

"Bee?" Ella repeated. "What's wrong? What's going on?"

"Nettie." I gasped. "She said—she said—"

"Said what?"

"She said I have a drinking problem." The words fell heavy from my mouth, and I was glad we weren't on a video call so Ella couldn't see my tears. There was a long pause before she burst into laughter.

"A *drinking* problem? What the hell is she talking about?"

I mumbled, "I don't know." I couldn't bring myself to tell her about how I'd blacked out and completely missed the majority of the task. That would be way too embarrassing.

I heard the Range Rover starting up. "Ignore her," Ella said with a sigh. "It's the Netties."

"But—"

"Come on, Bee. You know how she gets. Who knows what she's really upset about? She's just taking it out on you."

My breathing slowed. Ella was right. Annetta did have a tendency to clam up and get edgy about random things. Maybe this wasn't about me.

"Calm down," Ella said. "I'm coming to pick you up. You'll have some food. Then we'll go hang out with Roxanne."

I wiped my eyes, overcome with gratitude, already feeling better. "Okay," I said in a small, pathetic voice. "Thank you."

In the twenty minutes it took Ella to get to Winward Commons, I managed to brush my teeth, shower, and throw on some clean clothes.

"Hello, my darling," Ella said when I climbed into the Range Rover. A greasy bag of Cook Out was waiting on the passenger seat and a cold ginger ale was nestled in the cup holder.

"My savior," I gushed, and I kissed her. Everything was good again. I ate as we headed for Crystal Grove and Ella laughed again at Nettie's accusation.

"A drinking problem," she said, amused. "If you have a drinking problem, then we *all* have drinking problems. My sisters told me partying with the Serena girls is next-level. If anything, Nettie needs to get her stamina up and drop the attitude or *she'll* be the one getting cut."

I bit into my glorious cheeseburger and chose to believe her. I squashed Annetta's words until I couldn't hear them anymore.

I was fine.

By the time we reached the club, I was full and the rain had subsided. Ella did my makeup in the car. She was always taking care of things.

"I love you," I said as she carefully filled my lips with a peach shimmer.

"I love you too, Bee," she replied with a smile that rivaled the emerging sun.

CHAPTER 7

THE DAYS DRAGGED ON, and there was no word of any more Serena tasks. Ella and I tried to distract ourselves with work, but the high temps and sticky humidity made being at the pool a slog. One morning, on our long walk from the employee parking lot, Ella complained about the heat to her followers.

"Y'all, come save us," she whined to the camera before angling her phone so I was in the shot. I threw up a peace sign, and we giggled.

"Should we go to the beach later?" she asked the camera. "What do you think, Bee?"

I said, "Whatever you want, babe," because I knew her followers ate that shit up. She'd get at least five DMs telling us we were relationship goals before we even reached the pool.

"Y'all hear that?" she asked. "Baby said whatever I want." She tried to sip her iced mocha, but her lips missed the straw, so we had to shoot the whole thing over again.

The morning adult swim lesson was wrapping up by the time Ella and I entered the pool gates. Ella peeled off to the locker rooms, and I reluctantly headed for the Snack Attack Shack.

Todd, thankfully, was nowhere to be found. Tristan was thrashing around in the kitchen, grunge rock blaring from his headphones. Annetta was at the register, reading a book. When the door swung closed behind me, she looked up with a frown. We hadn't talked since the Serena Society task because she'd called out of work and ignored me and Ella's texts. Now a silence stretched between us and her words seeped into my skin.

I think you have a fucking drinking problem.

I slid onto a stool and tried my best to give her a casual smile. "Hey, stranger."

"Hey," she muttered. Then Mrs. Long walked up to the window and ordered a mango smoothie. I was grateful for the distraction. The skin on the back of my neck crawled as I threw the ingredients into the blender.

Clearly, Annetta was still mad. And for what? She was acting like she'd never had a wild night or two. I could easily remind her of the time she got so drunk with me, Josiah, and Ella that we mooned the club from the top deck of Josiah's boat. Or that time she blacked out sophomore year and made out with Josiah on a dare. Or—

"Blake."

"What?" I snapped. Annetta pointed to the blender. The top had slid an inch and the smoothie was dangerously close to flying out and splattering the wall. I fixed it, and my irritation flared again. When it was finished, I poured it into a cup and handed it off without looking at her.

"So now *you're* mad at *me*?" Annetta asked once Mrs. Long was gone.

"I'm not mad," I said as I rinsed out the blender jar. I could feel her eyes on my back.

"You sure?"

"*You're* the one who's been acting weird. We invited you over two days in a row and you ignored us."

"We need to talk about that night."

"What about it?"

"Blake."

I turned the faucet off and whirled around. "Fine. What do you want me to say? I'm sorry for drinking too much and messing up the puzzle. I'm sorry if I embarrassed you in front of the Serena girls."

Her face softened. "That's not what I'm upset about."

I opened my mouth, then closed it. My polo suddenly felt too itchy.

"I'm worried about you," Annetta said. "When you party . . ." She hesitated, searched my face. Tristan tapped out a beat on the grill with his spatula.

"What, Annetta? Say what you need to say."

"I think you drink too much."

I struggled to think of something to say, but nothing. There was nothing.

"Don't you remember what you said?" she continued. "The night of the first task?"

"I said a lot of things."

"You said you didn't belong there. You kept calling yourself a loser. And 'Bigfoot Brenner'?"

I reeled. "No, I didn't." There was no way. I would've remembered *that*.

"Yes, you did. In the bathroom. When I took you aside and made you drink water. You kept going on and on about how much you hated yourself and how much of a loser you were and how you didn't deserve to be there."

My throat constricted. "I . . ."

"You don't remember?"

No.

"Kind of," I said.

Annetta's fingers drummed the vape outline on her pocket. If she were a physical person, maybe she would've crossed the room and taken me in her arms. Maybe we would've hugged and forgot about this conversation. But Annetta had never been touchy-feely.

There was a burst of laughter outside, and soon four preteen girls were at the window ordering veggie wraps. While Annetta keyed in their order, I escaped to the bathroom, desperate to get away from her words and their weight.

I leaned against the sink and looked in the mirror and hated what I saw. My cheeks were red with embarrassment. I tried, I *tried*, but I couldn't remember saying any of that. But Annetta wouldn't lie. Would she?

I splashed water on my face and gathered myself. When I emerged, the order tickets had piled up, and we became too busy with the lunch rush to continue our conversation. But there was still a pile of shame in my stomach, no matter how many shakes I blended or dishes I washed.

An hour later, there was finally a lull. Annetta plopped on a stool and started up again.

"You're so mean to yourself when you're drunk," she said.

"Can you drop it?" I asked, glancing at Tristan. I barely knew him, but I still didn't want him all up in my business. "Or can we talk about this later?"

"When? When would be a good time? The next time you're blackout drunk?"

I sucked in a breath. It felt like a slap, and I could tell by the look on her face that she regretted the words as soon as they left her mouth.

"I'm sorry," she said. "I just—"

"Ella was right," I interrupted. "You've been so uptight lately. Like, I get that you're still pissed about your mom or whatever, but you don't have to take it out on me." God, I didn't mean that, and I hated how I felt when Annetta's face clouded over. But if there was one topic that would make Annetta shut up, it was Mrs. Jones.

"What does my mom have to do with this?" Annetta asked. "You're deflecting from the actual problem."

"There is no problem!" I yelled, just as Todd entered the shack. His pleated shorts were impeccable, per usual. Pinned to his polo was a cheesy FRANKLY? I'M WITH PETERSON! button.

"Ms. Brenner. Ms. Jones. If you have time to *lean*, you have time to *clean*," he said.

"I'm going on my break," Annetta mumbled, brushing past Todd.

"Annetta," I sighed, but she was gone.

"You need to focus on these crumbs instead of Ms. Jones," Todd said, thrusting a broom in my hand. "A clean store—"

"Starts with a clean floor," I mumbled. As I swept in wide arcs, he placed a couple of campaign buttons on the counter.

"Put this on your polo," he said.

I rolled my eyes. "I'm not wearing that."

"This is not up for debate, Ms. Brenner. Here at CGGYC, we support our members. Now please, button up."

Knowing he wouldn't leave me alone until I did it, I pinned one to my polo and asked, "Happy?"

"Delighted." Todd handed one to Tristan, who made the valid argument that literally no member would even *see* it since he worked the fryers and grill.

"Mr. Donohue doesn't care that no one will see you," Todd said. "And neither do I. Mr. Peterson is one of the club's most important members, and after the unfortunate incident with his yacht, we want to make sure he *remains* one."

My fist curled over the cut.

"Whatever, man," Tristan mumbled. He pinned it to his polo and Todd finally left. Before the door even closed behind him, Tristan tossed the button in the trash can. Though I was tempted to do the same, I sat at the register, annoyed, Mr. Peterson's goofy slogan right over my heart. There was a sour taste in my mouth thanks to the argument with Annetta.

Across the pool, Ella was applying sunscreen to her long brown legs. She was so beautiful, and she told me I didn't have a problem. Annetta didn't know what she was talking about. *Everyone* was drunk that night on the *Bewitched*. It wasn't just me! And when Annetta got super stressed out, her vape was practically glued to her hand. How was that any different?

I pulled out my phone and quickly typed in *Do I have a drinking problem?* I scrolled past definitions for alcohol abuse disorders, ads for treatment services. I found a link to a screening quiz. Simple yes or no questions. I clicked on it.

> Do you feel like a normal drinker?
> **Yes or No.**

Obviously yes. A lot of teenagers drank. Most *adults* drank. I wasn't any different from them.

> Have you ever awakened the morning after drinking and found
> that you could not remember a part of the evening?
> **Yes or No.**

I swallowed. Clicked yes.

> Has a close friend or relative ever worried or
> complained about your drinking?
> **Yes or No.**

A text from Leon appeared right as I was about to select an answer.

> Have you started packing up your room yet??

I closed my phone, pushed it away without answering. The quiz was bullshit. Ella was right. Annetta was tripping, clearly upset about her mom and taking it out on me.

When Annetta returned, she replaced me on register without a word. I wanted to fix things immediately, but I couldn't muster the guts to apologize first. She ignored me and I ignored her. She took orders and I made milkshakes and smoothies and restocked cups and washed dishes and avoided the ache in my stomach that was worried we'd ruined our friendship forever.

Finally, an hour before closing, Annetta cleared her throat.

"Hey," she said.

I set down the bag of Oreos I was refilling. The weight in my chest eased when I saw her soft expression.

"Hey," I said.

"I'm sorry I was so pushy." She folded her arms across her lime-green polo, and my ice melted. Annetta rarely apologized.

"I'm sorry, too," I said quickly. "I shouldn't have brought up your mom. Can we hug?"

She rolled her eyes. "As long as you take that damn button off first. I don't want contact with Frank Peterson in any way, shape, or form."

I laughed and happily obliged. I threw Mr. Peterson's button into the trash and fell into her arms, grateful. We were okay.

"I just worry about you," she said into my ear, and my eyes welled up because she cared so much and our friendship wasn't over and I hadn't ruined everything.

I pulled away, wiping my eyes. "I'm okay. I promise."

"Are you sure?"

A whistle trilled, and we looked out the order window. Ella, high above in her lifeguard chair. She pushed her sunglasses up and grinned. I managed a smile back, thankful the distance kept my watery eyes from being obvious. She held up her hand in a backward C, and I mirrored her, forming our heart. But my own heart felt splintered in my rib cage, beating overtime. There was relief there, yes. But there was also something else. Something underneath.

I ignored it.

"I'm sure," I said. We went back to work.

HOW TO BE OKAY

PROCEED AS USUAL.

Propose a beach night to celebrate a reinvigorated friendship. Loop your arms around your best friend and your girlfriend, tell them that you love them. Celebrate because everything is good again.

Go to your favorite beach, the one hidden away from tourists. Run toward the roaring ocean, inhale the salt-whipped air. Spread your blanket over the fine-grain sand and lay out the essentials: bubble-gum-pink speaker, Flamin' Hot Cheetos, a Polaroid camera to remember it all. Everything is good again.

Rest your head on your girlfriend's stomach; allow your best friend to lay her head in the crook of your knees. In this tangled triangle, under the star splay, gaze at the moon and watch the world soften. Say, *I wonder what moondust feels like* because tonight it's full and beautiful and shimmering silver. When your girlfriend says, *I wanna fuck the moon*, laugh until it hurts. Everything is good again.

Remember the old days. When you were freshmen, eager and so naïve. Before the divorce, before the social media hype. Tell them,

I barely remember who I was before y'all, but that's not true, is it? You remember. With a painful, biting clarity, you remember. That's why you want to forget. Imagine what you'll be like in college, first-years once again.

Still eager, one of you says. *Hopefully less naïve*, says another. You wish you met them in elementary school so your best friend could've braided your hair on the playground. Wish you could've watched your girlfriend's limbs lengthen in real time, sprout like a weed. Everything is good again.

Drive out to your favorite diner, the one with the turquoise booths and the checker-pattern floor and yellow pats of butter sliding down fluffy short stacks. You are eighteen and hungry and full of wanting. You may have grown up with a hole inside you, but the girls you're with fill it with laughter and inside jokes. Gorge on chocolate chip waffles and greasy bacon and sneak hits from your best friend's vape in the bathroom by the jukebox. Everything is good again.

Avoid your best friend's cautious gaze when your girlfriend proposes yet another night at the yacht club. Parties on boats with pretty girls and fruity drinks is what summer in Virginia Beach is all about. Play your best friend's favorite song in the car in hopes it will lighten her up. Everything is good again.

Party. Party the night away. Party like you'll never get this chance again. Impress the right people and you won't have to worry about that anymore. This life will be yours for the taking. You will no

longer be a plus-one, entering through a side door. You will belong.
You will.

Ignore the hushed insistence that something is wrong. Keep dancing.

You are fine.
You are okay.

JULY

CHAPTER 8

A FEW DAYS BEFORE the Fourth of July, I came down with a cold. The sniffles started right before my family's weekly dinner—taco night with store-bought hard shells and ground turkey. But after enduring yet another Make Sure to Pack Up Your Room and Be a Good Daughter lecture from Leon over ice cream, my throat was sore and I was sneezing.

Ella whined when I told her the news but, not wanting to get sick herself, refused to see me until I got better.

"No offense, Bee," she told me over the phone, "but I literally *cannot* get sick right now. Roxanne is throwing a party on the Fourth. You understand, right?"

Of course I did. So I called out of work and passed the time in bed, watching Ella's life play out online rather than by her side. Annetta and I traded silly memes, and I managed to convince myself that the world wouldn't end just because I was missing out on a few parties.

Ella loved me. Nettie and I were good again. Everything was fine.

But on the Fourth of July, when I still didn't feel any better, I had changed my mind. Everything was *not* fine. I was missing out on everything. It took all my strength not to burst into tears when Ella video chatted me before she left for Roxanne's party.

"Is this cute?" she asked, twirling around in a white crochet dress that barely contained anything. She was gorgeous, and I wanted to die.

"Bee?" she asked. "What's wrong?"

"I'm missing out on everything," I cried. I hadn't taken a shower in two days, my hair was a mess, and I was sniffling nonstop. I felt pathetic, but I couldn't hold it in anymore. "I miss you."

Ella laughed. "It's only been a couple of days."

"I know," I said limply.

"When you feel better, I'm gonna kiss you all over." Then she ran back to her closet, and I was left staring at Nina lounging in a wedge of sunlight on the bed. I burrowed under my blankets, clenched my soft jersey sheets. They smelled like the laundry softener Mom used, artificial roses blooming in May.

"Nettie's not coming, either!" Ella called off-screen. "She said she has other plans. Did she tell you what they were?"

"No."

She reappeared, this time in an aqua sundress covered in daisies. "Must be another case of the Netties. She's been *so* weird lately."

"I like the other dress better."

"Riiight? Ugh, thanks, baby, you're the best." She started yanking it over her head when she stopped and stared at the screen. "Hey, Bee, I gotta go. Roxanne's calling me."

I mumbled goodbye, and she was gone like a dying sparkler, lighting up my screen one moment, leaving nothing but black the next. I pushed my phone away and cried into my raggedy T-shirt, imagining Ella looking gorgeous and perfect, talking to Roxanne, who was also gorgeous and perfect, and picturing the two of them on the deck of the

Bewitched looking gorgeous and perfect together. In a hot, jealous flash, I hated both of them so much.

There was a knock, and when I emerged from my blankets, Mom was leaning against my door, a plastic shopping bag dangling from her fingers.

"Hey, sweetie," she said, looking around my junky room. "How are you feeling?"

"Awful," I mumbled.

"I brought you some things." She stepped inside, dodging stacks of books and piles of clothes. She sat on the edge of my bed and handed me the bag. Inside were throat lozenges, cold medicine, and a bag of Sour Patch Kids.

A lump swelled in my throat. "Thanks, Mom."

"Figured you must really be sick since this is the longest you've been home in a while." She cracked a weak smile, but my throat tightened as I remembered how much I'd be missing tonight. The inside jokes I wouldn't get, how this was one less chance to impress Roxanne Garcia. She was going to find another right-hand woman all because my ass had to catch a cold.

"How about a movie?" Mom asked. "I have some time before my shift."

"No, thanks," I said, struggling to hold back tears.

"Well, do you need me to get you anything else? You haven't gotten a new book in a while. I could run by the store for you—"

"I'm okay."

I could feel her pausing, waiting for me to change my mind. I was such a bitch. When I met her sad green eyes, my heart dropped even more, and my tears finally unleashed.

"Oh, baby," she said, and suddenly I was twelve again, sobbing into the crook of her neck when the bullying was at its most relentless.

"What's going on?" she asked, her voice muffled in my curls.

"I'm missing out on everything," I cried. "There's this . . . this party tonight, and I won't *be* there and . . ." The rest of my sentence drowned in a wave of hiccups. I could hear myself, could hear how *ridiculous* I must have sounded, but my head was pounding too hard to care.

"It's just one party," Mom said, and I flinched.

"It's not just about the party," I argued, pulling away.

"Then what's it about?"

How? How could I explain to her that a party was never just a party? Not when it came to something as exclusive as the Serena Society. Returning to the group after sitting out a couple of wild nights meant playing catch-up. It was going to be a relay race fueled by inside jokes and *Remember when . . . ?* and drama I'd missed. Ella and Roxanne waiting impatiently for me to pass a baton that kept slipping through my fingers.

"I just need to be there," I said instead, wiping my tears in frustration.

Mom sighed. "You need to be *here*." She pointed to the bed with a small smile. "You need to be resting. I wish you cared about yourself half as much as you care about your friends."

I looked out the window, angry that the sun was so hot and bright while I was stuck inside this room.

"You just don't get it," I said.

CHERRY COKE SLURPEES

And how could she get it? My mom was a white woman from Wytheville, Virginia, who'd had no meaningful relationships with any Black people until she fell in love with my dad. They'd met when Mom was eighteen and on vacation in Virginia Beach with her family. Dad was working at an old-timey photo shop on the boardwalk, peddling the promise of once-in-a-lifetime memories to sunburnt tourists. He'd convinced Mom to dress up like a flapper from the 1920s. Perched on a saloon bar with strands of pearls draped around her throat, Mom said she fell for him when he was carefully adjusting fake dollar bills in her garter. He smiled up at her, brown face stamped with dimples, and said, "I know this money's fake, but you *do* look like a million bucks."

"Dad with the corny pickup lines," Leon joked when our parents first told us the story when we were kids.

Mom blushed, and I thought about how pretty she must've looked in that maroon fringed dress, smiling at Dad for the first time.

"Corny or not," Mom replied, "I fell in love immediately."

The rest of her family, however, was less than thrilled. "They're racist, horrible people," Mom always said whenever Leon and I asked curious questions about them. "They never approved of my relationship with your dad. But I didn't care. I've never cared that your father is Black. I fell in love with a man, and that was that."

She never cared that our father was Black. "He could've been Black, white, purple, or polka-dotted, and I still would've fallen for him," she always, *always* said. She never cared that Dad was Black, so in a lot of ways, it felt like she didn't care that Leon and I were, too. We were just "her babies." We weren't Black or biracial or mixed to her.

We were just . . . Leon and Blake.

And maybe that worked for a while. But we could only live in Mom's World for so long before stumbling headfirst into the Real World.

Leon had our father's help to shape him into a young biracial Black man. Dad took Leon to Black barbers for his haircuts, taught Leon his rights early in life in case he was ever confronted by police. When Leon expressed a desire to pursue aviation, Dad shared all the insider knowledge one needed to know when joining a field that was made up of mostly white men.

Me and Mom on the other hand . . . we were different. She never knew how to style my hair, so I spent most of my childhood with my curls in a tangled ponytail. When I expressed a love for reading, she handed me books that were *her* childhood favorites, like *Anne of Green Gables* and *The Boxcar Children*. She always turned away from uncomfortable conversations about race, leaning on the flimsy sentiment that the world would be better if people just loved one another.

Anytime I wanted to see a reflection of myself, I was the one doing the research. I was the one awake at one a.m. rewatching hair tutorials, tearful and frustrated when my curls didn't come out looking like the girls in the videos. I was the one wandering off in the bookstore in search of characters who looked like me. I always knew my mom loved me, but it wasn't until I became friends with Ella and Annetta that I realized a mother's love also required effort. And that was something I wasn't sure she had always given.

By my sophomore year, sleepovers at Ella's and Annetta's had started to replace my 7-Eleven nights with Mom. But the rare times the girls had other plans, Mom would coax me into keeping her company "for old time's sake."

The night before my sixteenth birthday was one of those nights. It was February and rainy and cold and miserable and we'd seen two customers in the span of an hour. Mom was reading one of her paperback romances, and I was engrossed in a dishy celebrity memoir. We'd been sipping on cherry Coke Slurpees and giggling at how red they'd made our mouths.

"You used the wrong ratio," I complained since she was the one who'd made them. I'd just gotten my braces, and Slurpees and mashed potatoes were the only things my sore mouth could handle. "It's supposed to be seventy percent Coke, thirty percent cherry."

She made a face as she took another sip. "It's the opposite. Always more cherry than Coke."

"You're just wrong," I said, and we laughed and went back to reading. The radio behind the counter was playing hits from the nineties, and when Mariah Carey's "Fantasy" came on, Mom started absentmindedly humming along.

I set my book down. "I didn't know you liked Mariah Carey."

"Oh, yeah," Mom said with a soft smile. "I used to love her, but my parents refused to buy me any of her CDs."

"Why?"

"Because they were racist, horrible people," Mom said with an eye roll. "Even when I tried telling them that Mariah was only half Black, they still wouldn't budge."

In an instant, it felt like all the air had been sucked out of the store. Mariah continued to belt high notes and the Slurpee machine turned over, but I was frozen in place, waiting for her to realize what she'd just said. *Only half Black.* I stared at her, and she repeated, "They were racist, horrible people." And then she went back to her book, and I went back to mine.

I stared at the words on the page, but none of them made any sense. *Only half.* As if Blackness needed to be diluted in order to be tolerated. If Mariah's skin had been darker, would my mom still have defended her music to my grandparents? What did she think about me? Leon? A white mother wasn't supposed to say things like that to her mixed kids, right?

Was I just being dramatic?

I never asked those questions, so I never got any answers. At a quarter till midnight, a sleek black Range Rover pulled into the parking lot. Seconds later, Ella and Annetta were spilling into the harsh lights of 7-Eleven, armed with sparklers and ready to celebrate my birthday. They were as gorgeous as two full moons in an otherwise empty sky, and I loved them for saving me from the blooming cloud of discomfort that was apparently only palpable to me.

"Thanks, Mrs. B.!" Ella called as she and Annetta dragged me away in a haze of perfume and hairspray.

"Be safe, girls," Mom said. And to me: "Happy birthday, baby."

In the car, Ella drove twenty miles over the speed limit even though she still only had a learner's permit. She wasn't set to turn sixteen for another few weeks, but her parents had already gifted her the keys to the Range Rover. I told Ella and Annetta what my mom said, immediately feeling better when they rolled their eyes and groaned in all the right places.

"I hate it when people act like Blackness is only acceptable in light-enough doses," Ella said. "Kiss *only half* of my ass, ma'am. Ugh, I'm sorry, Bee. Your mom is so hopelessly white."

"Fuck her," Annetta muttered. By then, her parents were in the midst of their nasty divorce, spurred by Mrs. Jones's recent move to New York. Any soft spots Annetta once held for mothers had been iced over and frozen solid.

Before we reached the Spencers', Annetta climbed in the back seat and tied a fuzzy purple scarf around my eyes. Then the two of them guided me inside and down a flight of stairs, their hands on my arms somehow electric and soft at the same time.

"Surprise!" they chorused when Ella whipped the scarf off. "Happy birthday, Bee!"

The Spencers' rec room was filled with glittery balloons, a bloated *1* and *6* bobbing front and center. A gold banner that read HAPPY BIRTH-DAY, BUMBLEBEE! in shimmery black paint hung on the wall, and cutouts of chunky bumblebees dangled from the ceiling.

A surprise party. Just for me.

We welcomed my sixteenth year with ruby grapefruit hard seltzers, courtesy of Ella's older sister Sophie. They tasted like summer in the middle of February. I felt so loved sandwiched between my girlfriend and best friend, giddy with the knowledge that I was now someone worthy of a surprise party. Before them, I'd never even been *invited* to a party, let alone had anyone go through the trouble of planning one for me.

"You're not 'only half' anything here," Ella told me that night as we sat in a triangle painting one another's nails. We were tipsy, so the manicures were messy, but we covered everything in sparkles, so who cared? "You are perfect and complete and we love you."

I started crying, which made an already emotional Annetta teary-eyed, and soon the three of us were bawling and laughing and we didn't exactly know why.

All I knew was that I loved them, and they loved me.

They *got* me.

They saw me whole.

CHAPTER 9

AFTER MOM LEFT, I spent the rest of the afternoon in bed, sniffling and scrolling on my phone. I was watching Ella's latest upload—a clip of her and Roxanne opening a bottle of champagne too quickly, the foam spilling out in white puffy bubbles—when Annetta texted.

> How are you feeling?

> Like shit.

> Want me to come over? I'll keep my distance 😊

> You not going to the grove?

> I'd rather take a long walk off a short pier.

I laughed and rolled over in bed. My room was turning goldenrod yellow as evening approached. The sun hadn't set, but fireworks were already whistling and crackling all over Winward Commons. Dad was flying and Mom had just left for work, so I was going to be alone all night. Of course I wanted Annetta to come over.

Annetta had seen me in worse states, but I still managed to peel myself out of bed and take a quick shower. I was brushing my teeth when she texted saying she was here. I threw on a pair of old mesh shorts and a loose tank top and went out to the parking lot barefoot to meet her.

She popped out of her car with a six-pack of something in one hand and a box of sparklers in the other.

"Happy Fireworks Day!" she said with a giggle. She was wearing a pinstripe button-up and a pair of khaki Bermuda shorts, hair slicked into a low bun.

"You just get out of a real estate convention?" I asked.

"That's a nice way of saying 'Hey, thank you so much for coming over and keeping me company.'" She started around the side of our building, sidestepping gaping trash cans.

"I'm just saying, you look very Chadley right now," I said, following her.

"Fuck you very much," she said, laughing.

We lived on the first floor, so we were one of the lucky units that had a backyard instead of a tiny balcony. Still, it wasn't much to look at. A slab of concrete and a couple of lawn chairs, the folding kind you're supposed to use for camping but we used for everything. Annetta grabbed one and dragged it to one end of the patio; I sat on the other. The sky was now tangerine and alive with the hiss-smoke-pop of illegal fireworks. Annetta rummaged in her backpack and pulled out a ball of yarn and a cheap plastic bucket from the dollar store.

"Here." She tossed the ball of yarn to me while holding one end, and it unraveled in a multicolored blur. I caught the ball and cracked up when she slipped a bottle into the bucket, looped the handle over the yarn, and sent it sailing toward me.

"You are amazing," I said, grabbing the bottle. To my disappointment, it was sparkling lemonade. Nonalcoholic.

"We've gotta get creative in times like these," she said. She motioned for me to send the bucket back. When I did, she refilled it with a blue raspberry Bomb Pop, two sparklers, and a tiny neon-green lighter and shoved it back down the yarn. We laughed and unwrapped the pops and ate them before they melted in the humidity.

"Why *are* you so dressed up?" I asked when I'd made it down to the rough wooden stick. She'd already finished hers and had snapped the stick in half. She tucked her bare feet underneath her and shrugged.

"I just . . . am."

"Nettie."

"What!"

"Come on."

She groaned and tilted her face to the sky.

"I went on a date," she admitted.

"Bitch! What! And you're just now telling me?"

"Chill out. It's *not* that big of a deal."

"I want to punch you right now." I picked up the bucket and punched it lightly on the side. "There!" I said as I sent it back down the yarn. "Consider that a punch from me!"

"See, this is why I didn't want to tell you. I knew you'd make a big deal out of it."

"Nettie, you *never* go on dates." She'd attended senior prom at her private Catholic school with a group of friends. "Who was it? Tell me everything."

Night was nearing, and the fireworks were ramping up. A pretty silver one exploded in a metallic waterfall directly over our heads. Annetta watched it until it faded into smoke.

"We matched on an app," she said. "And they sent me a nice message."

"Okay, okay," I said. "Tell me more."

"They're in college. Well, culinary school."

"Okay, Chef!"

She giggled and cracked open her sparkling lemonade. I did the same. It was tangy and sweet, perfect for a night like this.

"Can I at least get a name?" I asked.

She shook her head. "It feels too new. Like it'd be . . . bad luck saying it or something."

I nodded gently. This was new territory for us. I'd never seen Annetta talk this way about anyone. Like this person was a rare butterfly and she was afraid they were going to fly away before she could take a picture.

"What did y'all do?" I asked instead.

"We were going to walk along the beach," she said, making a face. "But we couldn't even find parking. Too crowded. So we went to Mount Trashmore, but it was packed there, too." She laughed, twisting the broken Bomb Pop stick pieces in her hands. "I was ready to give up, but they were . . . great. None of the hiccups bothered them at all. We ended up wandering around Target and grabbing a bunch of random stuff." She motioned to the Bomb Pops with a dreamy look in her eyes. I wanted to squeal, but I bottled it up so I didn't freak her out.

"We were driving past the TCC campus and noticed it was totally empty. So we found a quiet spot under a tree and talked for hours. Next thing I knew, the sun was going down."

"What time did y'all meet up?"

She smiled coyly. "Eleven. It was supposed to be a lunch date."

I screeched. "Nettie! And you left them to come over here?" When she nodded sheepishly, I squealed again. "That's almost *eight* hours."

"I know, I know!"

"How did these Bomb Pops not melt? You sure you're not dating a witch?"

"They had a cooler and ice packs!"

"Come on, preparation!" I cheered. She covered her eyes with her hands, and we screeched as a siren-loud firework popped in the distance.

"I'm so happy for you," I gushed. "When are you going to see them again?"

She shrugged. "Between work and this Serena crap, I dunno. But soon, hopefully."

We settled into our lawn chairs as the sky darkened and filled with fireworks. We set off our sparklers, circling letters and hearts, spelling out smoky messages only we could see. Annetta vaped, and I thought about Ella partying it up with Roxanne. But every time I got on my phone, Annetta threatened to punch me via the bucket.

"Just enjoy the night," she said. "Don't worry about what Ella is doing."

"I'm trying." I shoved my phone in my pocket. "I really want to get into Serena."

"You will."

"Not if I keep missing everything."

"If you don't get in because you were sick and had to sit out a few parties, then is this really an organization we should be joining?" A red firework burst, and Annetta's face glowed in its splendor.

"What happens if you and Ella get in and I don't?"

She blew out a hazy cloud of smoke. "That won't happen."

"It might."

"If they don't pick you, then I'm walking. I don't want to join without you."

"Your mom would kill you," I joked. The minute the words left my mouth, Annetta's face fell. She looked toward the scraggly bushes lining our back fence. It'd been so long since we *really* talked about Mrs. Jones. I had no idea if she knew the pledge process had even started.

"She wouldn't care," Annetta eventually said, fiddling with her vape.

"Have you talked to her lately?"

"She called last week. She wants me to visit her this summer."

"Are you gonna go?"

She shrugged, still not meeting my eyes.

"Hug for your thoughts?" I asked. I picked up the yarn, hugged the bucket, and sent it sailing her way.

She shook her head.

"Come on, Nettie. Talk to me."

Another firework, royal blue this time. It burst into a star before fading into a shower of sparkles. Annetta stared at it as she spoke.

"I feel like she abandoned me. I still don't understand how she could just ... leave. Parents shouldn't be allowed to do that."

I wished I could hug her for real. She looked so sad and small in the lawn chair, folded into herself, arms wrapped around her knees for protection.

"It's silly," Annetta said, "but this whole time I've been trying to get into Serena ..." She scrubbed a hand over her face. "Never mind."

"Come on, nothing you have to say is silly. What is it?"

"I want her to come back, okay?" She sighed. "If I get into Serena . . . maybe . . . she'll be proud of me."

"She will be."

"But that still won't be enough, right? It won't make her come back to Virginia. She has a whole new life in New York. I just thought . . . if she sees me following in her footsteps or something . . . she'll remember what she left behind. Maybe she'll come back."

My eyes welled at the sight of Annetta's tears, and my thoughts drifted to my own mom. She was only across town, but there was still an indescribable distance between us. Maybe in my own way, I understood Annetta's ache. And I knew there was nothing I could do to make it go away.

"I love you," I told her, wiping my tears. "And no matter what happens with Serena, your mom will be proud of you. She *is* proud of you. Even if she doesn't show it."

"Yeah," she said quietly, voice thick. She sniffled. "I love you, too."

"And even if everyone else in the whole world fails us, *we* got us, right? Me, you, and Ella." The thought of Ella sent a tremor through my chest, knowing she was lighting up a room I wasn't lucky enough to be in tonight. But I resisted the urge to pull out my phone. We were okay. We would be okay.

"We got us," Annetta said. We tipped our sparkling lemonades to the firework-streaked sky in a toast.

CHAPTER 10

AFTER A FEW DAYS, I was feeling better and life went back to normal. My return to the Spencers' house was marked with a delicious dinner of Mrs. Spencer's chicken adobo and veggie pancit. I reluctantly returned to work and endured lectures from Pleated Todd about how I had "lost" my Frank Peterson button.

After a long, disgustingly hot day, Ella, Annetta, and I were walking to the employee parking lot when a cherry-red BMW convertible slowed beside us. The car belonged to Josiah Winters in all his blond frosted-tipped-head glory.

"Hey, you sexy bitches," he said. "Get in."

"JoJo!" Ella squealed. She ran around the hood of the BMW and jumped into the passenger seat without even opening the door. She kissed him on the cheek, loud and sloppy. If it were anyone else, I would've been jealous, but Josiah and Ella had been friends since elementary school. He was also gayer than the three of us combined. Annetta and I climbed into the back seat and he grinned at us in his rearview. His teeth were unnaturally white.

"Whale, whale, whale," he said, stepping on the gas. We flew forward in a wave of laughter. "Where you hoes been hiding all summer? Haven't really seen you since Big Bad Bee's paint debacle."

I flushed, but Ella laughed. "We've been busy with secret clandestine activities," she said, fluttering her eyelashes.

"Oh, I *heard*. I ran into Roxanne the other day and she filled me in."

"So much for clandestine," Annetta said.

Josiah blew past the valet stand and headed down toward the docks. Dozens of shiny summer-white sailboats and yachts bobbed like bath toys in the late-afternoon sun.

"Oh, please! Roxanne's yacht is *literally* right next to mine. Y'all can't hide shit," he said. He parked in a spot reserved specifically for his family and cut the engine. "But you *can* come enjoy happy hour with me."

"We just got off work," I groaned. We were tired and grimy and smelled like chlorine.

"I'll let you raid my sisters' closet," Josiah offered.

Ella, Annetta, and I exchanged a look. Josiah's older twin sisters were in the fashion industry. They were also expert thrifters, picking up the coolest clothes all around the world. Their closet was simply to die for.

"Y'all bitches coming?" Josiah asked.

The three of us scrambled for our door handles, exhaustion forgotten.

Josiah's family's yacht, *Byte Me*, reeked of new money. His parents had made a fortune in the tech boom and now owned a lucrative software company. They loved gadgets, so *Byte Me* was tricked out with every kind imaginable. Holographic displays that showed the weather and sailing conditions, televisions that morphed into beautiful art when not in use, voice-activated kitchen appliances. Ella, Annetta, and I didn't care about any of that, though.

We cared about the clothes.

"I still cannot believe this is their *overflow* closet," Annetta said.

We were in Jessica and Jillian's room. More specifically, their walk-in closet that was nearly the size of a studio apartment. We'd showered the pool away, slathered ourselves in Mrs. Winters's expensive serums and creams, and were now wrapped in waffle-knit towels, gaping at racks of clothes. Jessica and Jillian had eclectic taste, so everything from ten-thousand-dollar designer frocks to used overalls with patches sewed on the knees were at our fingertips.

"Hurry the fuck up!" Josiah's voice boomed through a hidden speaker. "I made daiquiris!"

"Calm your tits!" Annetta yelled. Then, to us: "You think he heard that?"

"Yes, I did." Josiah's voice oozed like syrup from the ceiling, and it was like God was speaking to us . . . if God was a gay white boy with frosted blond tips.

Ella let her towel fall as she grabbed a gorgeous royal-blue dress that looked like it cost my entire summer's salary. "How I wish I could wear you," she moaned, and I remembered the Serena Society's unofficial no blue rule.

"Well put *something* on so I don't have to stare at your damn bush anymore," Annetta said.

"Nice to know you're looking, Nettie," Ella purred.

I laughed, butted between them. "Let's just hurry up so we can—" I was going to say *go drink* but paused when I saw Annetta's face, remembered her biting accusation—

You have a fucking drinking problem.

"Enjoy the sunset," I said.

Twenty minutes later we headed for the top deck, feeling and looking gorgeous. Ella had selected a white tennis skirt that showed off her long brown legs and a vintage oversized maroon Harvard sweater; she looked like the prep school girl of my dreams. Annetta had said, "What the hell?" and decided to go for a formal three-piece suit. We'd called her dapper as we fussed over the sequined bow tie, making sure it didn't look wonky. And I had unearthed a floor-length ballet-slipper-pink dress that glided over my skin like water. Josiah whistled when we joined him at the bar.

"Ok*aaaaaaaay*! I'm loving the variety, loving the variety." Based on his red lips, he'd already helped himself to a daquiri. He looked Ella up and down like the catty bitch he was. "*Gossip Girl* extra . . ." He moved to Annetta: "Little Janelle Monáe . . ." Pointed at me. "And always the bridesmaid, never the bride."

"I *know* you ain't talking with your wannabe NSYNC Justin Timberlake ramen-noodle-head," Annetta shot back, and we all bust out laughing and everything was so good.

Josiah blended up strawberry daiquiris and topped them off with a thick rum floater. Annetta gave me A Look when the four of us cheers'd, but she thankfully didn't say anything. Soon we were dancing around in our bare feet and singing at the top of our lungs.

By the time the sun slipped behind the club and the globe lights flickered on, we were on daiquiri number three and our throats hurt from singing so loud. We collapsed in a knotted heap on the Winters's plush L-shaped sectional, Ella's head on my stomach, my feet in Annetta's lap, Josiah upside down and spread-eagle with his hairy toes near my face.

"Oh my GOD," Josiah scream-slurred, "I cannot believe I forgot to tell y'all about what happened with Mr. Peterson. It's the most ridiculous thing I've ever heard."

"More ridiculous than getting banned from Ocean Breeze for trying to have sex in the wave pool?" Annetta asked.

"That happened ONE time!"

"Yeah," I said slowly. "*Because you got banned*—"

"Hurry up and tell us, JoJo!" Ella interrupted. Her voice was deeper than usual. I wanted to bottle it up and drink it down, use it as an elixir to never worry about anything ever again.

"So him and the missus threw a party last night, right? My parents went. Tell! Me! Why!"—Josiah clapped between each word—"One of his mistresses showed up! And cussed him out in front of his *whole* family!"

"You lying!" Ella and I screamed.

"Swear on my ramen noodle hair," Josiah said, and Annetta laughed into her cup.

Josiah recounted the entire dramatic affair, and we drank and gasped and lost our shit. When the story was over, Ella curled a finger, beckoned me close for a kiss.

"See, baby?" she mumbled against my lips. "A little paint on his yacht was the *least* of his worries."

"You were right," I said, because she was, always.

After another round of drinks, Ella received a text that instructed us to look up. One slip over, Roxanne was waving from the top deck of the *Bewitched*, a cluster of girls behind her.

"Come over!" Roxanne called.

"Okay!" Ella yelled gleefully. She immediately got ready to leave, and I was about to follow suit when I noticed dread creeping across Annetta's face.

"You okay?" I asked. I was tipsy, but I was okay. See? I was being a good friend. I could handle my alcohol.

Ella slung her arms around our necks. "Come on, boos. Y'all missed the last bonding session. We should go."

"I'm tired," Annetta said. "We have to work tomorrow."

"And what do you think your mom would say if she heard you saying you were too tired for the Serena Society?" Ella prodded.

Something in Annetta shifted. She got a faraway look in her eyes, and I wondered if she was thinking about our Fourth of July heart-to-heart. How the thought of her mom not being proud of her made us both cry.

"Fine," Annetta relented, and Ella whooped and kissed our cheeks.

We said goodbye to Josiah, not that he noticed—he was too busy texting one of his playthings, trying to convince him to come over. We didn't have shoes besides the flip-flops and sneakers we'd worn to work, so we walked over to the *Bewitched* barefoot, stepping carefully to avoid splinters from the wooden dock. Roxanne greeted us wearing only a shimmering orange thong bikini, lazily gripping a bottle of white wine by the neck.

"Hi, my beauties!" Roxanne exclaimed. She welcomed us aboard, air-kissed our cheeks. She smelled like weed and lilies. She led us up to the top deck, where a Jacuzzi was bubbling and music was bumping. Half of the Serena hopefuls were also there. Keiko glared at me from the Jacuzzi.

"Did I miss the memo? Is there a Serena thing going on tonight?" Ella asked, slightly panicked. Roxanne looped an arm through hers, kissed her cheek again.

"No, no," Roxanne said, "this is just a chill hangout. I wanted to get to know some of the girls outside of the process. It can get so stuffy, you know?"

Envy seeped into my heart, but we couldn't really be mad since we started partying with Roxanne weeks before pledging began. So I forced a smile and waved to the girls on the deck, even Keiko.

Roxanne poured us glasses of sangria from a huge, sweating urn sprinkled with thick slices of orange and diced apples. Annetta and I squeezed on a chair together, but Ella remained by Roxanne's side in the center of the room. I watched them adjust each other's hair, pet each other like little cats. I drank my sangria.

"Hey," Annetta said in my ear. "You okay?"

"I'm fine."

"You sure?"

Roxanne pulled some other girl behind the bar to help her mix drinks and it felt like I'd been molly whopped. My absence at the Fourth of July party had finally come back to haunt me; I'd lost my place as Roxanne's right-hand woman.

"Blake."

"What?" I hissed, turning to Annetta. She raised her thick brows and looked at my drink, saying everything without saying anything.

"Not tonight," I said, low enough so only she could hear. "Please, let's just have fun."

We drank and danced and drank and introduced ourselves to the other girls again and drank and danced and drank. After an hour or so, the group moved to the main lounge because the top deck was getting too crowded. Near midnight, Alice arrived in black combat boots and shredded jeans, bringing along another group of Serena hopefuls. There was Khadija and Eden and Marisol and Zahra and Corinne and Quinn and I was on my fourth glass of sangria, so I immediately forgot who was who and mixed them all up. Someone suggested a game of Truth or Dare—Marisol, I think. Alice told us that it was a horrible idea considering how drunk we all were, so naturally that made us want to play more. We pushed aside the dining room table and gathered in a lopsided circle on the floor.

"Truth or Dare?" a petite Black girl with locs asked Roxanne.

Roxanne was sitting across the circle next to Ella. They'd been giggling to each other in their own little universe all damn night. I wanted to pull Ella away like a tide, tell her to pay attention to *me*, but I was stuck next to Annetta.

"Dare," Roxanne said confidently.

"I dare you to kiss someone in this room," Marisol said.

My chest tightened like sunburnt skin. I took another sip from my cup; the sangria had run out, so I'd switched to rum and Coke. I was pacing myself. I was chill.

"Okay," Roxanne said, and her lips twisted as she surveyed the circle, wondering who was worthy. Her eyes skipped right over me, and it felt like a punishment, yet another reminder that I was no longer her favorite. She kept going, considering each girl. I held my breath, hoping to God that her gaze would settle on anyone but . . .

Ella. Of course.

"What do you say?" Roxanne asked Ella, and I saw red.

Ella grinned. "Come here," she said, and their lips met like magnets on stainless steel. Everyone burst into nervous giggles and *Awww yeah*s, and Ella, never one to disappoint an audience, deepened the kiss. I watched in slow horror as their wet tongues collided.

"All right, that's enough," Alice said. She tugged Roxanne's shoulder to break the kiss.

Roxanne and Ella parted, and I wanted to slap the shit out of both of them. I boiled with humiliated jealousy. I was pissed at Ella for looking like she liked it so much. Infuriated at Roxanne for picking her in the first place. And, at the core of it all, mad at myself for missing the Fourth of July party. Maybe if I'd been there, I would still be Roxanne's favorite. Maybe she would've kissed me instead.

As if sensing my thoughts, Roxanne looked in my direction with a triumphant grin. I wanted to bash her pretty little head through a window. I chugged my drink till it was empty, till my chest didn't feel so tight.

"Don't be jealous, Bee," Ella called from across the circle, causing another round of giggles.

"I'm not," I lied. "I'm more upset about my drink being empty." That earned a louder laugh, and to prove my point, I rattled my empty glass. "Time for a refill."

The game continued as I headed to the kitchen in a white-hot daze. My hands shook as I yanked open the freezer.

Fuck them. Fuck them, I hate them all.

I hated Ella for enjoying the kiss and I hated Roxanne for picking her and I hated Marisol for suggesting the game in the first place. *Fuck Roxanne, Ella, and Marisol.* I angrily grabbed a frosty bottle of Bacardi and twisted the cap off, spouting curses to Roxanne, Ella, and Marisol so fast that their names began to blur.

Roxanne.

Ella.

Marisol.

Roxanne, Ella, Marisol.

RoxanneEllaMarisol

RoxEllasol—

"Hey," a low voice said behind me. It was Alice, tossing a beer bottle into the recycling bin. "You good?"

I nodded. Poured myself some rum.

She rounded the kitchen island and leaned against the refrigerator. We were roughly the same height, but when I looked at her, it felt as if she was peering down at me.

"I'm just asking because you don't seem good," she said. "In fact, you seem kind of pissed."

I sighed. "Oh, look, it's Annetta 2.0."

"What does that mean?"

"Forget it." I slammed the freezer and sipped my rum. Alice was blocking the Coke in the fridge, but whatever, I could go without it. "What do you want?"

"Not another repeat of the first task, that's for sure. Considering you passed by the skin of your teeth," she said. I froze, glass to my lips. "I know you didn't help with the puzzle. You were completely trashed before it even began."

"So what?" I hissed. In the living room, music abruptly switched on. Apparently Truth or Dare was over. "You act like I was the only one drinking."

"You don't remember me, do you?" Alice asked.

I searched her face. Hard brown eyes, a gleaming septum piercing. A scar on her chin she'd tried to cover with makeup. She was beautiful, but I didn't recognize her.

"What are you talking about?" I asked.

"Winward Commons," she said, naming the apartment complex I'd lived in my entire life. "I lived two buildings down from you. I was one grade below Leon. We all rode the same bus."

My heart dropped. *No.*

"I remember you in middle school," Alice continued, "and I remember how quiet you were—"

No.

Alice looked over her shoulder at the crowd of girls in the living room. They were drunk and screaming along to music, but my world was muted.

"Me and you, we're not like the rest of these girls," Alice said. "We didn't grow up with wealth. It's different coming from a family where everything isn't handed to you. I try to look out for girls like us."

My heart skipped a beat. *Girls like us.* Maybe she was talking about girls who grew up in Winward Commons or girls who took the bus to school or girls who'd never flown first-class. But I didn't hear that. All I heard was *I remember you in middle school* and I instantly was *that* girl again. Twelve-year-old Blake. Bigfoot Brenner. A girl who couldn't go one class without shouldering the weight of classmates' taunts and a girl who had terrible fashion sense and crooked teeth and bad hair. A girl who felt so lonely sometimes she wished her shadow had a mouth, just so she'd have someone to talk to.

Is that who Alice saw when she looked at me closely? Not the girl I'd fought *so* hard to become. But Little Blake waiting for the bus in Winward Commons? I thought I'd left her behind. I straightened my teeth with two painful years of braces. I discovered curly hair products and the wonders of a diffuser. I had a girlfriend, I could hold conversations, I had *friends*. I wasn't Little Blake anymore.

I reeled away. My hands could not stop shaking. "Why are you telling me this?" I asked. "I thought we were just having fun."

Her face clouded over. "You know these parties are about more than just having fun," she said. My thoughts drifted to the first task and the girls in blue who didn't even make it past introductions.

"You're trying to impress Roxanne, I get it," she said. "But I think

I should remind you that as the vice president, I also have a say in who gets in. Roxanne and I don't have the same set of standards."

My hands trembled as I met Alice's eyes. She felt so similar to Annetta, telling me to *watch myself* around Todd. Leon, telling me to *show up* for my parents. Like I was a child who constantly needed minding. In the living room, Ella's melodic laughter rang out above the music, and my heart fluttered before I remembered I was mad at her. I was so *pissed* and shaking and I had no idea what to do with myself, but unleashing my temper on Alice didn't seem like the wisest choice. I needed to chill out.

"I'm sorry," I said weakly.

"Don't apologize now," Alice said. "Say what you have to say."

I sipped my drink until there was nothing left but ice. The rum warmed my stomach and melted my anger. I looked Alice directly in the eyes, determined.

"I want Serena more than anything. I'm just doing what I have to do to make it to the end. I don't want to be a girl like *us*," I said. Alice's face remained cool. "I want to be a girl like them." Her gaze followed mine to the blur of beautiful bodies in the living room.

"I'm sorry to hear that," Alice said. She walked away without looking back, and I felt like I failed yet another test.

I drank and drank and drank, waiting to feel good but that feeling never arrived. Instead, I became a green-eyed monster, hungry for Ella's attention. Starved because she never gave it. I sulked in the corner and thought about what Alice said—

I'm sorry to hear that.

I drank and drank and drank and

Outside. Late. Heat. Annetta. Her arm around my shoulder.

"Let's go."

                                    You. Ruin. Everything.
          You fucking loser, you will never get into Serena Society.
          Roxanne hates you, now Alice hates you, and it's all. Your. Fault.
"Stop! Blake, I hate when you talk like that, please!"

"Did you *see* Roxanne and *Ellaaaaaa*. What are they, in *loooooove?*"

Then it was morning.

CHAPTER 11

WHEN I WOKE UP, the world was spinning.

I wasn't in Ella's bedroom. I knew the weight of Ella's body and the feel of her silk pillowcases and the sound of Nina's gentle purrs. None of those were present.

When I finally mustered the strength to sit up, I realized I was in Annetta's room. Next to me, Annetta was sleeping peacefully, hair covered with a satin bonnet.

I snuck out of bed and crossed the room in wobbly strides. Annetta's bedroom was the opposite of Ella's. It was simple and neat, everything chrome and silver and black. Shelves lined with nonfiction books about everything from astrophysics to old Hollywood floated on the walls. Sage and pine candles decorated the windowsills.

My feet got tangled up in something by her bathroom door, and I realized it was the baby-pink dress I'd been wearing last night. Now I only had on my lace bra and cotton underwear.

I barely made it to the toilet before I vomited. With each heave, the night came back in blurry, stuttering flashes.

Alice, in the kitchen. *I'm sorry to hear that.*

Flash.

Roxanne and Ella grinding in a tangle of red and brown hair, brown limbs, stiletto nails.

Flash.

A splintering crack.

Flash.

Tears.

Flash.

There was nothing left to throw up, but I couldn't move. I slumped next to the toilet, stared at the ceiling, willed the world to slow. I didn't know what time it was, but I could hear the coo of mourning doves through the window above the sink. It was the only birdcall I recognized because my ninth-grade science teacher once said it sounded like they were missing someone, and I'd always thought that was so sad.

I closed my eyes, and the next thing I knew, Annetta was there, helping me up.

"Easy," she said. Her hands were warm. I lifted to my feet, slow, afraid I was going to throw up again.

She got me back in bed. The alarm on her nightstand told me it was just before eight. She handed me a glass of water and I took a shaky sip.

"What happened last night?" I managed to ask.

She perched on the edge of her bed. "Oh, let's see. You got drunk off your ass and wanted to fight Roxanne and Ella because of the kiss."

"What?"

"Ella begged me to get you out of there before you got too sloppy. And thank God I did because in the car you were *wilding*. Talking 'bout how you hate Ella and Roxanne and Marisol." She cocked her head. "By the way, what the hell did Marisol do?"

I fell back against her pillows. *Fuck*. This was not good.

"You also destroyed your phone." Annetta handed me something off the nightstand. It was my phone, screen shattered and spidering into a million pieces. I tried turning it on, but it was dead.

"You dropped it on the dock and accidently stepped on it," Annetta said. "Then when you picked it up, you dropped it *again*, and it fell into the water. You almost jumped in after it, but I managed to grab it before it sank."

I didn't remember any of that. Tears blurred my vision.

You're so pathetic. You can't just handle your alcohol like a normal person, can you? Why can't you be a happy drunk? A funny one? Why didn't you stop before you got out of control?

"I had plans to grab breakfast this morning," Annetta said from inside her closet. "You can come with me or stay here and walk to work. Your choice."

I didn't want to face the daylight. I wanted to stay in bed and feel sorry for myself, maybe call out of work. Screw the Snack Attack Shack. Screw Todd.

But then I thought of Ella, perched in her lifeguard chair. Was she mad at me for how I acted last night? Was she with Roxanne? Did they spend the night together?

When I opened my eyes, Annetta was already dressed in baggy cargo shorts and a forest-green T-shirt with JAMESWELL across the chest.

"I'm leaving in ten," she said, slipping her bonnet off.

The only thing worse than facing the world would be staying in bed and letting my thoughts consume me. Plus, I *was* hungry. So I forced myself up, wincing when Annetta threw open the curtains.

In the car, I used Annetta's phone to text Ella. She didn't immediately respond, so I of course imagined her in Roxanne's bed, their limbs braided, laughing at how annoying and drunk I'd been last night. Her last upload was a selfie with Josiah, their cheeks red from rum, a full six-teen hours ago—anything could've happened since. I handed Annetta her phone back before my anxiety got the best of me.

Sugar Mama Café was in a strip mall near the oceanfront, wedged between a laundromat and a nail salon. Annetta parked and turned to me with a serious face.

"This is where Xan works," she said.

"Xan?" I racked my brain, going down the list of people we knew from Crystal Grove. Then I noticed the anxious tremble in her hands and remembered the Fourth of July date, the one that had her smiling like a goofball all night. "*Ohhhhhh. Xaaaan.*"

"See, this is why I didn't want to bring you. You don't know how to act."

"So why did you bring me?" I batted my eyelashes.

"Because you were there and I'm nervous as fuck, okay?" She whipped out her vape and inhaled, released the sweet smoke slowly. "I've been telling them I'm gonna stop by for breakfast one day."

"Are you sure you want me here? I could get lost." I spotted Perk-U-Later across the parking lot; I could wait there. A huge iced mocha sounded divine.

"No, I want you to come. You can be my buffer in case shit starts to get awkward." She shot me A Look. "It's the least you could do after I took care of your drunk ass all night."

I held my hands up. "I am here for your buffering services."

The moment Annetta and I stepped inside the café, I started drool-ing at the aroma of cinnamon and coffee beans and freshly baked bread. Old school R&B pulsed through the speakers, and nearly every table was filled with people working on their computers or hunched over books. I immediately started hunting for the mysterious Xan, but there was only a tall Black woman with a crown full of silver locs behind the counter, and she was old enough to be our mom. She was swaying her hips to the music while sorting through the cash register.

"Welcome to Sugar Mama!" the woman sang. Her yellow linen dress was covered in pink hearts. She was a burst of sunshine. "What can I get you?"

Annetta studied the list of specials. The woman didn't stop dancing, and a smile bloomed on my cheeks.

"Aye," she said with a wink. "You like this song?"

"Love it."

"So come on, then. Dance." She shook her hips harder and I laughed, protested gently. "No coffee until you bust a move!" the woman threatened, and that changed everything, so I half-heartedly shimmied my shoulders.

"CeeCee! Are you forcing patrons to dance in exchange for service again?" a voice called from the kitchen.

"You never let me have any fun," CeeCee huffed.

The kitchen door swung open, and even if Annetta didn't stiffen next to me, I would've immediately known that this person was Xan. Xan was a cool name, a chill name, and with their oversized tortoise-shell glasses and buzzcut and easy smile, this person was undoubtedly a Xan.

"Hey," Xan said breathlessly, grinning at Annetta.

"Hey," Annetta said.

They smiled at each other for a long beat. It was as if no one else in the café existed. The glass display case full of muffins and pastries could've spontaneously shattered, and they would've just kept on cheesing.

"You not gonna introduce us?" CeeCee asked, nudging Xan in the ribs. They had the same almond-brown eyes and wide noses. They must've been family.

"Oh, uh, Auntie CeeCee, this is AJ. AJ, this is my aunt CeeCee."

I glanced at Annetta. *AJ?* Since she was apparently too stunned to speak, I limply waved, hoping to hurry the intro along. I needed some damn coffee.

"I'm Blake."

"Nice to meet you, Blake and AJ," CeeCee said with a warm smile. "What can I get you?"

Annetta's voice returned, and she ordered a flat white and a slice of banana bread. I was desperately trying to bat away a hangover, so I ordered the biggest hazelnut iced coffee on the menu and a double bacon, egg, and cheese croissant.

In a quiet corner of the café, we settled on a worn couch nestled between a bookshelf overflowing with board games and a towering monstera plant. Annetta wasn't making eye contact, so I tapped her knee.

"So. AJ?"

"I'm just . . . trying it out," she mumbled.

"I like it."

"Yeah?"

"Yeah. You want me to call you AJ now?" I asked.

She shook her head. "Not yet. I dunno. It's silly."

"What's silly?"

She didn't get to answer before CeeCee appeared with our drinks. We thanked her and she sashayed away, singing at the top of her lungs.

"'*I WANNA BE DOWN!*'" CeeCee sang, then pointed at a white dude on his laptop. "You! Sir! Do you wanna be down?"

"I'm in love with her," I said. Annetta giggled into her cup.

"Don't tell Ella that."

"Like she can talk," I replied, and my anger from last night simmered again when I thought of her lips on Roxanne's, Roxanne's hand in her hair. "Be honest with me. Am I wrong for being mad?"

Annetta shook her head. "I would've been upset, too."

"Thank you! I don't understand why Alice was giving me such a hard time last night. She was trying to have this whole confrontation in the kitchen."

"What did she say?"

I sipped my coffee. "I don't know, it was so ridiculous. Did I say anything bad to Ella or Roxanne?"

"You were mostly just fuming in the corner," Annetta said. "Until we left. Then you ranted about loyalty until I was able to get your ass to sleep."

My face warmed. "I'm sorry."

Annetta set her drink on the coffee table. Her brown eyes were so sad, so worried.

"I'm saying this because I love you, Blake. I think you need to cut back on the drinking."

Angry tears pooled my vision. They were hot and sudden, full of shame and fury. "What are you talking about? I'm *fine*. I told you I'm fine."

"You don't seem fine to me. Blake, you say *really* cruel things when you're drunk. Like you're a loser and you hate yourself." She inhaled, like whatever she had to say was going to hurt. "And I don't think being around Ella helps. She doesn't see what I see. Or she's just ignoring it."

"One slice of banana bread and a Sugar Mama sammich!" a voice interrupted. Then, quietly: "Oh. Is . . . everything all right?"

I looked up through my tears to see Xan setting two ceramic plates on the coffee table.

"We're fine," Annetta said, and I wanted to scream, *LIAR!* Apparently, I wasn't fine.

"I can come back," Xan said quickly.

"No, stay," Annetta said. Then, almost as an afterthought, added, "If that's okay with Blake."

"It's fine," I mumbled. I struggled to shove my humiliation down. It was easier when I actually looked at Xan's warm brown face. Their smile was as gentle as a hug, and I immediately felt more at ease. "I just . . . had a rough night."

"I know all about those." Xan sat in a cushy armchair across from us. There was a smudge of flour near their ear, and that made me smile.

Annetta and I dug into our food. The croissant was fluffy and flaky, maple bacon seasoned to perfection. Annetta gave me a corner of her banana bread and we moaned as we chewed, much to Xan's amusement. At first, Xan and Annetta danced around topics like the weather and weekend plans. But there was an obvious chemistry between them, electric and sparkling.

After fifteen minutes, Xan reluctantly rose to return to work. They shook my hand, and I liked how old-school and polite it was.

"It was really nice to meet you," Xan said. "I hope your day gets better."

"Thank you." I bit back a grin when they hugged Annetta.

"Say bye before you leave," they told her.

Annetta nodded, and we watched them walk away, their cute butt plump in black jeans.

"I like them," I said, slurping the remainder of my iced coffee.

"Me too." She looked at me, and any hope that she'd drop our earlier conversation was doused by the sad, tired look in her eyes. I didn't want to talk about drinking or my behavior, but I was trapped. She was my ride to work, and it'd be impossible to avoid her during our shift inside the suffocating Snack Attack Shack. So I set my cup on the coffee table and leaned back against the couch. Stuck my arms out like *let me have it*.

"I think you should take a break from drinking," she said.

"What did you mean with that Ella comment?" I asked.

"Not you immediately deflecting."

"I'm not! I'm just trying to figure out what you meant by Ella doesn't see what you see."

"It means . . ." She hesitated.

"Nettie?"

"It means I care about you enough to recognize patterns. You drink and you're mean to yourself. You drink and you don't know how to stop. Either Ella doesn't see that or she doesn't care," Annetta said. "Look, Bee, I know we've all had our fair share of wild nights, but ever since we started partying with Roxanne, your drinking has spiraled out of control. And if being around those girls is what makes you act this way, then I don't know if it's what's best for you. What's best for *us*."

A lump swelled in my throat again. *No.* "What are you talking about? What about . . . ?" Everything. College. The society. It was supposed to be the three of us, together forever. Why was she trying to ruin everything?

"Do you really want to spend the next four years like last night? Begging for Ella's attention like a sad, drunk puppy?"

"I do not—"

"You do," she interrupted. "And frankly, I'm tired of being the one holding your leash."

I didn't know whether to be angry or embarrassed or hurt, so I settled for all three. "What the fuck is your problem?" I hissed. "Holding my *leash*? I didn't realize I was such a burden."

"Every night is the same. We drink, Ella kisses up to Roxanne, you get all mopey and whiny, and I'm the one cleaning up the mess." She shook her head. "My mom always talked about Serena like it changed her life, but that's hard to believe when all we've done is party on Roxanne's yacht all summer."

The walls of the café were closing in on me. I stood, shoving my sunglasses over my eyes to hide the angry tears threatening to spill. I walked to the front doors with my head down, somehow managing a half-hearted wave to CeeCee before stumbling into too-bright sunlight.

In the parking lot, I paced. I thought about calling a rideshare to work before remembering my phone was useless. Annetta's words ran on a loop, and they hurt so much I couldn't see straight. Any relief the coffee had on my hangover receded, and by the time Annetta joined me outside, I was dizzy and deflated.

She unlocked her Mini Cooper, and we got inside. I fiddled with the air vent, my heart pounding overtime and desperate for something to hold on to.

"I'm sorry," she finally said. "I was harsh. All of this has been on my chest for a while."

"We're supposed to be friends forever," I said quietly.

I still couldn't look at her, but I heard the tremble in her voice.

"I thought so, too. But this doesn't feel good, Blake. Friends don't treat each other like Ella treats us."

"What are you *talking* about?"

"Do you remember when she slapped me last summer?" Annetta asked.

It took me a moment, but when the memory resurfaced, my heart dropped. "That was just a game, Nettie."

"To y'all. It was a game to *y'all*."

I finally mustered the strength to look at her, and she was my best friend and a stranger at the same time. She looked older. Tired. Our anger was stifling, and the air conditioner wasn't cooling anything. I rolled down the window, but the air was stagnant and hot outside, too.

"She apologized for that," I finally said. "We both did."

"*Did* she?" Annetta asked. "God, Blake, it's more than that. Look at us. All Ella cares about is getting into Serena. Partying every night is getting old."

"Then what do you want us to do? Play chess on Friday nights? Be in bed by eight?"

"I don't know. I just feel like you're forming some bad habits and I'm the only one who cares."

"I care!" I yelled. "I do. This is just pledging! Things will be better once we're finally in."

"What if they're not?" she snapped. "What if we get in and nothing changes? Or it gets worse? I'm not going to spend the next four years of college watching you get shit-faced every weekend."

"How is my drinking any different from your vaping?" I shot back. "I sit in clouds of smoke every day and I don't give you shit for it."

She hesitated. "That's . . . different. It helps my anxiety."

"And drinking helps mine," I said. I crossed my arms across my chest, shot her a look of defiant triumph. She responded with her own stern expression. She looked just like her mother, cutting into your scheduled programming to drop breaking news.

"Fine," she said. "You stop drinking and I stop vaping. At least until we get through the pledge process."

I was stunned silent. I was sure pulling out the vaping card would get her off my back, but no.

"Please," she said. "Blake, please. I can't keep doing this."

My mouth dried. I couldn't imagine it. This thing she was asking, it felt impossible. I needed alcohol. I needed it like thirsty crops after a drought. How would I douse my anxiety without it? How could I prove that I belonged in the society if I wasn't the life of the party? How could I transform into Big Bad Bee if I was sober? I couldn't picture myself clutching a club soda while the rest of the Serena pledges downed shots of tequila.

But I also couldn't picture losing Annetta. And she was right in front of me, hopeful and waiting for my answer.

"Okay," I said. "Deal. I won't drink."

"You promise?"

I nodded, and everything inside me curdled like rotten milk.

LEMON DROP

If there was a holiday the members of the Crystal Grove Golf and Yacht Club enjoyed more than the Fourth of July, it was Labor Day. It was the last official weekend of summer, the dying days of the pool. Everyone wanted to close the season with a bang. And the Labor Day before senior year, Annetta, Ella, and I did just that at one of Josiah's infamous parties on his yacht, *Byte Me.*

Annetta had finally started coming around again after her parents' divorce was finalized. For months, it'd been nearly impossible to get ahold of her. She dodged our texts and calls, kept her curtains closed when we came over. She'd abandoned social media. But somehow, we'd gotten her out of the house for the last party of the summer.

Josiah taught us how to make lemon drops and we were instantly obsessed with the tangy mix of vodka, lemon juice, and triple sec.

"We're cosmopolitan girls," he announced, and we held our martini glasses up in toast, lemon wheels teetering dangerously on the rims.

"To Annetta!" I said, catching her eye across the circle. I'd missed her so much.

"To Annetta!" Ella and Josiah echoed, and Annetta laughed and said, "I missed y'all."

We toasted to the beginning of senior year, which led to toasting just because. We drank lemon drops, and they were so sweet and addicting that we didn't realize how easily we'd skidded from tipsy to drunk. Everything was good again.

For a little while, at least.

Halfway through the night, Ella and I were sitting on the top deck railing, balancing like drunken clowns. Annetta scolded us, told us to come down.

"'*Get down*,'" Ella mocked. "Glad to have you back, Nervous Nettie!"

I remembered laughing with Ella. I remembered Annetta's face clouding over. We climbed down when Josiah suggested a game of Truth or Dare, and we all know how well *that* game goes over. But Annetta must've been grateful that Ella and I were no longer in danger of injuring ourselves because she agreed to play. We squeezed into the hot tub with Josiah and a couple of guys from work. We ran out of lemon juice, so we switched to screwdrivers. As the vodka flowed, secrets were revealed, kisses were swapped, dares were dealt.

"I dare," Josiah started deviously, "Annetta to slap Ella."

There was a roar of protest from Annetta and another server. "Why would I do that?" Annetta kept asking.

"You're being dramatic," Ella said, sitting forward in the frothy bubbles. "It's just a game. Come on, Nettie. Hit me."

Annetta refused. "I don't play games like that."

"You don't even register pain when you're this drunk," I said loudly. To demonstrate my point, I insisted Josiah slap me. When he did, stars sparked and twinkled. The next morning, I'd have a bruised, aching cheek, but that night I was happy, happy, so happy, and ready to keep the party going. "See? It's fine!"

Annetta still refused.

"Oh my God! Here!" Ella leaned across the hot tub and slapped Annetta so hard her entire head snapped to the left. Everyone burst into laughter as Annetta brought a hand to her cheek.

"Are you okay?" I asked once I saw the tears in her eyes.

"Awww, babe, I'm sorry," Ella said, attempting to wrap Annetta in a hug. "It didn't hurt that bad, did it?"

"Fuck you," Annetta said. Which sent Ella and Josiah into another round of giggles. When Annetta climbed out of the hot tub and ran inside to grab her clothes, no one followed her. I didn't follow her. I stayed with Ella.

"She's such a drama queen," Ella said with a sigh.

I kept waiting for Annetta to come back to the party, but she never did. It would take weeks for her to forgive us, and only when we kept annoying her and showing up at her house with her favorite maple bacon doughnuts. Our relationship was never really the same after that. Something shifted, so slight that you would only notice if you were truly looking. Like how a tree sheds its leaves in the fall, slowly, one day at a time. But you don't notice until it's completely naked and you're wondering how winter snuck up so fast.

That night, we were too drunk to think about repercussions.

"To Annetta!" Josiah toasted as he worked open another bottle of vodka. And a cheer rose into the steamy night air.

"To Annetta!"

CHAPTER 12

WHEN WE PULLED INTO the employee parking lot, Ella's Range Rover wasn't there. My anxiety simmered when we walked into the pool area and there was a stocky blond guy in the lifeguard chair where she normally sat.

"Ella texted back," Annetta said, and I lunged for her phone.

> I'm off today! Teddy and I switched shifts.
> Come by after work xo

I sighed in relief. She gave me an *xo*, so maybe she wasn't mad. Maybe everything would be okay.

It was some brat's birthday, so once the snack shack opened, we were busy our entire shifts. It was for the best. Our conversation at Sugar Mama had left me bruised. I was ashamed of how I'd acted at the party. I was mortified of having to promise I'd stop drinking in the first place. But, worst of all, I was terrified at the prospect of our friend group fracturing for good.

Four years, we'd been a trio. We balanced each other's scales: fiery, wild Ella; sensible, responsible Annetta; and whatever the hell I was. I'd grown up with them. They were closer to me than my actual blood family. Around them, I didn't worry about how Dad had been keeping me at arm's length ever since I'd come out. I didn't care about not meeting Leon's expectations. Whenever I remembered Mom's "half" comment, they were there, filling me with light, making me whole.

We were Ella, Annetta, and Blake. I didn't know how to make sense of any other configuration.

After work, Annetta gave me a ride to Ella's. She shook her head when I asked if she was coming in.

"I don't want to be around Ella right now," she said. She felt so far, and I didn't know how to reel her back.

Ella was in her bedroom, fresh out of a shower and rubbing baby oil on her legs. Her face lit up when she saw me, and I was so, so relieved.

"Hey, Bee! How was work?"

I tugged off my lime-green polo. "Okay. How was last night?"

"Good," she said. I tried to hug her, but she wrinkled her nose. "You smell like corn dogs. Go take a shower."

I stripped. Let Ella run me a warm shower. She added a eucalyptus tablet, and soon her entire bathroom smelled like a greenhouse. She applied her facial products while I scrubbed the day away. When I stepped out, my skin was red and I smelled like a peach. I wrapped myself in one of her fluffy towels and joined her at the mirror.

"Look . . . I think we should talk about last night," I said.

She paused with her eyelash curler halfway to her face. "You were fine, Bee, if that's what you're worried about. I made sure Nettie got you out of there before you got too sloppy. Where is Nettie, by the way? Bitch couldn't come in and say hi?"

"She wanted to be alone."

Ella rolled her eyes and continued primping. "Figures. Typical case of the Netties."

I watched as she curled her already long lashes. She was so beautiful, and I was happy she wasn't mad at me. But there was a desperate little voice in my head, remembering the way she and Roxanne kissed, and it was a reminder that maybe *I* was mad at *her*.

"Can we talk about the kiss?"

She froze. "What kiss?"

"You know . . . you and Roxanne." I steepled my fingers and flexed them twice. "Kissing."

She laughed. "Oh, Bee, *that* kiss. It was a dare."

"I know—"

"We were playing Truth or Dare. You can't pass down a dare."

"I *know*—"

"So what's the big deal, then?" She turned to me. "Don't tell me you're jealous." My eyes trailed down, down, down. She was wearing my favorite lacy red underwear.

"A little," I admitted. "You guys, like, used tongue."

Ella threw her head back and laughed. I immediately felt childish for even bringing it up.

"Awww, Bumblebee, you're *jealous*," she squealed. Then she kissed me with the same lips she kissed Roxanne with. Still, I melted. I couldn't help it.

"It's cute when you're jealous," she mumbled against my lips.

"You wouldn't be upset if I kissed someone else like that?" I asked when she turned back to the mirror. "What are you getting ready for, anyway?"

"Roxanne invited us to the beach. And no, if you were playing Truth or Dare and someone was dared to kiss you, I would not be jealous." She was starting to sound irritated. "I know how to play a game." She slapped my butt before heading for her closet. "Get ready! We're meeting Roxanne at seven."

"Do we have to go?" I mumbled. I slathered on lotion and imagined punching Roxanne in the face and throwing her into the ocean. Let a shark swallow that bitch whole.

When Ella reappeared, she had on a silky red dress that matched her hair. I was perched on the edge of the bathtub, still wrapped in a towel and picking at my nails.

"You should be thrilled Roxanne still wants to hang out with you," she said sharply. "Seriously, Bee, get ready."

"Or what?"

She raised an eyebrow, and I immediately regretted my words. She had her fighting face on now, and after four years of loving this girl, I knew she liked to cut deep.

"What are you, six years old?" she snapped. "Are you forgetting that we are trying to get into the *Serena Society*?"

"You'll get in. Why are you even worried?"

"Excuse me?"

"You'll get in," I said louder. My heart pounded in my chest like it did before every fight. Normally, I would be the first to let it go and want to smooth things over, but not this time. Not today. "You're a legacy," I went on. "Your mom is the *advisor*. You'll get in. I don't see why you have to kiss Roxanne's ass all summer."

Ella's mouth dropped. "Are you serious right now?"

I rose shakily. I felt exposed wearing only a towel. Clothes. I needed clothes. I tried to brush past her, but she yanked my arm and twisted me around. Fury stormed across her face.

"Kiss Roxanne's ass? Did you *really* just say that?"

"Let go of me."

Ella's eyes flashed, and she flung my arm away in disgust. I hurried across the room, dodging Nina, who was snoozing in a sunny spot on the floor. On top of Ella's dresser were the bouquets of calla lilies her parents had gifted us the night of the first task. They were dead now.

I opened a drawer and searched through clothes I'd left behind after countless sleepovers, my hands shaking. I shouldn't have said anything, why why *why* did I say that? I was yanking underwear on when her slick voice slid down my back.

"For your information, I *have* to impress Roxanne. Do you know why?"

I stayed silent, let the towel drop as I threw on a pair of shorts. My eyes welled. *No, no, no.* I didn't want to fight, but I'd started it.

"Because of *you*, Blake. Because I'm trying to make sure *both* of us get accepted."

The admission nearly knocked the wind out of me. I slowly put on a T-shirt, wishing I could rewind time and take back my words.

"Being a Serena woman is an honor," she continued. "An honor Spencer women know very well. My mother was the *first* Filipina to pledge the society, did you know that? Then Sophie and Ariana."

"I get it." I whirled around and she was still at the bathroom door, glaring at me. "Forget I said anything. Let's just go to the beach."

"You're so ungrateful," she said, eerily calm. It was frightening how she could say the most hurtful things with a face like a beautiful frozen lake. "Do you know how many girls would love to be in your position right now?" I stared at her fingernails, tapping away on the doorframe. "How many times have I told you I want us *both* to be in Serena?" *Tap, tap, tap.* "It's like you don't even care anymore."

"I care," I said, and suddenly tears spilled over. Ella was my family, the Spencers were my family, I couldn't lose them. And if I didn't get into Serena, I was going to.

"I'm sorry," I cried.

"Oh, now you wanna cry?" she said with a mean, hard laugh.

"I want Serena, you know I do," I said. She glared at me with such heat that I had to look away. "I'm sorry, I was just upset about the kiss—"

"You're so dramatic," she snarled. "All this over one little kiss?"

"I'm sorry, El," I pleaded. I crossed the room and reached out for her. I needed her to hold me, forgive me, tell me everything was going to be all right. "I'm sorry, I'm sorry, I'm sorry." I repeated the words like a chant, a reverent prayer, and she finally opened her arms and let me fall into them. She felt like home, and it was a reminder of the home I was running away from. That empty apartment in Winward Commons. Little Blake haunting the halls like a lonely, insignificant ghost. Ella was right. I was being dramatic. I was about to ruin our future over a silly game of Truth or Dare. The vision of me and Ella basking in golden autumn light on the front lawn of the Serena Society house sparked and burned.

"I'm sorry," I whispered. "I'm sorry."

She stroked my damp hair, kissed the top of my head. "My mother is perfect," she said into my hair. "My sisters are perfect. *I* have to be perfect."

"You are, El," I said tearfully.

"I feel like I'm busting my ass trying *so* hard to impress Roxanne, and I still don't know if it'll be enough. And now I have to worry about you, too?"

I shook my head against her chest. I was sorry, so pathetic. I needed Ella. I needed the society. They were all I had.

"I love you," I whispered. "You don't have to worry anymore. I'll chill out."

"I love you, too," she said. When I peeled away, her face was no longer a crystalline lake. She was a warm fire, crackling, winter night comfort. I loved her. I was so lucky to love her.

"Come on," she said. "Let's go to the beach."

And everything was good again.

A few days later, all of the Serena Society hopefuls gathered for an afternoon of community service at the food bank. As we checked in, I realized this was the first time I'd seen Roxanne outside of a party or the country club. It was strange. She actually looked like a responsible adult in her short-sleeve button-up, checking names off a clipboard. Alice stood beside her, divvying us up. Some girls were going to the dry goods storage to pack boxes while the other half would be heading to the refrigeration room to organize their newest shipment. Ella and I were split up again, to my disappointment.

"Text me," Ella said before peeling off to join her group. She nodded at the new silver iPhone in my hand. She'd gifted it to me this morning, and I was grateful to have a phone again.

"Love you till the world stops turning," I said.

"Love you till the sun explodes," she replied, and we giggled. Our fight a few days prior didn't matter anymore. Everything was good again.

Annetta and I were in the same group. I caught up to her as we made our way to the chilly refrigeration room.

"Hey, Nettie," I said.

She nodded. There were dark circles under her eyes.

"You look tired. Xan been keeping you up?" I whispered.

"No." But she was smiling. "Okay, fine. *Yes.* We've been out every night this week."

"Ahh! You'll have to tell me everything," I said. "I've missed you."

"Missed you, too," she said, and my heart swelled.

An older man with a jolly smile and a salt-and-pepper beard passed out thick gloves to keep our hands warm while handling the food. Annetta and I worked side by side, far enough away from the rest of the girls that we had some privacy.

"So are you and Xan in *loooove* yet?" I asked.

"No." She smiled. "I really, really like them, though."

"And I can clearly see the feeling is mutual."

Her smile faded as she neatly stocked rows of frozen sausages.

"What is it?" I asked.

"I don't know," she said, but her eyes searching around the refrigerated room told me she *did* know, but she was trying to find the right words.

"Tell me what's going on, Nettie," I coaxed.

"You wanna know why Xan called me AJ? That morning at Sugar Mama?"

"Yeah?"

"Because when I met them online, I'd been using a whole new profile. I called myself AJ, said I was nonbinary, and put *they/them* pronouns in my bio. But now . . ." Her gaze flickered to my face and she looked so lost. "Now *none* of that feels right, but I don't know how to tell them. I don't want them to think I'm a liar."

"You're not a liar, Nettie," I said. "Sometimes it takes a while to figure these things out."

"Xan is just so cool and knows who they are, and I don't," Annetta said softly.

"Do you think you're trans? Do you have new pronouns you want me to use?"

"No. I've never felt like a guy. But lately I haven't felt like a girl. And being somewhere in the middle feels so damn scary." She groaned.

"Ugh, I wish I could just wake up and be thirty and know what the hell I'm doing with my life. Like that movie with that white lady."

I smiled. "I think the whole point of that movie was that she didn't exactly know what she was doing, either."

"Well, I'm tired of this." Annetta broke down an empty box, the tape making a loud screech as she yanked it. "I'm tired of all these uncertainties. I just want to know . . . something."

"It seems like Xan is wild about you."

She blushed. "Yeah . . . but they don't *really* know me."

"I'm sure they'll be equally as wild about all versions of you."

She smiled at me gratefully. "Thanks. Don't tell Ella, though? Not yet."

I crossed my heart. "I'll take it to the grave."

When we finished our shipment, we joined Khadija and Eden, who were sorting through packages of bacon on the verge of expiration. We chatted about weekend plans and the upcoming school year. Khadija was a rising junior and had been trying to gain admittance into the Serena Society for the past two years. Eden was a fellow freshman like me and Annetta.

"I feel like the second task is gonna be any day now," Khadija said.

"What do you think it'll be?" Eden mused.

"Anything but a puzzle," Annetta said, and everyone laughed except me. I couldn't have another night like the first task, not when Ella and I were back on track. I refused.

"They've been a lot more ridiculous this summer than the previous years I've pledged," Khadija said, glancing around to make sure Roxanne and Alice weren't lurking nearby. "There was way more community service and fewer parties."

"Do you think it's because Roxanne is president now?" Eden whispered.

"Definitely," Khadija said. "Roxanne was in the theater program with me when I was a freshman, and no one partied harder at cast parties than she did. Girl is *wild*."

My face flushed as I thought back to my blackout nights. How so much of that was fueled by a desperate desire to keep up with Roxanne, show her I was worthy of being her right-hand woman. I didn't want to think about it, so I asked Khadija about Jameswell's theater program.

"It's fantastic," Khadija told me. "You have any interest in acting?"

Picturing myself onstage under an array of lights almost made me break out in hives. I thought back to my freshman year in high school when I was briefly convinced Drama Club was my ticket out of my loner hell. As an actor, I could be anyone. Anyone besides dorky, quiet Blake. But then I choked during my audition and hadn't really thought about it since.

"Maybe," I said with a shrug.

"Well, college is a time to do whatever you wanna do," Khadija said. "And if you decide to try out theater, you already know someone in the program."

"Thanks," I said. A strange excitement bubbled in my chest as I pictured the Jameswell campus in the fall, shrouded in gold and auburn leaves. A fresh chance to start over, Annetta and Ella at my side, the three of us snug in sapphire-blue sweaters.

Later, Annetta and I found ourselves alone again when we had to organize a shipment of frozen breakfast items. While double fisting bags of frozen fruit, Annetta proudly said, "I haven't vaped in three days."

"Look at you!" I said.

"The withdrawals *suck*. I've been going through a pack of gum a day to cut the cravings." She pulled out a pack of Trident and offered me a stick. I happily accepted.

"What about you?" she asked. "Have you kept *your* promise?" Her tone was teasing, but I remembered her serious expression at Sugar Mama. The promise we'd made.

"Yes, Mom," I said, my heart picking up speed.

She raised an eyebrow. "Really? You haven't drank?"

"Nope," I said, and guilt seeped in my chest. I'd had four or five glasses of sparkling wine on the beach the other night with Ella, Roxanne, and a handful of other pledges. I *had* to in order to be around Roxanne all night without thinking about her lips on my girlfriend's. But I'd paced myself and didn't black out, so did that really count? I was good. Everything was fine.

"How are you and Ella?"

I focused on a box of frozen waffles. I didn't want to tell her about the fight. It felt like that'd give her more proof. Something she could point to and say, *See what I mean? Friends don't treat each other like Ella treats us.*

"We're great," I said. "She even bought me a new phone."

Annetta hummed.

"Things have been really good," I went on.

She hummed again.

We didn't speak for the rest of our shift, but she did agree to grab lunch afterward with me and Ella. At our favorite diner, we shared a plate of chili cheese fries and talked shit about Todd and fantasized about Jameswell. Things were okay again. They had to be. This was just the ebb and flow of friendships. After all, we were Ella, Annetta, and Blake. *We got us.*

We could survive anything.

CHAPTER 13

ON THE NIGHT OF the second Serena task, there were no yachts. There was no music, no dancing, no strobe lights. There was also no bar, which I was relieved to see when Ella, Annetta, and I arrived on the outskirts of the Great Dismal Swamp Wildlife Refuge just before midnight. Under a sliver of moonlight, the remaining twenty girls and I were stripped of our backpacks and phones and led to a dark pavilion nestled in a thick tangle of woods.

The roofed pavilion housed eight benches. Roxanne and Alice stood on top of one, decked in black from head to toe. The ends of Roxanne's two braids grazed the middle of her back, and I couldn't stop staring at them as she conferred with Alice quietly. There wasn't a hair out of place, her part razor-thin down the middle. I wondered if I would ever look that put together if—*when*—I joined the society. My hatred of her had dampened over the past couple days, leaving behind only the familiar need to impress her. Ella was right. As the president, Roxanne had the most influence over who got in and who got cut. So if ass kissing was what it took, ass kissing was what she'd get.

I was sandwiched between Annetta and Ella, huddled in nervous silence. All around us were the equally eager faces of the girls who'd survived the first night, attended the community service event, and were ready for more. When we arrived, Keiko scowled at me as she climbed out of her car. I wanted to tell her the puzzle night was a fluke. I was worthy and ready this time.

"All right, everyone!" Roxanne yelled. "How are you all feeling about the second task?"

My and Ella's cheers got lost in the cacophony of voices. Annetta remained quiet, studying the scene with an unreadable expression.

"I love the enthusiasm," Roxanne said. She motioned toward the dark woods behind her. "Anyone want to take a wild guess as to why I've dragged you out to the Great Dismal Swamp this fine evening?"

No one said anything. Even Keiko, Queen Know-It-All, was quiet.

"I figured we'd need a little history lesson before we began," Roxanne said. "Alice, would you do the honors?"

Alice stared down at us from the bench. "There was a sign we passed on the way to this pavilion. Anyone remember what it said?"

Ella's hand shot up first. "The Underground Railroad Pavilion."

"Very good, Ella," Roxanne said with a proud smile.

"Indeed," Alice said. "The land we are standing on is an official Underground Railroad Network to Freedom site. Enslaved people used this swamp as an escape route when fleeing plantations. Some of them lived within the swamp itself for years." She paused to let her words flow over us. "I want you to think about that tonight—what it took to survive out here."

The dark night was alive with insects. I wrapped my arms around myself and shivered.

"These woods also signify hallowed grounds for the Serena Society," Alice continued. "We've talked about Serena's eleven founders."

"Can anyone name all of them?" Roxanne chimed in. Keiko smoothly launched into the list of names, and I prided myself on recognizing all of them.

"Very good, Keiko," Alice said. "Indeed, those eleven women are the reason we're all standing here. They were leaders in every sense of the word. But you'll notice none of them are named Serena. Anyone know why?" Roxanne handed her a lit white pillar candle, and the flame flickered as the wind picked up.

"The twelfth founder died before the society documents were officially drafted," Alice said. "Her name was Serena Wake. She is the Lost Girl." The candlelight danced under Alice's chin, and goose bumps sprouted on my arms.

"Serena died in the summer of 1950, mere months before the society was officially chartered on Jameswell's campus," Alice said. "She was killed by an abusive boyfriend." There was a soft collective gasp, and Alice met all of our eyes seriously. "She was found two days before her twentieth birthday, dead in Lake Drummond."

My stomach turned. I was grateful Ella and Annetta were there to prop me up.

"Even though all the evidence pointed to Serena's boyfriend, he was never charged," Alice continued. "Imagine that. The police not giving a shit about a Black girl like Serena. The founders realized that in this racist, misogynistic world, women of color have to look out for ourselves and one another. We have to make our own way. The founders made it their mission to honor Serena's life in any way they could. She is the reason we wear sapphire blue, as it was her favorite color. It signifies wisdom and strength. Tonight, we honor and remember the Lost Girl of Serena, the twelfth founder." Wax dribbled over Alice's fingers, but she didn't even blink. "Tonight is all about the number twelve."

Roxanne stepped out of Alice's shadow.

"There are one hundred pennies in the swamp," Roxanne said. "Your job tonight is simple. Bring us twelve. You'll be broken into the same three groups from the first task. The first two groups to bring me and Alice twelve pennies will move forward in the selection process. The rest of you . . . unfortunately, your journey will end here." When Roxanne's eyes met mine, I set my jaw. I was going to show everyone I belonged in Serena. I wasn't just Some Drunk Girl who was the laughingstock of the rest of the pledges.

I mattered.

"Oh, and by the way," Roxanne said. "Be careful out here. There are snakes . . . and bears." She and Alice grinned at each other, then yelled, "On your mark!"

Alice lifted the candle. "Get set!"

"Go!" Roxanne finished.

I didn't even have time to be disappointed that Ella and I were separated again. She immediately took off down a darkened path, red hair flying, bellowing for her group to follow. Keiko quickly copied her.

"Group two!" Keiko shouted. "Group two, over here!"

Annetta and I followed Keiko's voice to the edge of the pavilion.

"I think the best course of action is for us to split up," Keiko demanded. "We'll divide the woods into sections, start on the outskirts, and work our way inward."

"That's ridiculous," Khadija said. "This swamp is huge, and we don't have our phones. How are we supposed to find each other if we split up?"

"Yeah, Khadjia's right," Annetta said. "We should stay close. What if half of us find the pennies before the other half? Then what?"

"We don't have time for this!" Keiko snapped. "All in favor of splitting up, raise your hands." When only two hands rose—including her own—Keiko sighed. "Fine, we'll stay together. Now, let's go! We're already behind!"

We took off, Keiko sprinting down the wooden boardwalk back to the main road, as Annetta and I brought up the rear. Trees towered above us, obscuring all moonlight. The sounds of nocturnal animals were thick in the swamp beyond.

"What is the likelihood of us finding twelve pennies in the pitch dark with no flashlights?" I panted, hot on Annetta's heels. My lungs were already burning, and we'd barely started.

"About as likely as us getting eaten by a bear!" Annetta yelled over her shoulder. "But hey—if we fail, we fail together!"

"We're not going to fail!"

"Says the slowpoke of the group!" Annetta pumped her legs harder, and I grinned at her back. I could barely make out Keiko's orange sweatshirt far ahead, but it was all I focused on as we ran deeper into the swamp.

The energy of our group began to wane after thirty minutes had passed and there was no sign of any pennies. Khadija and Eden thought they found one, but it was only an unusually shiny acorn. We were afraid to veer off the road and boardwalks into the actual swamp since no one knew what was lurking beneath the water's surface.

We finally reached Lake Drummond, and it was eerily calm, an inky void in the middle of the swamp. The night air was sticky and hot. It smelled like dirt. Impending rain. Annetta and I volunteered to search the pier that stretched over the lake.

"Oh, look," Annetta said after carefully searching the pier railings. There were countless initials carved into the wood, but no pennies. "Here's some water. And more water. And dirt!"

"I'm just grateful we haven't run into any bears," I said.

Annetta popped her gum. "This is a joke. An absolute joke. *Pennies?* What the fuck does finding some pennies have to do with the Underground Railroad and a dead girl in the lake?"

I crouched to check around the base of the observation binoculars that overlooked the lake. "We're doing this to become a part of the Serena Society," I said, more for my benefit than Annetta's. "There will be an abundance of opportunities at our fingertips. Unparalleled mentorships, sisterhood—"

"A sweet-ass bracelet," Khadija yelled farther down the pier, and everyone laughed except Keiko.

Our group wandered along the edge of the lake before turning back to the woods. Annetta and I trailed behind again, far enough away that the other girls couldn't hear Annetta grumpily mumbling under her breath. I whacked her shoulder lightly.

"We're gonna get through this," I said. "Serena's worth it."

"Oh, please," she said. "This task is bullshit, and you know it. Seriously, what does finding pennies have to do with sisterhood and community service?"

I paused near an uprooted tree and sat on its trunk. I motioned for Annetta to join me, which she did reluctantly.

"All right," I said. "Dr. Blake is in the house. What is going on?"

"I don't know," she said with a sigh. "I'm just so . . . grumpy. I think it's the withdrawals. Everything's pissing me off lately."

"Clearly," I said, amused. "You need a hug?"

She dragged a boot through the dirt. "I think so," she mumbled, so I hugged her, laughing.

"I don't know," she said in the crook of my neck. "Lately I've been thinking that maybe I don't want to be a 'Serena Society Woman.'"

Then, so quiet I almost didn't hear her, she added, "Maybe I don't want to be a woman at all."

We pulled apart. "Do you want to talk about it?" I asked.

"Every day I wake up more confused," she said. The voices of the rest of our group were fading fast. "I want to talk to Xan about it, but I'm afraid."

"Of what?"

"Things have been so good between us! I don't want to mess anything up. And besides, what happens if we talk and I have some light bulb moment that I'm *not* a woman? What does that mean for all of this?" She gestured around the trees, the star-studded sky. "Can I be in Serena if I'm trans or nonbinary—" Her voice snagged on the word, and she groaned. "Fuck, I don't know what I am."

I smiled. "You know I love you, right?"

She blinked away tears. "I know."

"What if instead of thinking about this uncertainty as something bad, we make it exciting instead?" I suggested. "Like, how cool is it that you want to explore your gender? That's fun!"

She shot me a watery smile. "It'd be a lot more fun if I wasn't so worried about my mom."

"You don't think she'd accept you?"

Her eyes were sad as she looked around. The endless dark woods, no sign of any pennies. "I don't think so. She's all, *strong woman* this, *Black girl magic* that. I feel like becoming a 'Woman of Serena' is the last common thread we have." She wiped away a tear and whispered, "I'm so tired of trying to prove my worth to her."

"Oh, Nettie. You *are* worthy. I'm sure your mom knows that."

"Easy for you to say," Annetta muttered. "Your mom's never left you."

I swallowed, thinking of my mom and the distance that'd somehow formed between us through the years. Then Keiko's sharp voice sliced through the trees.

"Annetta! Blake! If you're done with your social hour, will you *please come help us!*"

"Another hug?" I asked as we stood. She nodded, so I crushed her into a smothering one, hoping it was enough to squeeze the pain away.

"I love you," I told her. "We got us, remember?"

"We got us," she whispered.

"And now they're hugging!" Keiko yelled.

"We're coming!" I hollered.

"She's almost worse than Ella," Annetta joked.

Another half hour passed, and our group was still empty-handed. I couldn't tell how far we'd wandered from the starting point. Every tree was beginning to look the same, all paths led nowhere. Annetta and I searched high and low around trees and grassy patches. Eden stumbled across a bird feeder, and we all held our breath as she climbed on Khadija's tall shoulders. When the search yielded nothing, Keiko cursed under her breath and demanded we trudge forward.

"This is miserable," said a short curvy Black girl with microbraids whose name I didn't know. I nodded in agreement, then turned my attention to the algae-coated creek that paralleled the road.

"I'd take the puzzle over this any day," the girl continued. "I'm kind of good with puzzles."

"I'm not," I snorted. Maybe it was the late hour or maybe I had just grown frustrated, but I no longer cared about trying to pretend like the first task never happened. Everyone in the group had witnessed my drunken spectacle, anyway.

"You were just out of it," the girl said, and I looked at her in surprise. She smiled warmly. "Happens to the best of us."

I was stunned by her thoughtfulness. Annetta clapped my back. "Corinne's right. Happens to the best of us!"

I stuck out my hand. "I'm Blake."

"I know," Corinne replied, still smiling. "We've already met. Several times."

My cheeks burned. Of course we did, and I didn't remember. But Corinne's voice held no scorn or mockery, and my nerves settled as we continued our hunt.

After another thirty minutes, everyone was on the verge of quitting. It was beginning to feel like Roxanne and Alice had sent us on a wild-goose chase with no geese in sight. When the sound of distant traffic neared—indicating we were close to the bounds of the swamp—Keiko turned to us, her black-lined eyes brimming with tears.

"I give up," she said. "I have no idea what to do. It's been at least two hours and we haven't even found *one*. How the hell are we supposed to find twelve? We're going to lose."

While the girls in our group rallied around Keiko, echoing hollow affirmations, Annetta, Corinne, and I hung back. A life without Serena was quickly becoming a reality, and I imagined Ella's face when my group returned empty-handed. How disappointed she'd be. I envisioned her breaking up with me, how she'd claim she didn't see a future with someone who wasn't as ambitious as she was. I had to look away. In the distance, there was a pinprick of neon and the occasional swing of passing headlights.

Keiko was full-on blubbering now. "I applied to Jameswell *just* to join Serena." Tears streamed down her porcelain face. "This is my dream!"

I couldn't tear my eyes from the road. That light. It was so familiar. I took a couple of steps forward, twigs crunching beneath my sneakers, and my heart pounded wildly. When I realized what I was looking at, I nearly wept.

"Follow me!" I shouted.

"Why should we follow you anywhere, after what you pulled last time?" Keiko snarled.

I didn't wait to see if the group was following as I took off in a full sprint, eyes trained on the lights. I knew those lights. I laughed as I raced down the gravel road, brushing past drooping branches and dodging uneven earth. I sailed, lungs burning, and the lights brightened. I focused on nothing else as I ran. Closer, closer, closer.

Those lights were home.

"What the hell?" Keiko screamed. As we closed in, I heard the distinctive richness of Annetta's laugh when she realized what had captured my attention.

The seven of us broke through the wood's clearing, and the lights were unmistakable now. Fluorescent white, green, and orange, the number seven lit up like a beacon of hope.

It was 7-Eleven. And in the parking lot, my mom's sedan.

"Blake, you're a genius," Corinne squealed.

"What does 7-Eleven have to do with anything?" Keiko asked.

"I would *die* for some nachos," Khadija said, and the girls laughed.

We approached the building from the side, and my heart almost burst at the sight of Mom behind the counter. She was leaning against the register, thumbing through a paperback, a wall of cigarettes and chewing tobacco behind her. I yanked open the door, and she looked up in shock.

"Blake!" She set the book down, surprised. I could only imagine what we looked like stumbling in her store in the middle of the night, squinting against the harsh light, covered in dirt and grass. She circled around the counter. "What on Earth are you doing here?"

"Can we talk about it later?" I asked. "Right now we need some pennies."

"And food," Khadija moaned.

"Help yourself to whatever you want," Mom said, waving us inside. Everyone took off down the aisles.

"And here I was thinking this was going to be a slow night," Mom said.

"You're a miracle worker." I wrapped my arms around her tight. She stiffened before hugging me back.

"Seriously, Mrs. Brenner," Annetta said through a mouthful of frosted chocolate doughnut. "You have no idea how happy we are to be in your fine establishment this evening."

"I'll pay you back for all of this," I said.

Mom quirked an eyebrow. "Where are your wallets?"

"Can we file that under the 'Later' category as well?"

She chuckled. "Let me go get you those pennies." She went behind the register, and Keiko appeared at my side, shaking her head.

"This isn't going to work, Blake," she said. "Roxanne said the pennies were *in* the woods. This is cheating."

"Do you have any better ideas?" I suppressed a grin as her mouth twisted into a frown. "Look, the way I see it, isn't this something a Serena woman would do? Alice was talking about how they had to make their own way." On cue, the cash register popped open and Mom started counting out coins. "We're making our own way."

Keiko considered this as Mom pushed the pennies across the counter with a dull scrape. When I pocketed them—twenty, just in case—Keiko nodded. "I hope you're right about this."

Once everyone had their snacks, I looked to Mom for one final favor and asked to borrow her car. The starting point had to be miles away, and I didn't want to risk not making it back in time now that we were still in the running.

"I promise I'll return it," I said as she offered me her keys. "We're in a time crunch."

"I'm going to assume you're desperate, seeing how you're trying to squeeze seven people into my sedan that seats five," Mom said wryly. "Please, don't do anything illegal. I get off at eight."

"I owe you," I said, already taking off. "I promise!"

"Just get that room packed up soon!" she called. "Then we'll be even!"

The seven of us hurried out to the car. Being the tallest, Khadija called shotgun, and she was tearing into her nachos before she even opened the door. Keiko, Annetta, Eden, and Corinne squeezed into the back seat, and Bianca draped over their legs, making her already petite body as small as possible. The energy in the car was rejuvenated as I pulled out of the parking lot, everyone munching on their respective snacks.

"Blake, if this works, we might just have to forgive you for passing out on us last time," Khadija said before taking a long sip of her blue raspberry Slurpee.

"Yeah, seriously!" Eden piped up. "You were straight-up comatose."

"It's going to work!" Annetta declared. "Lay off my girl, y'all."

"Blake got me a chili dog," Corinne said, her mouth full. "So in my eyes, Blake is the shit!"

"Blake, Blake, Blake!" Annetta cheered. The rest of the car joined in, even Keiko. I was smiling and laughing so hard that I nearly missed the road leading back to the swamp.

"This is either going to go well," I said, "or it's going to blow up spectacularly in our faces."

"Have a little faith," Annetta said. I smiled at her in the rearview, and we held our breath as we parked and raced back to the pavilion.

Which was . . . surprisingly empty, save for Roxanne and Alice. In the time we'd been searching, they decked out the pavilion in Christmas tree lights, washing everything in a red-and-green haze. They were lounging on the same benches, scrolling through their phones. They sat up as the sound of our footsteps echoed down the wooden boardwalk.

"Moment of truth," Corinne whispered.

"Feel like we're walking into our doom," Keiko moaned.

"Only one way to find out," I said. I reached into my pocket to make sure the pennies were still there and rubbed them for good luck.

"Well, well, well," Roxanne said, standing. "What do we have here?"

I pulled the pennies out of my pocket and counted out twelve. I dropped them in her outstretched palm and held my breath. Behind her, Alice sat on the bench cross-legged, a slow grin spreading across her face.

Roxanne considered the pennies. She looked up with a glint in her eyes. "Did you find these *in* the swamp?"

I lifted my chin. "We did not."

Roxanne looked over her shoulder at Alice. "What do you think, Allie?"

"I think we asked them to go into the woods for pennies," Alice said, "and they came back with snacks."

"*And* the pennies!" Corinne piped up, still munching on her chili dog. Annetta laughed silently, and Corinne shrugged. "What? I'm just saying."

Roxanne smirked. "Would you consider this cheating, Blake?"

My lips twitched. I couldn't tell if this was a trick question. I thought back to one of the first nights I hung out with her—the night of the paint debacle. How delighted she was when I decided to take justice into my own hands. If that act of defiance appealed to her, then there was no reason why another one wouldn't. So even though I was stone-cold sober, I channeled Big Bad Bee and held my head high.

"Absolutely not." I clasped my hands behind my back to hide the shaking. "You asked us for twelve pennies. You didn't *explicitly* say they had to come from the swamp."

Roxanne nodded. Out of the corner of my eye, I noticed Alice's smile widening.

"Where did you get these pennies?" Roxanne asked.

"7-Eleven," I replied. "The snacks, too."

Alice threw her head back in laughter, startling us. Roxanne's smile looked forced. "I'm glad you find this amusing, Alice."

"They're geniuses," Alice said, clapping. "Every last one of them."

I relaxed, nearly cried with relief. Roxanne sniffed and said, "Well, group two, it seems you have impressed Alice. That's not a small feat."

"They got chili dogs," Alice cackled. "Holy crap."

"And Slurpees!" Khadija said, boldly holding her cup up. Alice laughed harder. Even my own composure started to crack. I smiled, but Roxanne leveled her gaze at me.

"You were calculating," she said to me, and the group fell silent at her frosty tone. "You took the task and completely bent the rules. You took the easy way out." Then a genuine smile crossed her lips. "Or, depending on how you look at it, the smart way. It's precisely what a Serena woman would've done. Well done."

Keiko gasped. Everyone else burst into excited whispers, and I melted against Annetta.

"Congratulations, group two!" Roxanne said. "You have officially completed the second Serena task!"

We cheered, our voices ringing out into the night. Annetta clapped my shoulders and started her chant again.

"Blake, Blake, Blake!"

The rest of the girls in my group joined in, and my heart filled like a balloon. How I'd managed to pull that off, I wasn't sure. But I'd done what I said I was going to do. I'd earned my place. I was more than some drunk girl from the first task. My plan was working.

I was worth something.

"Blake, Blake, Blake!"

I loved the sound of my own name.

"This calls for a celebration!" Roxanne exclaimed. She headed for the corner of the pavilion, toward a dark mound that hadn't been there earlier. She whipped off a blanket, revealing a navy blue ice chest. My heart skipped a beat as she flipped the lid and pulled out a dark green bottle of sparkling wine.

"To Serena!" Roxanne cheered.

"To Serena!" group two chorused. Everyone except for me and Annetta. Her hand flew to steady me as I stepped back, still staring as Roxanne twisted the cap off the sparkling wine. When it popped open with a magnificent flourish, another cheer rose and I could do nothing but stare at the excess wine oozing down the side of the glass bottle.

CHAPTER 14

SPARKLING WINE

THE FIRST TIME ELLA and I went all the way, we were drunk.

Spring break, freshman year. At a mere fifteen, I'd found something I loved almost as much as Ella Spencer. It was a green bottle with a white label, a wire cage under sparkly gold foil.

Sparkling wine.

"It's *not* champagne," Ella would tell me, Annetta, and Josiah as we sipped the bubbles that made our throats tickle. "Champagne only comes from a certain region in France. Everything else is sparkling wine." She sounded like her mother. I didn't care what we called it. I just knew that I loved it.

By that point, alcohol was a permanent fixture in our social gatherings. It seemed as if everyone except me had access to their parents' abundant supply. Josiah would snag a bottle from his parents' yacht here, Annetta would steal some of Mrs. Jones's wine coolers there. And we would hang out in the Spencers' rec room or on Josiah's yacht and consume until our young limbs didn't feel awkward and gangly, until the words we spoke rang sophisticated and intelligent. We would watch bad movies just for the sex scenes, sipping drinks that ranged from light and fruity to strong and burning.

The night Ella and I went all the way, our drink of choice was sparkling wine. We'd downed two bottles that were left over from the Spencers' Easter bash. Her parents were in Milan, and Ella's older sister Ariana was tasked with watching us—which was, quite frankly, a joke. She was a junior at Jameswell at the time, and after making sure Ella's debit card had enough money for a week's worth of food, she promptly left for the Serena Society house on campus with little more than a *See ya!*

Josiah and Annetta fell asleep halfway through *Blue Is the Warmest Color*, slumped together on the couch. Ella and I sat in front of the screen in rapture, watching two girls have wild, passionate sex. I couldn't imagine being so naked and exposed, especially since I'd barely even explored myself. The women seemed so confident with their heads thrown back, gasping in ecstasy. Sweat. Heat. Desire. It didn't matter it was an unrealistic fantasy directed by a man's hands. It didn't matter they were actors. With burning cheeks, I poured more and more wine until those feelings of insecurity vanished and only confidence remained. Before the credits rolled, Ella and I were rushing upstairs to her bedroom.

She pushed me down onto her window seat and ravenously discarded my clothes piece by piece. Up until this point, we hadn't gone further than that first night at the Crystal Grove holiday party. We'd kissed. Made out. Let our hands roam under shirts or up skirts. But we'd never seen each other naked, and we were growing antsy.

"I don't know what I'm doing," I admitted, half terrified, half elated. Ella unclasped my bra, and when it fell to the floor, she stared at me in reverence.

"You're beautiful, Bee," she said, voice wine thick. "I love you."

"I love you, too," I said.

She slid off my shorts. I faded in and out as I fumbled with her clothes, trying to yank them off before she kissed my inner thigh and pushed me back against the cushions.

"Trust me," she said, and when her head dipped between my thighs, the room spun. The entire night flashed before me. Every sip of wine had led to *this*. Not even a year prior, I'd been a loner who could barely utter a sentence. Now I went to parties, I had rich friends, a *girlfriend* who had her head between my legs. When my breath grew ragged and I couldn't take it anymore, Ella's hand pressed against my lips to silence me.

"Your turn," she whispered when I finished, and we sank to the floor together. I made my way down her chest, leaving a trail of sloppy wet kisses. The next morning, I wouldn't remember anything after that, except for the heat and the pain when her hand tangled into my curls as she cried out my name.

Blake, Blake, Blake.

I loved the sound of my own name.

I felt so powerful and wanted. In that moment, it felt like nothing could stop us.

Like nothing in the entire world could ever make me feel as good as Ella and drinking.

Now a wave barreled toward me. My throat dried as I stared at the bottle in Roxanne's hand.

I can't drink. I shouldn't drink. I can't—

But it's a celebration. You're being celebrated. Haven't you earned it?

Roxanne poured sparkling wine into plastic champagne flutes, handed them out like trophies. The girls in group two chattered like little birds, their fears over not passing the task shedding like falling leaves.

"It's okay, Blake." Annetta's voice was low as I turned away from the excitement. "We won't drink together, okay? I'm here with you."

"Okay," I said quickly. My throat was dry.

Alice made a beeline for me and Annetta. I couldn't take my eyes off the glasses in her hands.

"Congratulations," Alice said, handing me a flute. It felt heavy, filled with lead. "That was genius. Roxanne and I fully expected to be out here until dawn."

"Are there really a hundred pennies out there?" Annetta asked as she accepted her sparkling wine. "Because we couldn't find shit."

Alice smirked and said something, but I couldn't hear her. The entire world was muted. My palm was clammy holding the flute. If I couldn't drink it, then I wanted it as far away from me as humanly possible.

I looked around the pavilion, at the easy way the girls tipped their heads back and let the wine celebrate them. How Roxanne held her glass, gesturing wildly as she talked. No one was overthinking this like I was. Why was I being so dramatic about this? Was it really that big of a deal? Maybe I could just have *one* . . . I felt my resolve floating away, like a balloon released from a child's hand and well on its way to the heavens.

"Blake." This time, the low voice belonged to Alice.

I shook my head. "Sorry. What were you saying?"

"It's okay." Alice nodded at my flute. "It's just sparkling cider."

I finally looked down at the bubbles that I'd assumed were sparkling wine. I brought it to my nose, not believing her, and sniffed. It didn't smell like booze at all. It smelled like sweet autumn apples. I looked at her.

"Um," I said slowly. "Okay."

"I didn't want a repeat of the previous nights," Alice said, holding her glass out. "Figured you should take it easy on the drinking. So. Congratulations." I limply clinked it with my own, my cheeks growing hot.

How did she know?

I waited for Alice to walk away before yanking Annetta's arm. "Did you tell her?" I whispered.

"Ow!" Annetta pulled her arm away. "Tell her what?"

"Sparkling cider? Why would she give me sparkling cider?"

"Jeez, I dunno, Blake, did it ever occur to you that Alice has eyes?" Annetta asked. "I'm not the only one who notices how shit-faced you get when you drink."

My happiness from leading the group to victory fizzled like flat soda. "Did she say something to you?"

"No."

Even if she wasn't lying, I felt betrayed. And humiliated, remembering how Alice sought me out in the *Bewitched*'s dark kitchen.

Girls like us . . .

"Well, that's great," I said. "Nothing screams 'I want to join Serena' like the vice president thinking I'm a raging alcoholic."

"Will you cut it out? Alice is cool. It actually sounds like she's trying to help you."

"I don't need help," I said sharply. "I have everything under control."

"News flash. There's nothing wrong with needing help. Remember how I was after my mom left? How I needed a therapist? How I *still* need one?"

"That's different," I said.

"You turn into a completely miserable person when you're drunk." Her brown eyes searched mine intensely. "I'm on your side, Blake. Don't you trust me?"

I nodded, my embarrassment waning. But I also trusted Ella, and she'd said I didn't have a problem.

So who was the liar?

"We've got to look out for each other," Annetta said. "We got us, remember?"

I said nothing. I reluctantly followed her back to the group when Corinne called us over. While the rest of the girls laughed with Roxanne and Alice, I hid in Annetta's shadow, swirling my flute around and around. I couldn't focus on anything besides how awkward I felt taking sips of sparkling cider. Only Alice and Annetta knew what was truly in my cup, but it still felt like the entire world was laughing at me, telling me I couldn't handle it. Despite Annetta's words, I felt like a toddler sitting in the corner with a sippy cup while the real adults danced through life, all smiles and glitter and cocktails.

Ten minutes later, there was a shout in the distance. I recognized the voice, but I didn't truly believe it was Ella until I saw her red hair flying behind her as her group thundered out of the woods. Her fist was curled in the air, and as she grew closer, we could make out her breathless screams.

"We found them! We found them!"

Roxanne and Alice clapped when the group made it to the pavilion, haggard and elated. When Ella's eyes met mine, there was a flicker of shock. Probably because she wasn't used to coming second in anything.

"Well done!" Roxanne cheered as Ella dropped a handful of pennies in her palm. "You passed! Come, come, celebrate!"

The girls in Ella's group squealed in excitement and helped themselves to celebratory wine. Roxanne handed Ella a glass filled to the brim, and the two of them joined me and Annetta.

Ella kissed me on the cheek. She smelled like pine trees and sweat. I hoped Roxanne was watching. *Bitch*.

"Look at you, Bee," Ella said. "Coming in first."

"Blake led us to victory," Annetta chimed in.

"It was quite impressive," Roxanne added with a smirk. "She showed some ingenuity."

"Cheers to that," Ella replied, and my heart pounded with her approval. She frowned when she looked in my glass. "You're empty. I'll get you another one."

"No," Annetta and I said at the same time. I cleared my throat, feeling Roxanne's gaze on my temples. "No, I'm fine."

"Don't be silly," Roxanne said. "This is a celebration." She headed for the cooler and Annetta glared at Ella.

"Why isn't one 'no' enough?" Annetta asked.

Ella shrugged. "It's just a little sparkling wine. Calm down."

"Don't tell me to calm down," Annetta said.

"Chill, y'all," I said quietly. People were starting to stare.

"What the hell is your problem, Nettie?" Ella hissed.

"Why can't you just listen? Blake said she didn't want to drink," Annetta snapped. There was an awkward silence until Roxanne returned with a fresh bottle.

"Cheers, bitches," she said, filling her and Ella's empty flutes. Annetta shook her head when Roxanne offered the bottle, and I mustered up the strength to do the same. Roxanne smirked at me. "What, you're too good for André now?"

My cheeks flushed. "No."

"'Cause you had no problem drinking an entire bottle by yourself the other night at the beach," Roxanne went on. Annetta stiffened next to me, and my heart dropped to my damn toes. Then Roxanne turned to Ella and said, "Let me go break out the Cristal since Blake is too good for the cheap shit." Ella laughed uneasily, and I wanted to throw up.

"I'll be back," I mumbled. I walked away before anyone could try to stop me, weaving between girls laughing and sipping and existing so easily. But I couldn't outrun Annetta. She caught up with me at the edge of the pavilion.

"Why did you lie to me?" she asked. The question was like a knife jab to the ribs.

"I don't know," I said, throwing my hands up in exasperation. "Maybe because I knew you'd flip out."

She glared. "Are you serious?"

"You weren't even *there*, Nettie," I pushed back. "I didn't black out or cause a scene, so can you please let it go?"

"I've been dealing with fucking nicotine withdrawals for *days* because we made a deal," she said. "I've had constant headaches, mood swings, I can't sleep! But you couldn't even try?" The lights in the pavilion flickered red and green. Their shadows danced across Annetta's face—*Stop. Go. Stop. Go.* The disappointment in her eyes almost rivaled my brother's. Or my dad. I was always letting people down.

"Everything okay over here?"

Alice.

I swallowed and nodded. "It's fine," I said. "Everything is fine."

She handed us our phones; they'd been taken at the start of the task. "You two did really good tonight," she said. "I'm proud of you."

"Thanks," Annetta mumbled. "It was mostly Blake."

Alice appraised me like a proud older sister. "Way to go, Winward Commons." Annetta looked confused, so Alice asked, "What, Blake didn't tell you? We go way back."

"Blake doesn't tell me a lot of things," Annetta said. Another jab. She walked away, and I was too empty, too *tired*, to call her back.

Alice tilted her head. "So. What were you *really* arguing about?"

I nodded to the sparkling cider in our champagne flutes. "My drinking. She was lecturing me like my damn brother."

Alice rolled her eyes. "Oh, boo-hoo, people care about your well-being. You know she and Leon just love you." She smiled when she said my brother's name, and I squinted.

"What about Leon?" I pressed.

Her face flushed. Not even the darkness could hide it. "So I'm assuming he hasn't told you," she said, sipping her cider.

"Hasn't told me what?"

She shrugged. "We've been talking."

For a split second, I was terrified they'd been talking about *me*. But Alice looked smitten, not judgmental.

"You like my brother," I said in awe. "*Ew*."

Alice laughed, and it was such a rare sound that all the girls in the pavilion looked our way.

"He mentioned he started dating someone," I said, recalling his lovesick faces at all our family dinners. I'd gotten so good at tuning him and Dad out that I didn't remember any details. "How long?"

"It's still pretty new," she said. "About two months."

So Leon had been hooking up with a Serena Society girl before my pledge process even started. "Small world," I said, sipping my cider.

"About as small as Winward Commons," Alice said, shrugging. "I was home visiting my mom and we ran into each other in the parking lot." She smiled and added, "I was mostly curious if he was still as dorky as he was in high school."

"Trust me, he is," I said, and we laughed. I felt like I was floating.

Maybe *this* was the key to Serena I'd been so desperately seeking. Clearly, I was no longer Roxanne's favorite—but maybe that didn't matter anymore. If Alice and my brother were a thing, maybe she'd start looking out for me like an older sister.

Yet my happiness faded when I caught a glimpse of Ella and Roxanne over Alice's shoulder. They were talking in the corner of the pavilion, just the two of them, lost in their own little world. I thought I was over the kiss, but jealousy still ticked like a metronome in my chest.

I excused myself from Alice and made a beeline across the pavilion, eyes locked on Ella and Roxanne. They looked like they were . . . arguing? But when I closed in, Roxanne stopped talking and eyed me like an annoying party crasher.

"Everything okay?" I asked Ella. I slipped my arm around her waist and her face lit up.

"Bee! Yes. Everything's fine," Ella said. She tipped her flute back and downed the rest. "Ready to go?"

"So soon?" Roxanne asked frostily.

"I need to get my mom's car back," I said, and Ella nodded and set her empty glass down.

"Let's go," Ella said, and she started leading me away from Roxanne without even saying bye. It was a beautiful little victory—Ella was always choosing me.

Annetta was waiting for us by the Range Rover. She shot me a look that singed my heart and didn't say a word to either of us. I couldn't apologize for lying now, not when Ella didn't know I'd made—and broken—the promise to not drink in the first place.

They followed me as I drove Mom's car to 7-Eleven. Then I climbed into the Range Rover and drifted in and out of sleep as Ella recounted how her group stumbled across a stash of pennies in an abandoned boot.

We took Annetta home, and she barely mumbled goodbye when she got out of the car. Ella rolled her eyes as we watched her disappear inside her house.

"The Netties strike again," she said with a sigh. "Y'all won the task, what is she pissed about now?"

"I don't know," I lied.

"You want to sleep over?" Ella asked as we backed out the driveway.

I nodded. I didn't want to be alone.

By the time we pulled into the Spencers' driveway, dawn was blooming. In the amber light of Ella's bedroom, we stripped out of our clothes, took quick showers, and crawled into bed. We faced each other, heads on her silk pillowcases.

"What were you and Roxanne arguing about?" I asked. "In the pavilion?"

She brushed a curl away from my face. In the golden dawn, without the face full of makeup, I recognized her as the girl I fell in love with at fourteen. "We weren't arguing."

"Looked like it."

"What were you and Annetta arguing about?"

My heart dropped. I thought she hadn't noticed. "Nothing," I lied.

Her fingers trailed my temple, down the curve of my jaw. "Really?"

I didn't know what to say. I thought about her lips on Roxanne's. Her angry fingers wrapped around my wrist. Annetta's disappointment.

But I didn't want to spoil the moment. The clean sheets, her soft skin—it all felt like slipping into a warm bath, and I didn't want the water to run cold. So instead of answering, I kissed her.

She rolled on top of me and kissed me back. Her weight pressed down, down, down, but it wasn't heavy enough to squash the flurry of memories cycling through my mind. Her tongue slipped into my mouth, and all I could think about was her laughing when I told her Annetta thought I drank too much.

I cupped her chin and thought about us fighting in her bathroom.

Her lips moved to my neck. In my mind, fingers tapped Morse code against the doorframe.

Oh, now you wanna cry?

I took off her shirt, and it slid off her body like warm butter.

Shouldn't have mixed the light and dark liquors?

I tried to kiss the thoughts away. I tried to think of nothing. I tried to relax into her like I always did, but Ella's tongue tasted like wine, not her. I tried to let my hands speak for me, hoping that I could feel my way back to the magic of us. I tried, I tried, I tried.

Be happy, Blake! Be happy!

Why wasn't I happy?

I stared at the ceiling as her lips made their way down my body and hoped she wouldn't notice my eyes brimming with tears. More than anything, I wanted to down an entire bottle of whiskey, sparkling wine, rum, tequila, *anything*. Anything to take me out of my jumbled mind and back to a place where I was comfortable and I could drown out these doubts. Back to a place where Ella and I made sense and there wasn't a question mark where there should've been an exclamation point. I wanted everything to go back to the way it should've been. When Ella and Annetta laughed like old friends. When everything felt easy, felt like glow.

With every kiss, every curve of our bodies, every flicker of joy, I tried to climb outside of my own head. I tried to find my way home. But I was stumbling around in the dark, searching for a door I couldn't find.

CHAPTER 15

"WOW," DAD SAID AS he leaned against my doorframe. "You've really made progress."

My gaze traveled over the mountain of boxes lining the taupe wall of my bedroom. "I guess so," I said, dropping another book into the box near my feet. I wasn't sure how long I'd been packing. Once my hands got ahold of the tape and boxes, I hadn't been able to stop. Dad looked impressed as he wandered inside to examine my work.

"What's your system?" he asked.

"System?"

"You know." He rummaged through a box filled with fantasy books. "What are you giving away, what's going with you to school?"

I stared at it all with dull eyes. I felt nothing. "I'm donating everything."

Dad brushed his hand over the frilly quilt I'd had since middle school. "Isn't that a bit dramatic?"

My shoulders clenched at the word. *Dramatic.* "Fine," I said. "I'll keep this one." The packing tape made a horrible screech as I sealed up another box. I had to keep my hands moving. I didn't want to think about the society or Ella or my broken promise to Annetta. All I wanted was the satisfying feeling of packing my life away slowly, but surely. I grabbed a marker and scrawled BOOKS on the side of the box.

"We're really going to miss you, kid," he said as I slid the box toward my closet.

"I'm going to miss you, too," I said to the wall.

"Your mother told me all about that craziness with the sorority the other night." Dad chuckled. "I'm glad you're going to have a group of girls for your stand-in family. As long as you're still getting your work done." His peck to the back of my head came so quick I didn't have time to react. He was halfway out the door when he added, "Don't forget about Busch Gardens on Monday."

"I know."

He sighed as he ambled off, no doubt grateful to be walking away from our stiff conversation and toward the baseball game on television in the living room.

I padded across the room and checked my phone. I scrolled through the unanswered texts from Ella that'd been collecting over the past couple of days. Texts asking where I was, why hadn't I been to work, what was my problem? She even stopped by, but I told Mom to tell her I was asleep. I'd watched the Range Rover pull out of the parking lot through the cracks in my blinds, a hollow ache in my chest.

I couldn't pinpoint why I felt so empty. Ever since the second Serena task, there was a gaping hole where my heart should've been. For the first time in my life, being at the Spencers' didn't felt like a safe haven. Between Ella constantly talking about the society and Mrs. Spencer's daily live streams taking over the kitchen, I couldn't find a corner in that house where I could just *breathe* and quiet my mind. So now I was in my childhood bedroom in search of . . . something. Clarity? Peace? A sense of home?

Whatever it was, it wasn't here, either. I hadn't felt this lonely since middle school, when I was hidden away in a corner of the library, desperately tuning out my classmates' taunts.

I threw my phone to the side and buried my head in my hands. I could just imagine Leon's eye rolls or Ella's snickers at my dramatics, but the tears formed anyway. I wanted to crawl outside of my skin as the seconds ticked by.

I missed the way things used to be. I missed the parties, I missed feeling alive and watched and wanted. I missed Big Bad Bee. I hadn't had a drink in days, partly because there was no alcohol in my house but also because I still felt horrible about breaking my promise to Annetta. She hadn't replied to the numerous apology texts I'd sent her, and I didn't blame her. I wanted to go back in time, when everything was fun and life made sense and I wasn't a liar who broke promises to my best friend.

My phone buzzed. Ella, again.

> I didn't know the Netties were contagious.
> Seriously B wtf is going on?

I deleted the message. Strode to the other side of my room. Went back to packing.

Sunday mornings after church were always a busy time at Crystal Grove, and it felt weird arriving alone. I knew from Ella's socials that it was her day off, and Mrs. Spencer had taken her dorm room shopping. Thank God. We were due for a massive fight whenever we eventually talked. I'd taken the bus to the outskirts of Crystal Grove and walked the mile to the club in the center of the neighborhood. As I passed the golf course, none of the members called out to me. I was invisible without Ella shining next to me.

At the pool, moms lazed in their lounge chairs like sunning seals, the screeches of their children undoubtedly muted by whatever was sloshing around in their chilled tumblers. As I strode to the Snack Attack Shack, I eyed Mrs. George lazily flipping through a magazine, taking sips of a minty mojito. I looked away, only to find Mr. Sanderson and his grown son chatting near the deep end, gesturing with cans of beer from a local brewery. I gritted my teeth and sped up, feeling ridiculous for being jealous.

I didn't even *like* beer. Why was I so testy?

Inside the shack, Annetta was sipping on an iced coffee. When our eyes met, it felt like a standoff in some old Western, minus the tumbleweed. I busied myself by clocking in as slow as possible. My heart pounded in my chest, wondering who would crack first.

"Hey," she said.

"Hey," I replied. I looked into her eyes, hoping to find softness, only to be met with stone.

"You really fucked us over by not showing up to work the past few days," she said, frowning. "We've been busy as hell."

My shoulders drew together as if there were magnets on my spine. In the kitchen, Tristan smacked a spatula on the grill top in an erratic beat. A symphony of fans whirred over our heads, but it was still steaming hot.

"Well, sorry," I muttered, heat creeping up my neck. "I've been busy."

"Busy," Annetta echoed. "What, partying?"

"Fuck you," I spat. Shock crossed Annetta's face, but my irritation didn't allow me to feel any guilt. Before, I was empty.

Now I was angry.

"I'm sorry—"

"All you do is judge me," I interrupted. Something inside me was screaming, clawing. I ignored it.

"What do you expect after lying directly to my face?" she snapped back. "God, you and Ella really are two peas in a pod."

"This isn't about Ella," I said. "It's about me. And I want you to leave me alone."

Annetta looked hurt, so hurt, and bile rose in my throat. Why was I being such a bitch? *Make it stop, make it stop.* But no. I couldn't. A child had their grubby fingers on a pull string on my back, and every time they yanked, something nasty came out. "Why don't you just mind your business?"

"Did you have a fight with Ella?" she asked. "Is that why—"

"Ella has nothing to do with this!" I screamed. Annetta shrank against the slushie machine, and I had to make it stop. *Make it stop, make it stop.* But my mouth was moving and I was saying words and I couldn't—

"Stop trying to control me. Stop acting like my mother just because your relationship with *your* mom is so messed up," I said, even though I had no fucking right and I felt horrible as soon as I said it and Annetta's face shattered and why *why why* was I doing this?

The order bell tinged, and Brayden Peterson's stubby pruned fingers slapped the counter, the laughter of his friends echoing behind him.

"Hey, loser," Brayden jeered. "You going to take my order or just sit there all day?"

"Haven't you ever learned any manners?" I snapped at him. I turned back to Annetta, the storm brewing in my gut, knowing I needed to apologize. Annetta was my friend. I needed to make this right.

"Look," I said with a sigh, only to be interrupted by the order bell pinging in quick succession.

"I am a paying customer," Brayden taunted. "Don't ignore me!"

"Jesus," Tristan moaned from the kitchen, pulling out one headphone. "Take this kid's order so he can go away."

"I have money to spend," Brayden said.

"You mean your dad's money," I said.

Brayden's cheeks reddened. His friends cackled like sunburnt hyenas.

"Do you want to get fired?" Brayden asked. He crossed his arms across his bare splotchy chest. "You should already be in trouble for not wearing my dad's button. *All* club members are supposed to wear them."

"Oh, boo-hoo, I'm so afraid," I said. Annetta tugged my arm, undoubtedly trying to save me from myself yet again. But I was rooted and ready to take someone down.

Brayden glared. "Fries. Chocolate shake. Now. Or my dad will make sure you don't have a job tomorrow."

"Oh yeah? Your dad? He's going to make time for that between painting his face black and cheating on your mother?"

This time, Brayden's friends didn't laugh. Their eyes widened and Brayden's mouth dropped.

"Blake." Annetta's voice, a warning. One I ignored.

"You're such a miserable brat," I barreled on. "Does this make you feel better, being a nightmare to people serving you?" Brayden started to sputter, and I leaned closer, making sure to enunciate every word. "Instead of threatening to have me fired, maybe you should be more worried about the fact that your father is a racist piece of shit." I smirked as Brayden reeled.

"Ms. Brenner!"

I froze. The voice didn't belong to Annetta or Tristan. Time slowed as I turned, already picturing the pleated shorts and deep frown of my boss.

Todd stood next to Annetta, his mouth a thin line of disgust. He pointed to the stockroom.

"Step away from the window. Now."

I was fired immediately.

Todd didn't need any excuse, and I didn't have the strength to make one up. Without a word, I handed over my name tag and register key card while he scolded me about Crystal Grove club ethics. CGGYC employees would *never* shame or embarrass any member, no matter how unpleasant they were. It was simply unforgivable.

"He is a *child*," Todd said as I gathered up my things. Tristan and Annetta watched with grim expressions. "How could you say those things to a child? I'm so disappointed in you, Ms. Brenner."

I didn't answer him. Shrugging my backpack over my shoulder, I met Annetta's eyes. She looked like she didn't recognize me.

"I was already going to fire you after you completely failed to show up for your shifts this week," Todd said, following me out of the shack. On the other end of the pool, Brayden was ranting to his mother and pointing in my direction. Mrs. Peterson looked at me with murder in her eyes, and I glared back. I was ready to burn this whole place down.

"Don't worry, Mrs. Peterson!" Todd called, trailing behind me, sneakers squishing on the damp concrete. "I have it all under control!" In a lower voice, he said, "You're fortunate you lasted this long, Ms. Brenner. If you didn't have the good word of the Spencers, I would have let you go a long time ago. You have completely tarnished the good name—"

"Fuck you and your pleated shorts, Todd." I felt an immense satisfaction as his footsteps abruptly stopped. Over my shoulder I called, "I'll see myself out!"

I walked away, ripping a FRANKLY? I'M WITH PETERSON! sign off the pool gates for good measure. I tore it to shreds. Threw it in the air like confetti.

I walked through the Crystal Grove neighborhood in a sun-hot daze, mind oscillating between *What the fuck did I just do?* and *How could I say that to Annetta?* and *My life is officially a dumpster fire.* I didn't know where to go, what to do. Sweat pooled under my pits and on my forehead, and I was so *pissed* I could hardly see straight. I was using my shirt to wipe my face when a familiar Audi slowed, and suddenly there was Mrs. Spencer with her signature red lip. In the passenger seat, Ella lowered her phone and shot me a withering glare.

"Blake!" Mrs. Spencer called. "What are you doing?"

I could make out my warped reflection on the Audi door, and I imagined what I must look like to them, trudging through their neighborhood filled with million-dollar homes in my lime-green Snack Attack polo. My gaze swept to the ground. "Uh . . ."

"Get in," Mrs. Spencer said. "It's hotter than Hades out there."

If Mrs. Spencer noticed the coldness between me and Ella as I carefully climbed into the back seat, she didn't say anything. As she glided through the neighborhood, I sank into the buttery leather seats amid a sea of shopping bags. In the passenger seat, Ella scrolled through her phone without acknowledging me. I deserved it for ignoring her for days. Our fight was brewing like a category five hurricane.

"If I'd known you were getting off this early, I would've invited you to go shopping with us," Mrs. Spencer said as she turned onto a leafy tree-lined street. "There were some lovely sales going on."

"Looks like it." I took in the massive amounts of knickknacks and gold décor and twin XL bedsheets.

We entered the Spencers' cul-de-sac, and I felt like I was falling into a black hole as we descended down their driveway. The reality of everything that happened this morning settled on me with a horrifying weight as we shuffled the shopping bags inside the house. Mrs. Spencer began prepping for a haul video, so Ella and I went upstairs to her bedroom.

Ella sat on the edge of her bed. The sadness in her eyes nearly knocked me backward.

"I'm sorry," I said quickly. "I know I've been distant."

"Aren't you supposed to be at work?"

I couldn't stop staring at her lips, pouty and full. I swallowed. "I got fired."

She snorted. "Yeah, right."

I shook my head. Her eyebrows raised, and I spat out a condensed version of the morning's events. Her face morphed from confusion to horror to utter elation. She flopped back onto the bed in a fit of giggles.

"You really told Todd to fuck himself. And of *course* I wasn't there to witness it!"

I cringed. "It wasn't one of my finest moments."

She waved her hand. "Whatever. That job was a joke, anyway.

There's only a few more weeks before we start at Jameswell." She sat up on her forearms and narrowed her eyes. "But why have you been ghosting me?"

I sat on the edge of the bed. I tried not to think about how I snuck away while she was sleeping the last time I was here.

"I just feel so sad," I whispered. I stared at my hands, flinching slightly when her warm palm rested on my elbow. "I don't know . . . I don't—"

She frowned. "What is it, Bee?"

"I just . . ." I paused, voice cracking. I focused on the lines on my palms, noting the way they dipped and intersected and fell off the sides of my hands. "I can't stop feeling like Annetta was right. Maybe I *do* have a drinking problem."

She snorted. "Are you serious? *That's* what you're upset about?"

My heart fell, deeper and deeper and deeper, a little girl tumbling into a well. I didn't know why this was so hard to say. Ella had always been my confidant. We wanted the same things. She always chose me.

"I've noticed that I'm so mean to myself when I drink," I said slowly. "And I don't know when to stop. Once I start, I just keep going and going until it spirals out of control." I couldn't stop looking at my hands, but I heard the frown in her voice.

"I think you're overexaggerating, Bee. You're fine."

"I don't feel fine," I whispered.

"Then how do you feel?"

Lonely. Confused. So nervous and full of shame. But I could see Ella batting away all those emotions, telling me I was being dramatic.

"I blacked out during the first task, Ella. And the night with the yacht and the paint. *And* that night Annetta had to take me home."

"So?"

I swiveled around. She was a lioness, perched in the middle of her bed in jean shorts, red hair spilling over her shoulder. "'So?' You don't see anything wrong with that?"

Her laughter filled the entire room. "Bee, you've got to be kidding. The paint was *hilarious*. Frank Peterson is a dick. You *still* feel bad about that? And who cares about the first task? You killed the second one." She patted the space next to her, the curtain-filtered sun shining on her bare shoulder. I crawled to her, and her eyes searched every corner of my face. Searching for something familiar. I wanted whatever she found.

"You don't have a problem, my Bumblebee." Her finger traced my jawline. "It's not like you've gotten a DUI or killed someone—"

"I just lost my job," I pointed out.

"Yeah, because you told a spoiled little brat about himself, not because you were stumbling in drunk." I shivered as her fingers made their way to the nape of my neck. I loved her so much. "It's not like you're doing meth or something. You just drink like every other normal person. It's not something to be worried about, though." She waved her hand toward the corner, as if Annetta were there and staring at us in disapproval. "Whatever Nettie said has clearly gotten into your head. And she's wrong."

My heart thudded. "What if she's not?"

"You don't have a drinking problem." Her forehead rested on mine and her fingers entangled in my curls, deeper and deeper. "All this back-and-forth isn't good, it's making you miserable. You *don't* have a drinking problem."

I felt the stinging burn of tears. I closed my eyes, and they dribbled down my cheeks.

"I care about you, Bee." She kissed each cheek twice, catching the tears before they dropped to her comforter. "You have nothing to be worried about. You're beautiful, you're smart. We're going to Jameswell and we're going to be in the Serena Society, and everything is going to be fine. I wouldn't let you get in over your head. You trust me, right?"

I nodded, swallowing the rest of my tears. She kissed me some more, and my body softened into the bed. After the stagnant nothingness, the overwhelming shame and loneliness . . . I liked *this* feeling the best. Assured. Someone whispering in my ear that everything was going to be okay. I didn't have a problem.

I was normal.

And she was right, wasn't she? Her parents drank regularly, and they had the world at their fingertips. They had a house with sweeping water views. They traveled the world. And Ella herself was destined for greatness, too. Maybe—just maybe—it truly *wasn't* that big of a deal. I had a few bad nights, but Ella wouldn't lead me astray. We were in this together.

So I kissed her back. Unlike the previous night, my body didn't respond with a rush of bad memories at all. Instead, I thought of that first night at Crystal Grove. The two of us twisted together on an exercise bench, tipsy and full of wanting. I thought of how full I felt. The opposite of empty.

Ella got up and locked her door, and we had sex right there in the middle of the afternoon. It was the opposite of the sex we normally had. Instead of letting Ella take charge, I climbed on top of her, wielding her small purple vibrator with ease, finding every spot on her that she always found on me. She looked at me in surprise, stifling gasps, but I didn't stop. I kept going, so sure that this was okay and this was what I wanted.

Everything was good again.

That night, there was a gathering on the *Bewitched*. Just a couple of people, according to Ella. Nothing special. Still, we followed the agenda.

We got ready. Ella did our makeup. We made out between shots of tequila, giggling into each other's spicy mouths. That Feeling welcomed me back with open arms. I was home.

We drove to the party on the same road we always took, passed the same security guard we always passed, parked in the same spot we always parked. As we made our way down the docks, I opened my phone and saw texts from Annetta asking what was I doing, was I okay?

I didn't answer.

I was more than okay. I focused on Now.

Now I felt good.

Now I felt amazing.

Now I felt alive.

There would be no starting over. I didn't have a drinking problem, and everything was good now.

Now.

My vibrant and beautiful and brilliant Now.

CHAPTER 16

BUSCH GARDENS WILLIAMSBURG WAS regularly touted as one of the most beautiful theme parks in the world, and I already wanted to go home. The boisterous music and screaming children would've been too abrasive, even if I weren't hungover. While security searched Mom's backpack, Leon and I waited by a bubbling fountain. Dad studied the park map, bald head covered with a Nationals cap and a fanny pack snug around his waist.

"So I'm guessing this is the England section of the park!" Dad announced, twisting and squinting at the map. Leon and I glanced up at the dozens of UK flags that crisscrossed overhead and the red telephone booths scattered around the plaza. We held back our laughter.

Mom joined us, reapplying sunscreen even though she'd already put on a layer in the car. I couldn't see her bright green eyes behind her black sunglasses. "This is so exciting," she said. "I don't even know where we should start!"

The park was divided into villages that mirrored various European locales. Soon we were leaving England and entering Scotland. Bagpipes blared, and I rubbed my temples. Leon fell in step beside me, smiling like a goofball. It was the first time I'd seen him since I learned about him and Alice. I was waiting for the perfect moment to bring it up, but he was making it hard to keep quiet by how freaking happy he looked.

I even caught him *humming* when we were waiting in line to get our entry tickets scanned.

"You okay?" he asked.

I nodded. "I'm fine. This is just . . . weird."

Leon chuckled. "For real. How many times did we beg them to take us here when we were little? Better late than never, I guess."

I nodded. I didn't know what—if anything—my parents were trying to accomplish with this family outing. I couldn't remember the last time the four of us had gotten together simply for fun's sake, but they couldn't have picked a worse day to do so. I was recovering from what Ella had fondly dubbed a "Termination Celebration," a wild party on the *Bewitched* that I could barely remember thanks to copious tequila shots.

"Such beauty!" Dad exclaimed. Mom nearly ran into the back of him as he stopped to admire the view. Several roller coasters stood prominently in the distance, and screams emitted from plummeting riders.

While we waited in line for the first roller coaster, Leon and Dad chatted about work. Next to me, Mom studied the park map. I leaned against a railing and checked Ella's socials. She was working today; in her latest upload, she was in the Crystal Grove locker room, blowing a kiss in a full-length mirror.

"So how are things going with the Serena Society?" Mom asked.

"Mom!" I glanced around wildly, as if a group of women with sapphire bracelets were going to charge out of the bushes and tackle me. "I'm not supposed to talk about it all out in public like this."

"Oh, sorry. I forgot." She pretended to zip her lips. We inched forward in line, and she tried again. "How are your . . . clarinet lessons going?"

"They're good."

"When does it become official?" Mom asked.

"Before school starts," I said. *A month*, I realized with a jolt. Summer was flying by. These weeks used to feel endless when I was little.

"So you and Ella and Annetta will be the cool girls on campus?" Mom asked.

Her words were like a slap. Annetta and I hadn't talked since I got fired, and it felt like lifetimes. I shoved that anxiety away and thought about Ella instead. Ella, beautiful Ella. My girlfriend. I pictured her lips on my neck. Us giggling in the closet with the bottle between us like a beating heart. Her whispered assurances—

You don't have a drinking problem. You don't have a drinking problem.

"Something like that," I said quietly.

"First in the family to go to college." Mom beamed, and I managed a weak smile. "I'm so proud of you, Blake."

"Thanks, Mom." I didn't hear praise from my family often. So before her words faded, I snatched them out of the air. Sat in their glow for a while. Felt golden.

It took nearly an hour to reach the front of the line. By that point, my parents were losing their enthusiasm, and my headache was pounding. When the four of us climbed into the coaster's green-and-orange striped cars, I was more excited to sit down than I was for the actual ride. My parents took the row in front of us, and Leon and I nestled behind. A bored-looking guy with a smattering of pimples checked to make sure our harnesses were secure.

"Ready for this?" Leon asked.

"I was born ready," I replied. My parents turned to smile at us. They looked so dorky and full of life. A slow grin crept across my face. There was a hiss, and the coaster glided forward, metal clanking beneath us.

We climbed higher. The sky stretched forever. My heart quickened. Mom threw her hands in the air, already screaming. Dad's laugh carried in the wind.

"Here it comes," Leon said, and I held my breath. This was the moment of stillness I dreaded. I knew the plunge was coming, and it was too late to turn back now. Then we lurched, and I gasped as we hurtled toward earth, rushing toward the inevitable.

After the first roller coaster, I was addicted. I hadn't been on one since my eighth-grade class trip to Kings Dominion, and exhilaration surged in my blood long after the ride. I took over and led my family through the Scotland and Germany sections of the park, making sure to hit every attraction in between. It was well after noon when Mom dragged me away from the tallest roller coaster, claiming we were all going to pass out if we didn't eat soon.

"We have the rest of the day," she insisted. "The rides aren't going anywhere."

We stopped for lunch at Das Festhaus, a huge indoor eating facility that was a replica of a traditional German tavern. We grabbed plates of bratwurst, potatoes, and red cabbage and settled at one of the long wooden tables.

"We missed the noon show," Mom said, motioning to the large stage in the center of the room. "But they have another one starting in thirty minutes. Should we stay? The program says the dances are based on famous fairy tales."

Dad balked, probably already dreading having to watch people twirl and high-kick while he was eating. But something in Mom's tone must have got to him, so he said, "Sure. It'd be nice to take a break from the heat."

As we ate, people in dirndl and lederhosen marched between the aisles, dancing and filling the air with trumpets and horns. Leon and I cackled as a busty girl sashayed in our direction and batted her eyelashes at us. At one point, Dad grabbed Mom's hand, and they joined other couples awkwardly dancing near the stage.

"They actually look like they like each other," I mused. Not like strangers who slept in the same bed on occasion. And thanks to Mom's night shift schedule, they barely did that.

Leon swigged his lemonade. "Yeah. They're cute."

"Kinda like another couple I know."

His eyes bulged. "What are you talking about?"

"You and *Aliiiiiiice*."

His smile was so wide I could see his molars. "I've been waiting for you to bring her up."

"I've been waiting for *you* to bring her up!" I said, shoving his shoulder playfully.

"We're not official," he said, but I could tell by his lovesick expression how much he wanted to change that.

"Well, don't be an asshole and break her heart," I said. "Or you'll ruin my chances getting into Serena."

"Whatever," he said. "I don't know anything about that whole process. I didn't even know she was *in* some secret society until she mentioned that you were also trying to get in." He looked at me curiously. "What's the big deal about this club, anyway?"

"It's not a club," I said. I watched as Dad dipped Mom on the dance floor, and her surprised laughter echoed throughout the dining hall. She looked twenty years younger, and I couldn't help but smile. I remembered when I was in middle school and Mom was my only friend. How close we used to be. But that inevitably ushered in another memory—my sixteenth birthday and a passing comment that'd stuck to me like flypaper for over two years now.

Even when I tried telling them that Mariah was only half Black, they still wouldn't budge.

Even when I tried telling them that Mariah was only half—

Only half—

There were a million reasons to join Serena, but in that moment in Das Festhaus, I could only think of one. I pushed around a pile of hot red cabbage.

"Aren't you in a group for Black air traffic controllers?" I asked.

"Yeah," Leon said. "What's your point?"

"Serena is my version of that. I'll get to be around women of color. They'll be my mentors. They'll guide me . . ." My gaze lingered on my parents. I hoped that Leon could hear what I was unable to say: *They'll be able to guide me in a way Mom never has.*

"Blake?"

Leon and I looked up, and there was Cody Fisher, a lock of black hair matted to his greasy white forehead. Cody used to work the fryers at the Snack Attack Shack, and he was a frequent fixture in our post-work gatherings last summer. That was before he was fired for dealing molly to some of the club members' kids.

Cody wiped his nicotine-stained fingers on his apron and thrust his hand toward Leon. After they introduced themselves, Cody grinned at me. "How's life at the Grove, Big Bad Bee?"

My relief at being saved from the memory of my mother's

microaggression fizzled. I hadn't told Leon or my parents I'd been fired yet. "You know. Same old shit."

"Dude, the Grove blows," Cody said. "Come on, I can give you the exclusive backstage tour. I'm on break for the next fifteen minutes."

"The show's starting soon."

Cody smirked. "You scared to see what a real kitchen looks like or something?"

I laughed, a stream of memories from last summer at the Snack Attack rushing in. Annetta, Cody, and I used to pass the lazy hours by coming up with ridiculous backstories about different club members. We'd experiment with the blender and dare each other to drink whatever the disgusting concoction of the day was. Cody probably would have been cheering me on when I confronted Brayden Peterson, unlike Annetta.

"Go on," Leon said. "Bring me back some cake."

So that was how I found myself following Cody into the kitchens of Das Festhaus, watching as he swiped a slice of triple-layer chocolate cake from the frosty walk-in.

"I'm a real kitchen man here," he said, sweeping an arm over the stainless-steel appliances that seemed to stretch forever. "None of that rinky-dink shit from the shack." The kitchen was loud, full of clanging pans and sizzling grills as the chefs worked to replace the dwindling supplies of sausages and burgers and roasted chicken. No one batted an eye as Cody and I slipped out the back door into a small courtyard with a patch with dead grass and a couple of sagging plastic chairs. The humidity felt like a dense fog, and I immediately wanted to go back inside. Cody lit a cigarette, got comfy in one of the chairs.

"How's Nettie?" Cody had always had a crush on Annetta, even though she shuddered anytime someone mentioned it to her. He held out the cigarette, but I wrinkled my nose.

"She's fine."

"And Toddy boy?"

I snorted. Now that we were in the stillness of the courtyard, I felt comfortable enough to share the truth. Cody, out of all people, couldn't care less.

"He fired me, actually."

Cody's eyes lit up. "No fucking way. What the hell happened?" I told him the story, and his laughter punctuated all the right spaces. When I was done, he reached inside his chef's jacket and pulled out a small silver flask that glinted in the sun.

"That's the Big Bad Bee I know," he said, untwisting the flask and swigging. I awkwardly held the cake. The chocolate frosting was melting in the heat. "You want some?"

My knee-jerk reaction was no. But it was fleeting, as if cool, nonchalant Big Bad Bee had rested her hand on my shoulder.

Have fun. Focus on Now.

I took the flask, balancing the cake in my other hand, and waterfalled some into my mouth. Whiskey, of course. It was surprisingly cool, but it still burned. I liked it.

"Drinking on the job?" I handed it back and wiped my mouth.

Cody took another swig. "Some things never change, Bee."

We passed the flask back and forth for the next ten minutes. While Cody blathered on about life at Busch Gardens, I downed three shots of spicy whiskey. My limbs grew languid. With the heat on my face, it felt like last summer. I closed my eyes and saw me, Ella, Cody, and the rest of the Crystal Grove crew on the docks, playing cards and drinking.

The door to the courtyard banged open, and two guys in chef coats stumbled out. Cody swiftly tucked the flask into his pocket without missing a beat.

"Yo, Fisher!" the older one shouted. "Get your ass back on the line!"

"Duty calls," Cody said, leading me back inside. "It was dope catching up with you."

I nodded, my head light.

Cody led me back to the serving lines. "Enjoy the show. I've slept with half the chorus line." He waggled his tongue before disappearing into the kitchen, and my skin crawled. Cody was right. Some things never changed, including his disgusting comments no one asked for.

I bought a Sprite before heading back out, hoping the soda would mask the whiskey. The lights had dimmed in preparation for the show, and I stumbled over someone's purse strap as I made my way to my family. Leon raised his eyebrows as I plopped into my seat and passed him the cake.

"You almost missed the beginning," Mom whispered.

I mouthed an apology as a brilliant burst of music flared and dancers took to the stage. Leon dug his fork into the cake and shot me a look.

"What?" I hissed.

"You've got to be kidding me," he mumbled. He glanced at our parents, but they were completely enraptured by the show.

My stomach sank. "What?"

But he just glared at me and turned to face the stage.

By the time the show was over, I'd passed the edge of tipsy and was flirting with drunk. I thought I could swallow it down, drown it out with Sprite. I even went to the restroom twice, but splashing water on my face didn't help. When my family and I stepped out of Das Festhaus, the sunshine world was a little tilted, a little off.

I was screwed.

"All right, Blake!" Dad said. "Where to next?"

My mouth was dry, so I pointed to a sign announcing another roller coaster. My parents headed in that direction, Mom still humming the show's theme song. Leon and I dragged behind, and I braced myself for his lecture. We only lasted a minute before he cracked.

"Tell me I'm imagining you're drunk right now," Leon said. We dodged a toddler having a meltdown. The little girl's screeches followed us around the bend.

I stared ahead and said nothing. I guessed our brief moment of sibling bonding was done.

"You came back to the table smelling like booze and cigarettes."

"Cody had a cigarette," I said. "What's the big deal?"

"Are you serious?"

I scoffed. "Jesus, Leon, *you* were the one who told me to go with him! Now you wanna be all annoying." I threw my hands up, gesturing to the rows of beautiful flowers lining the walkway. "We're having a 'nice family outing.' Why are you trying to ruin it?"

"Don't bullshit me, Blake," he said in a low voice. My parents walked hand in hand a few yards in front of us, oblivious to our bickering. If my brother weren't annoying me, I would've marveled at the way Mom smiled up at Dad, like they were those teenagers from the old-time photo shop. But Leon's voice was cutting in my ear.

"Were you drinking with that guy?"

I whirled to face him, fists curling. The same rage that simmered when I got fired was threatening to erupt again. "And so what if I was? Who cares!"

"*I* care," he snapped. "And I think our parents would, too. This day was supposed to be special."

"God, you're *so* dramatic," I said, smug that I was able to throw his favorite insult in his face before he could use it on me. "News flash, not everyone lives in a boring little bubble like you. Some people actually know what it means to have *fun*."

Leon looked like he'd been slapped. I walked away, a fire at my heels.

"I know what fun is," he said behind me, and I stifled laughter. "Blake, I'm serious. I just didn't know your definition of fun included getting drunk when you're supposed to be hanging out with your family. What are you doing?"

"I'm growing up," I said. The heat and the whiskey blew on the flames of my anger. "Do you think I'm still thirteen? Sitting in the house all by myself with no friends? Is that what you want?"

"No," he said. "That's not what I want, but—"

"Just drop it," I said. "I'm fine. For real."

I caught up with my parents before he could reply, and we joined a snaking line for a roller coaster named Verbolten. While we waited, Leon scrolled through his phone, sulking like a child, and I studied Mom's park map over her shoulder. She hadn't stopped smiling since we left the show. Anytime we inched forward, she did so with a little extra pep in her step.

"Someone's happy," I observed, trying to focus on anything but Leon's words.

"I *loved* the show," she gushed. "Didn't you? All the music and dancing!" She had a faraway look in her eyes, one that was usually reserved for when she was absorbed in a novel. My gut pinched, but I shook it off.

"It was great," I lied. I actually thought the costumes were ugly and the dancers had no rhythm, but I wasn't going to prove Leon right. This was probably the most excitement Mom was going to have all summer. I couldn't ruin it.

The line for the coaster moved swiftly, and we were at the front in no time. It wasn't until we were rolling away from the station, secure in our lap belts, that I thought, *Maybe this wasn't a good idea.* I could've kicked myself for pulling a stunt so mindless—honestly, shots with Cody Fisher?—but it was too late.

The train picked up speed, twisted around bends, and there was no way out. Mom squeezed my hand as we launched full speed into a tunnel of flashing lights.

I couldn't open my mouth, even as Mom's screams swelled. Acid bubbled in my throat as we plunged, twisted, curved, defied gravity. The darkness was disorienting, and I couldn't tell when the next whiplash curve was coming. *Stars.* There were so many stars. I squeezed my eyes shut, but that only made them burn brighter. I wrangled my hand out of Mom's death grip and covered my mouth. My stomach churned faster. Another dip, I peeled one eyelid open. Mistake. The lights were a psychedelic trip, neon green and azure blue. Leon's and Dad's cheers intermingled with thunder sound effects. A big bad wolf chuckled in the darkness.

There was an abrupt stop, and that was all it took. I dropped my head and retched into the bottom of the car. Mom gasped.

"Blake! Oh, sweetheart!"

The coaster shot forward into glaring daylight. My stomach clenched, and I threw up again, gagging at the whiskey's reappearance. Bits of food clung to my sneakers, and I felt sick—so fucking *sick*—I could only sit there and cry like a child with vomit on my shoes. Mom held my curls away from my neck. The car lurched and slowed before the final drop. I gagged and Mom whacked me on the back so hard it stung.

"What the fuck!" I screamed, and Mom yanked her hand away like she'd placed it on a hot burner. I could barely make out her stricken expression through my tears.

"I'm sorry," she stammered. "I thought you were choking!"

We plunged to the earth. There was nothing left to throw up. I cried as we snaked over water, between trees, around a final bend. Then we finally, *finally*, slowed, and I heard Dad asking if I was okay.

"Blake got a little sick," Mom replied. My fingers curled around the safety bar, and I took slow, labored breaths. My vomit was already starting to stink.

"It's okay," Mom said. Her hand did a nervous dance before settling back on her lap. "It's okay. This probably happens every day. We'll get you cleaned up, and everything will be okay."

I stared at my knuckles as we arrived back to where we started. A peppy girl over the loudspeaker boomed, "*Welllllcome back, thrill seekers! How! Was! Your! Ride!*"

"Eww!" The voice came from the crowd of people waiting to ride. "That girl puked all over herself!"

I pushed on my lap belt, cheeks burning, but we were still locked in. I looked off to the side, to the faces of three horrified preteen girls. The girl in the middle had a long curtain of blond hair and was clearly the ringleader. I pushed on the lap belt again.

"That's, like, so gross," she announced. I looked away, but I could still hear her friends tittering in agreement.

This damn belt. I almost ripped the bar up with my bare hands when the hydraulics hissed and we were free. I stumbled over Mom trying to get out.

"Blake, wait!" Mom called.

"Bathroom," I choked out. I couldn't look anyone in the eyes.

Especially not Leon. Not after our conversation. I could picture the gloating look on his obnoxious, smug face, and I couldn't stand it. I had to leave.

I ignored scandalized looks as I barreled into the closest restroom. I grabbed a handful of paper towels, ran them under water, and locked myself in a stall.

I yanked my vomit-streaked T-shirt over my head and shoved it into the tiny wastebasket bolted to the wall. My chest was bare and sticky in my thin tank top. I wiped my legs and shoes, grateful the damage wasn't any worse.

"Blake?"

Mom's voice echoed through the restroom. Balancing on the toilet seat, I pulled my feet to my chest and held my breath.

Please don't find me. Go away.

"Blake? Are you in here?"

I could hear Mom's soft footsteps darting around people washing their hands at the sink. Could hear her gentle voice saying, "Excuse me, excuse me." Glimpsed her through the tiny crack in the stall as she called my name again.

"Blake? Sweetheart, are you in here?"

I stayed quiet.

She left.

I remained locked in the stall for five minutes, trying not to cry. I should've just gone out there, rejoined my family, and bought a new T-shirt at the souvenir shop so we could get on with our day. But I was frozen. I checked the time on my phone, ignoring the messages from Mom and Leon. It was barely four. We still had hours.

I called Ella. When it went to voice mail, I cursed, remembering she was working the afternoon shift at the pool. My thumb hovered over Annetta's name, but I couldn't bring myself to press it. I needed to get the fuck out of there. I needed someone with a car who had nothing better to do.

Josiah.

He picked up on the first ring. "My darling, to what do I owe this pleasure?"

"I need a rescue mission. Bad."

"Oh, thank God. I was beginning to think I was going to *die* of boredom today! We'll come back to the boat," he said, thrilled. "Have a girls' day."

"I love you," I said breathlessly. "And bring a toothbrush."

We hung up, and I let my legs drop to the ground. I did a sweep under the door, and when I didn't see Mom's smudged white tennis shoes, I emerged from the stall. I washed my hands, washed my face, rinsed my mouth out with tap water so lukewarm it almost made me gag again. Then I went to the entrance and hovered in the doorway, searching for my family.

I didn't see them. They were probably still at the roller coaster exit, waiting for me. I slipped into the crowd and walked quickly, head down. My phone buzzed in my back pocket, and when I pulled it out, an all-caps text from Leon greeted me.

WHERE ARE YOU?!

I kept walking. I cleared Bavarian Germany and wound up in Italy. The scent of cotton candy and churros swirled in the air, and I pressed on, past a group of kids all clad in the same red T-shirt like a shifting human stop sign. I glanced over my shoulder, certain Leon would be there. But there was only a sea of strangers as I made my great escape.

CHAPTER 17

SALVATION ARRIVED IN THE form of a cherry-red BMW. A blond white boy at the wheel, a travel toothbrush, toothpaste, and a bottle of water riding shotgun.

"Do I wanna know?" Josiah asked in amusement as I quickly brushed my teeth.

I spat onto the concrete. "Dental emergency," I said, and he hummed sympathetically.

When I climbed into the passenger seat, I tossed my phone in the cup holder. The screen was lit with an incoming call from Leon.

"You gonna get that?" Josiah asked.

"I'll text him."

Josiah nodded, not needing any further explanation. If I hadn't smelled like vomit, I would've thrown my arms around him in gratitude.

We blasted music as we merged onto the highway. It was the perfect antidote. I didn't need anyone looking at me, looking *for* me, worrying about me. I just needed the music turned up so loud I couldn't hear myself think. I sent a quick text to Mom and didn't give myself any time to consider how ridiculous it sounded.

> I'm fine! I forgot I had to go to my friend's thing but they picked me up, love you!!

My friend's thing? Whatever. I turned my phone off and threw it in the back seat. Sang louder. I imagined Josiah and I were in a music video. His bleached hair, skin tan from too many hours on his yacht's sundeck. Me, wild curls, sexy and carefree. On our way to our favorite hiding place.

We drove past the pool really slow, creeping along until Ella noticed us. From her lifeguard chair perch, she lowered her sunglasses.

"Be jealous!" Josiah screamed.

I could see her dazzling smile from the road. I loved her. Everything was good again. With a cackle, Josiah sped toward the docks.

Once aboard *Byte Me*, I waited impatiently while Josiah blended strawberry daiquiris.

"What are we toasting?" Josiah screamed over the roar of the blender.

I spun on the stool, kicked my legs in the air. I was so ungraceful I nearly toppled over. Josiah and I howled with laughter. He handed me a daiquiri, bright red with a thick layer of rum on top.

"We're celebrating life!" I cheered, and we clinked our glasses in celebration.

> *Please feel something. Let this work.*
> *You're such a fuckup. Just pathetic.*

I sipped. Pushed the thoughts out of my head. Drank more when they fought their way back in.

You ditched your family at an amusement park?

After getting drunk?

To go drink more?

Who does that?

"Cheers, bitch," Josiah said. We took our drinks and the half-empty bottle of rum and sprawled on the sectional. The daiquiri was cool, refreshing, everything I wanted. I wasn't trying to get shit-faced. Just enough to stop beating myself up.

I drank more.

Everything was going to be okay. I didn't have a problem. Ella told me so. And Josiah could drink me under a table. He was already almost done with his daiquiri. I had to catch up.

We listened to music. I drank more.

"God, whoever said the summer before college was supposed to be magical was full of shit," Josiah whined.

"Maybe it's because all your friends have jobs besides you," I teased.

"Oh, excuse me, Miss Bitch." Josiah uncapped the rum and topped us off. "Word on the street is that you're no longer employed, either."

My cheeks flushed. I drank more.

"Oh well." He settled into his lounge chair and wiggled his hairy toes. "That just means the two of us will be having fun while the rest of our chump friends waste the rest of the summer away."

We cheers'd to that. Drank. Josiah twirled his straw around in his melted mixture. "How was Busch Gardens?"

I took another sip. Felt the sting of vomit hurtling up my throat.

Heard the echo of Mom's voice in the restroom. Searching, searching. Never finding. Another sip.

"It was fine. I saw Cody."

Josiah squealed. "Gay Cody? Used to work at Snack Attack?"

I scoffed. "He is not gay."

"Oh, honey." Josiah smacked his lips, made an *ahhhh* sound. "Everyone is a *little* gay."

I took another sip, but my glass was empty. I beat Josiah to the bottle and refilled myself. "Cheers to that," I said.

And we drank more.

By the time Ella got off work, Josiah and I were full-blown drunk.

"So y'all got the party started without me?" Ella asked. She kicked the empty rum bottle and sent it skittering under a lounge chair. Then she nestled next to me, smelling like chlorine and sunscreen, and sipped my drink. She said something about a fundraiser dinner and her parents. I could barely hear her. She took another sip, and I yanked my cup away.

"Get your own," I said, and we laughed and laughed and laughed.

The Crystal Grove club looked regal in the amber light of the setting sun. Like a castle. Ella and I were princesses. I loved her. I wanted all of her and I tried to show it with one urgent kiss after another. My princess.

"Y'all are nasty!" Josiah called from the bubbling hot tub. I had no idea how he could stand being in there in this humidity. I imagined flesh sizzling off his bones and burst out laughing.

"What's so funny?" Ella asked, lips grazing my collarbone.

I steadied myself on the rail. "I have no idea."

I never said I was someone to be proud of.

This is you. Look at yourself.

Bathroom. I clenched the sink and stared at my reflection in the mirror. Red cheeks, low eyes, greasy hair.

"You're a fucking mess, Blake," I said to my reflection. I sounded like my brother. I scrunched my face up in my best Leon impersonation. "Hi, I'm Leon Brenner, and I constantly look like I need to take a shit."

Someone pounded on the door.

Josiah's drawl: "Blake! Hell you doing in there, bitch?"

"I don't know!" I screamed, and we cackled together through the closed door. I fiddled with the lock. I freed myself. Josiah, also red-faced, giggled against the wall.

"I don't know," I repeated, and he stumbled past me into the bathroom.

There was a crowd of people aboard *Byte Me*. Full-grown adults. Who the fuck were they? Someone's hand on my arm.

"Excuse me, excuse me, coming through!" Josiah. Why did he sound so damn chipper?

I ran into someone. There was a gasp, followed by shattering glass.

"What in the world?" a woman cried out.

"So sorry, Mrs. Long!"

All I could make out was a smear of a face, a prim scowl.

"Get your shit together, Big Bad Bee," Josiah whispered singsong in my ear. "Act sober for the nice rich folk."

"Where are we going?" I mumbled.

"Roxanne's."

"Got you food. Come on, sit up for me."

Fries. I smelled fries. My eyelids fluttered open.

Ella. She looked so different. Gone was her bare face and damp hair, replaced by glittery, smoky eyes and blown-out waves. When had she left?

"Where did you go?" I asked.

"I told you about the fundraiser dinner." She waved a fry in my face. I bit and tasted truffle oil.

"You went to dinner?"

She laughed, pink lips parting over bone-white teeth. "Yes, silly. I told you that. My parents missed you."

I shoveled more fries in my mouth. "They asked about me?"

"Of course they did."

"I could've come."

She laughed again. Fed me another fry. "I don't think so, my Bumblebee."

I stared at her. Stared past her. The room looked familiar. "Where are we?"

"Roxanne's. In one of the cabins."

"Who's upstairs?"

"Everyone."

We were missing the party. I sat up, too quick. My head hated me.
I hated me. "Let's go."

"You sure?" Ella asked.

Wasn't I always?

Someone was cheering my name. Josiah.

"Tell everyone how you got fired," he demanded.

"Did you really tell Todd to fuck off?" someone asked.

I choked up a laugh. "Uhhh, yeah?"

A cheer rose. The room was blurry, too many faces, I couldn't focus
on anyone . . . except . . .

Roxanne. Glaring at me from across the room.

                    What did I do? What did I do what what what what—

"You are so wild, Bee," Ella said. I loved her. She steered me to the
kitchen as the crowd chanted, "Big Bad Bee! Big Bad Bee!"

I loved it, I loved it so much.

"Give her a kiss!" someone demanded, and we obliged, our mouths
hot and wet and sticky and—

Applause. I loved it. I deserved it.

Then Roxanne appeared. She didn't look mad anymore. Had I
imagined it?

"Look at the cute couple," she cooed, pinching my and Ella's cheeks
like we were precious toddlers. Ella laughed nervously and swatted her
hands away.

Roxanne pulled on one of my curls. She was smiling. She liked me
again. Maybe I could be her right-hand woman again. Maybe—

"Blake, what are you drinking?" she asked.

My mouth was a barren wasteland. "Um . . ."

"Rum!" She started picking through bottles. "Do you have a preference? White or gold? Spiced?"

"I don't know . . ." She wasn't listening to me. Another drink appeared in my hand. The world tilted.

I was in the kitchen. I was dancing with Ella. My vision was going in and out.

"*I love you,*" Ella sang into my ear. She twirled around like a ballerina in a music box. "I! Love! My! *Bumblebeeee!*" Her red hair slapped me in the face like seaweed.

"I'm gonna be sick," I said. Or whispered. Either way, she didn't hear me. She kept spinning.

I wriggled out of her grasp and clutched the counter. I stared at a pile of dirty dishes in the sink, begging myself to focus on one thing so the world would stop spiraling. There was a bowl filled with soapy water, something crusted around the rim. The smell of it nearly made me vomit. I backed away, ran into Ella.

"Whoa there." She giggled. "Where you headed in such a rush?" She pulled me close. Her breath smelled like wine.

"I'm so drunk," I moaned.

She laughed. "Me too."

"I need to go lie down."

"I'll come with you," she cooed.

We stumbled down to the lower deck. We passed Alice on the way, and I gasped when I saw her. "My brother's girlfriend!"

She looked surprised. "What are you doing here?"

"Come on, Bee." Ella tugged on my hand.

Alice placed her hands on my shoulders, stopping me. Her gaze seared into my soul. "I thought you were supposed to be with your family today."

"I was," I said, half laughing. Ella's grip tightened around my wrist and we continued our sloppy descent.

"Blake, stop," Alice said. She sounded so disappointed. It felt worse than Leon's fury. But I was in too deep. There was nothing I could do.

I'm having fun, I'm having fun, I'm having

"Oh my God," Ella said with a sigh. "Allie, you need to lighten up! So freaking uptight."

Alice was lightning quick. In one swift movement, she pinned Ella against the wall.

"What the fuck is wrong with you? Seriously? What. The. Fuck. Is. Wrong. With. You?"

"Get off of me!" Ella tried to push Alice away, but her movements were slow and careless.

"After what I told you?" Alice growled. "After what we *talked* about?"

Ella pushed her off. "You're a psycho," she spat, chest heaving. "Come on, Bee." She yanked my hand again, and I stumbled. My left knee struck the bottom stair with a crack. They helped me up, still bickering.

"Look at what you did! Bee, are you okay?"

"Who let her drink this much? Why is she like this, Ella?"

"What are you talking about?"

"You know damn well what I'm talking about."

My knees wobbled. "Stop. Fighting. I'm fine."

"We're going to go lie down, Bee," Ella said. "Come on." She snaked an arm around my waist and guided me into the closest cabin.

It was dark and mercifully quiet. I collapsed onto the bed with a soft thud and buried my face into the feathered pillow. There were muted footsteps on the other end of the cabin.

"I told you." Alice. "I told you I was worried about Blake's drinking and you told me you'd look out for her. You told me—"

"Oh my God!" Ella yelled. "What is your problem? We're literally just trying to go to sleep and you're, like, all up our asses!"

"You should be ashamed of yourself."

I twisted my head toward Alice's voice, but she was gone. Ella slammed the cabin door and stumbled to the bed next to me. I focused on her silhouette, swirling in the dark.

"What was that about?" I mumbled.

"I don't know," Ella said. Her voice trembled, and then she was crying.

"It's okay," I whispered. "It's okay." She melted into me. I stroked her hair, and she cried harder.

"I'm sorry," she sobbed. "Bee, I'm *so* sorry."

"You didn't do anything."

"I'm sorry," she repeated. Her chest racked with sobs. I held her tighter. "*God*, I fucked up and I'm so sorry."

I closed my eyes as the room spun. I didn't know what time it was. Where was my phone? Were my parents still looking for me? Another flash of my mom's smudged sneakers, walking up and down the restroom tiles, trying to find me.

"Let's just go to bed," I mumbled.

"Yeah." She nodded against my neck, tears smearing my skin. "Yeah. Yeah, okay."

Ella and I woke up with our limbs still tangled together. I squinted against the sunlight. My mouth felt like someone had shoved cotton balls in it. I was still drunk.

"Fuck," Ella said. "Last night was crazy." Her laugh was hollow. There were mascara streaks under her eyes.

"Are you okay?" I croaked.

"Besides being painfully hungover?" She curved her body into mine, making me the big spoon. "God, I'm so glad I have today off."

My knee throbbed, and it caused a memory to resurface. Alice and Ella, facing off.

"What were you and Alice fighting about?" I asked.

"Fighting? What are you talking about?"

"El, Alice literally had you pinned against the wall. Then you were crying and—"

"Oh my God, right? She freaking snapped."

I licked my dry, cracked lips. "What was she talking about? She told you she was worried about me?"

"I don't know *what* she was talking about," Ella said. She peeled herself out of my arms. "You wanna go get breakfast?"

"I have no idea where my phone is," I said. "Did I tell you I ditched my family at Busch Gardens?"

She snorted. "Only a million times yesterday. You kept going on about your mom's shoes for some reason." She stood and crossed the room. She pulled something out of her purse, and my cell phone came flying through the air. It landed near my foot. "Josiah gave it to me. You left it in his car. Didn't want you drunk calling anyone."

I was afraid to turn it on, but I was only delaying the inevitable. When Ella disappeared into the bathroom, I powered it up and waited for the messages to pour in. My phone whistled repeatedly as they did, and my heart sank lower than I ever thought possible. They were mostly from Leon.

> I can't fucking believe you.

> Do you know how much mom paid for these tickets?
> She saved up for this!

> You just left?! Where the fuck did you go?!

> This day meant so much to mom and dad.
> How could you do this?

> You're a fucking mess. I knew you were drinking.

My throat constricted. Each text felt like a hundred knives stabbing between my ribs.

I closed Leon's thread. There were no messages from Dad, but he'd called twice. And from Mom, just one text in response to my sorry excuse.

> OK, sweetie. Love u 2.

HOW TO BE A DISASTER

ERASE THE TEXTS. Try not to cry. When your girlfriend emerges from the bathroom, laugh at the toothpaste she missed on her chin. Climb out of bed. Wince when you put weight on your left knee.

Get dressed. Resist the urge to vomit when you look at yourself in the mirror. Splash water on your face. Wipe away the night.

Follow your girlfriend to her car. Walk slow because it hurts. Listen to her fuzzy version of the party. Curl your fists when she jokes about how drunk you were. Wonder if you're still drunk. Wonder if she should be driving.

Go to the fancy country-club restaurant overlooking the bay, even though you really want Waffle House. Roll your eyes when your girl-friend says she can't stand Waffle House because it's so dirty. Tell her it's part of the experience. Don't argue when she replies, *Not my experience.*

Sip coffee. Order a stack of pancakes, nothing else. Lose your appetite by the time they arrive. Observe the steady stream of Jet Skis and yachts criss-crossing the bay. Consider jumping off the balcony, right between the couple drinking Bloody Marys and the wrinkled man reading the newspaper. Reconsider when the fall won't be far enough, water not deep enough.

Stall. Say yes when she asks if you want to go back to her house. Spend the rest of the day in bed. Ride the hangover out. Ignore your phone. Pay no attention to the way it lights up with messages from certain people you've disappointed. Be grateful when your girlfriend doesn't press further. Realize she rarely does.

Remember your best friend's hopeful face when you made a promise. Think about how you immediately broke it. Question why you're so weak, why you can't do one fucking thing right. Feel horrible when you remember just how deep you cut your loved ones. Feel worse when you can't think of any way to make it better.

Tell yourself you could stop drinking if you wanted to!

(do you want to?)

No.

Have amazing sex with your girlfriend. When her lips are on your rib cage, try to name five things you love about your relationship. Panic when the answer isn't immediate.

Say yes when she suggests, *We should get tattoos.* It sounds like a good idea to take your mind off things. Plus, every moment you're with her is one you're not facing your family. Giggle on the way to the tattoo parlor as you come up with one ridiculous ink idea after another.

An octopus snaking around the left butt cheek.

French fries adorning the big toe.

A tube of lipstick across the forehead.

Think about flaking when you pull into the parking lot. Follow her into the shop. Peruse the books filled with intricate designs and wonder how anyone commits to anything forever.

Let her go first. Watch as the needle digs into her hip. Hold her hand while she winces in delight. Believe her when she says it doesn't hurt. Brace yourself when it's your turn. Focus on the artist's gloved hand as the needle pierces you. Wonder how it'll look in fifty years when you're old and wrinkly. Squeeze your girlfriend's fingers when the needle skirts around bone.

Admire yourself in the mirror when it's all over. Laugh at the cat outline on your girlfriend's hip. Smile at the small planet on yours.

(breathe a sigh of relief they're not matching)

Spend another night out. Let people check out your fresh ink. Ignore your best friend across the room, who frowns every time you have a drink in your hand. When your girlfriend asks, *What the fuck is her problem?* drunkenly spill a secret you swore you'd take to the grave.

When you finally go home two days later, marvel at the emptiness. Run your fingers over the boxes scattered around the living room. Lock yourself in your bedroom. Sink to the floor and cry.

Apologize to your mother when you run into her in the kitchen. Feel your heart sink when she averts her eyes so she doesn't have to look at you. Watch as she stirs cream into her coffee with shaking hands.

Let yourself say the words *I'm sorry*. Feel worse when she says, *It's okay*.

Act like you don't know why your brother is there when he appears in your bedroom a few days later. Stare out the window like a sullen child while he tells you—

This isn't okay.

I'm worried about you.

Alice is worried about you.

Can't you see how this is hurting Mom?

Can't you see how this is hurting you?

When he says your girlfriend is a part of the problem, snap. Tell him he doesn't know what he's talking about. Defend your relationship. It's the only thing in your life that feels right.

Contemplate how you can be in a downward spiral when the end result looks like nothing but *up*. Envision the cocktail parties, the country-club dinners with crisp white tablecloths, a fine-ass girlfriend who will become a wife. Circle your wrist where the society bracelet will rest.

Zone out in front of your laptop. Binge your favorite show, the one where teens run New York City like it's a sandbox. Salivate whenever there's alcohol in a scene.

(cry when you realize this is not normal behavior)

Dig deep. Question everything. Hold your past up to a magnifying glass.

Was it the plane ride?

The loneliness?

The bullying?

Your parents?

Ella?

Roxanne?

All of the above?

WHAT IS THE REASON?

(isn't there supposed to be one?)

Spend the next few weeks in a cycle. Drink with your girlfriend because you're bored. Drink because you're celebrating whatever. Drink because everyone else is doing it. Drink because you love the way it lifts the veil of sadness and guilt, at least for a little while.

Jump into pools fully clothed because *I can't fucking believe you* sounds so much nicer when it's wrapped up in delight. Dip the words like tie-dye. Make them something new.

Feel the layer of frost thicken between you and your family, you and your best friend. Know that it's all your fault. Realize you've become somewhat of a black sheep. That friend.

Some Drunk Girl.

Say fuck it.

Drink.

AUGUST

CHAPTER 18

BLOODY MARY

ON THE MARCH AFTERNOON Ella and I received our Jameswell acceptance letters, Mrs. Spencer was filming a video about Bloody Marys.

The video was a part of *Maricar Mixes*, a series dedicated to Mrs. Spencer adding her own twists to classic cocktails—vodka martinis dashed with lychees, whiskey sours with calamansi honey and ginger. She was in the middle of making a Bloody Mary with mango juice when the *Welcome to Jameswell* email landed in our inboxes, and Ella and I flew downstairs to the kitchen like banshees. Crying, laughing, screaming, "*We got in! We got in!*"

Mrs. Spencer must've sensed the once-in-a-lifetime moment because she frantically waved us over in front of her still-recording camera.

"You got into Jameswell?" Mrs. Spencer asked, on the brink of tears.

"Yes! Mommy, we did it!" Ella cried, and the three of us fell into a crushing group hug full of *Oh my God*s and *Salamat sa Diyos!*

The video went viral. It seemed like the entire world was rooting for us, congratulating us. How charming it was to see the normally composed @MamaMaricar completely caught off guard. Our unabashed joy, jumping around a kitchen island cluttered with tomato juice and citrus and highball glasses.

After she stopped recording, Mrs. Spencer made us virgin Bloody Marys to celebrate.

"Mom, we literally just got the best news of our lives," Ella joked. "Don't you think we've earned a little vodka?"

"Well, all right," Mrs. Spencer relented with a cheeky smile. "Just a little. It's a school night!"

But who cared? We were Jameswell girls now. One step closer to becoming Serena women. We added dashes of vodka to our Bloody Marys and cheers'd. The tomato juice made me want to gag, but it was a celebration and I didn't want to be difficult.

That's the thing about loving Ella. I didn't just love her—it was a family affair. And I loved how Mrs. Spencer's excitement eclipsed my mom's. When I called her later that night to tell her the news, she said, "Congratulations!" before we settled into a weird, awkward pause. She finally managed to say, "I'm proud of you," but it felt like an afterthought. Like there was supposed to be a *but* behind it, and I could only fill in the blanks myself.

I'm proud of you, but how are you going to pay for a school like that?

I'm proud of you, but why didn't you apply to the community college like I suggested?

I'm proud of you, but why did Mrs. Spencer get to know first?

And if she'd asked that, maybe I would've been honest. Maybe I would've said, *Remember that time at 7-Eleven? "Only half Black"? Do you know I still carry that memory around like a bad habit? Do you know that I'm still mad at you?*

Instead, I said, "Thank you," and we hung up and Ella and I made another round of Bloody Marys. Annetta came over later, the news of her own Jameswell acceptance letter displayed in her deep dimples, and we danced and screamed ourselves hoarse. Mr. Spencer ordered in hundreds of dollars' worth of sushi, and we had a feast fit for royalty.

Afterward, we were too excited to sleep. We had our future in our inboxes, but we needed to see it in person. So Annetta drove us out to Jameswell, so deep in southern Chesapeake we could practically kiss the North Carolina border. The campus was a redbrick, ivy-coated dream. Even the stars seemed closer there. We wandered through the main quad filled with weeping willows and pressed our palms to their rough bark. We nervously hid behind their trunks whenever we spotted campus security, terrified that we were going to get caught trespassing and have our offers rescinded.

We eventually ended up on Greek Row and Ella led us past pillared colonial homes adorned with Alphas and Omegas, to a large white farmhouse partially obscured by a tall line of bushes. It was the opposite of the traditional fraternity and sorority houses—tucked away instead of proudly hugging the curb, no letters on the outside to give off any indication of what lay beyond the front door.

"This is the Serena Society house," Ella whispered.

"Holy shit," I said, because all at once I could *see* it, this future I so desperately wanted. A sapphire bracelet around my wrist. Surrounded by women who could finally teach me how to exist in this world. Belonging. Known. Containing multitudes, not being only half of anything.

"We're going to Jameswell," Annetta said in awe, and the three of us stared at the house like hungry seedlings, ready to bloom. Ready for spring.

Now, in the dog days of summer, the remaining pledges and I stood in front of the Serena Society house in all its glory. School would be starting soon, and we all wanted to be the lucky ones walking through the front doors in early September for the induction ritual.

"Good morning, my beauties!" Roxanne chirped. "You all did such a great job on campus cleanup! Give yourself a little round of applause."

A polite golf clap arose from the fourteen of us on the lawn—we were exhausted from picking up trash all morning in the hot August sun. But Roxanne had promised a relaxing afternoon tea party for all our hard work, and the idea of catching a glimpse of the Serena Society house had us eager nonetheless.

Roxanne blathered on about sisterhood and community service and my eyes flickered to Annetta. We hadn't spoken since I was fired. It'd been nearly three weeks, the longest we'd ever gone. I knew from her socials that she had gone to New York to visit her mom, and it seemed to reignite something in her. After returning to Virginia, she was at every community service event and party with a determined look in her eyes. Every time I tried to talk to her, I felt sick to my stomach, full of apologies I couldn't find the courage to say.

Because only official Serena Society members were allowed inside the house, Roxanne and Alice led us to the enclosed backyard. The perimeter was dotted with towering oak trees with comfy hammock chairs and string lights suspended from their thick branches. Explosions of flowers bloomed in bright patches everywhere: fragrant lavender bushes, ivy twisting up trellises, bloodred roses with spiky thorns. And in the heart of it all was a long wooden table covered in dainty sandwiches, sliced fruit, veggie quiches, and citronella candles to keep the bugs away. Bottles of sparkling wine and rosé chilled in ice buckets at opposite ends of the table.

There were place cards at each seat, and Ella was predictably near the head of the table by Roxanne. My heart sank when I spotted my name in looping calligraphy right next to Annetta's. We took our seats, and she refused to look at me as she splayed a linen napkin across her lap. Corinne and Khadija sat opposite of us.

"Did you ever tell your mom thanks for saving our asses?" Corinne asked me.

I laughed, but the mere mention of my mother sent a lump ricocheting up my throat, as I remembered how I'd abandoned her at Busch Gardens. Her gentle pleas as she searched for me. Leon's fury.

Someone put some music on and we loaded our plates. Drinks started flowing. Annetta handed me a bottle of rosé without looking at me, and I sank lower, lower, lower. I poured myself a hefty glass, hot anxiety spreading through my body like a wildfire.

"Hey," I said quietly, nudging her side. "Can we talk?"

Her jaw worked overtime as she chomped on gum. "Now is not the time."

"Nettie. Please?"

She discreetly spat her gum into a paper napkin. I took her silence as permission to keep talking.

"I'm sorry about what I said the day I got fired. I wasn't . . . in the best headspace."

"No shit."

I took two huge gulps of wine. The rosé was sweeter than anything I deserved in that moment, but it gave me the courage to keep talking.

"Nettie, I'm sorry," I said. "What can I do to make it right?"

"Nothing," Annetta said quietly. "You don't want me to act like your mom anymore, then fine. I'm done cleaning up after you."

I swallowed. "I'm sorry."

Annetta looked at Roxanne and Ella, who were laughing and topping each other's glasses off with fresh bubbly. "You're going to drive yourself into the ground," Annetta said, and the bluntness of her tone nearly made me drop my drink. "And she's just going to sit back and watch you do it."

I faced my plate, deflated. I drank and finished my glass and poured another because it was the only thing I could think of that would make me feel better.

We went through the motions. My world became a carousel of partying and drinking and sleeping. But the end was in sight—halfway through August, we woke up to another text.

> CGGYC Ballroom. 8/20. 9pm.
> Dress Code: All black.
> SS

This was "The Big One" according the Ella. The Final Night. The night that would determine if we were going to join the ranks of the society or be forced to wait another year to begin the pledge process again. Ella had the inside knowledge that the final night involved extensive quizzing from scores of Serena women, so we spent our days reviewing the society's history facts. I wanted to get in so bad it hurt, a desperate need to accomplish *something* like a drumbeat in my chest. I couldn't afford any distractions, and my family was by far the biggest.

I'd been dodging them for weeks. After Busch Gardens, every time I entered Winward Commons, guilt shrouded me like a fur coat. The Awful Thing Blake Did was expressed in the dim disappointment on my parents' faces whenever our paths crossed. I used to hate being home alone when I was younger. I craved it now. At least when the house was empty, I could pretend like everything was fine. I continued to pack up my room in an oblivious little bubble, one that was swiftly popped when Leon unexpectedly showed up and cornered me into a guilt trip. Since then, I'd been staying at the Spencers', hoping he'd leave me alone for good.

I should've known better.

One afternoon while Ella was still at work, Leon texted me. He was outside the Spencers' house. Knowing he wouldn't go away until I talked to him, I skulked out to the driveway. The asphalt was hot beneath my bare feet, but the look in Leon's eyes chilled me instantly.

"Let's get this over with," I said with a sigh.

He pushed away from his car. Then the gap between us vanished as he crushed me in a hug. To my horror, he started *crying*. I couldn't remember the last time Leon cried, and it scared the shit out of me. Something must've happened to Mom, something must've happened to Dad.

"Leon, what is it?" I kept asking. "Is someone hurt?"

"Yes," he said, his voice muffled in my hair.

I pushed away, images of a plane crash or a gas station robbery gone wrong immediately flooding my brain. "Is it Mom? Dad?"

"No," he said. "It's you." He threw his arms up, and I looked toward the sky. But he was motioning to the house. To the Spencers.

"All of this," he said, his voice raw. "All of this."

"All of *what*?"

"Blake, I'm so fucking worried about you."

I reeled. "Is this about Busch Gardens? Because I already apologized to Mom—"

"I'm sorry," he interrupted. "I'm sorry I snapped at you. I'm sorry I said all those things."

I blinked. Shook my head. We must've been in an alternate universe if Leon was apologizing to *me*.

"I have no idea what to do anymore," he continued. "Alice is worried about you. I'm worried about you. Mom, Dad, we're *all* worried about you."

"I'm fine," I said, but I was instantly irritated that Alice had been talking about me behind my back again. *So much for sisterhood.*

He shook his head. "You're not. Blake . . . none of this is okay. Blowing off your family at an amusement park? Taking fucking whiskey shots in the middle of the day? Being hard on you isn't helping. So what will?"

An embarrassed heat churned my stomach, as I remembered how I'd run like a coward at Busch Gardens. *No.* I couldn't spiral now. I had to focus.

"So where are they?" I asked.

"Who?"

"Mom and Dad. If they're so worried, why haven't they said anything? Why are *you* here instead of them?"

His eyes searched my face, and I knew from the helpless look in them that he couldn't answer me.

"They love you, Blake," he said. "And so do I. But they're busy with the move and you keep pushing us away."

"Pushing you away?" I laughed. "Was I pushing Dad away when I came out to him and he could barely utter a 'Yay'? Face it, Leon. The minute Dad found out I had no interest in following his footsteps and being a pilot, he started focusing all of his attention on *you*."

"That's not—"

"And Mom," I barreled on. "Did I push her away during the years she couldn't be bothered to talk to us about race? When she referred to another mixed person as 'only half-Black' in front of my face?"

He rolled his eyes. "Come on. She's a white woman. Of course she says shit like that sometimes."

"Leave me alone, Leon." I was already turning back to the Spencers' house. Back toward my *real* future. I was so close. So close to becoming a part of something that made me feel whole. He couldn't ruin this for me.

"I know you care about this society," he said, "but there are other ways to accomplish your dreams. You don't have to act like this."

"Like you would know," I seethed. "You didn't even go to college."

We stared at each other. The silence stretched. A sprinkler ticked.

He didn't try to stop me as I made my way to the front door.

On the morning of August twentieth, Ella was up by dawn. She gently pulled on a curl near my temple and whispered in my ear, "Waaaake up. Today's the day."

I groaned. "Let me sleep, woman."

"We're going to study allll day. They'll have no choice but to welcome us with open arms."

"The only arms I care about are yours."

She bit my neck, and I giggled and enjoyed it when she bit harder.

We spent the morning in the Spencers' sun-drenched kitchen, quizzing each other about Serena Society history facts and munching on blueberry bagels with strawberry cream cheese. When Mrs. Spencer emerged from the garage, sweaty from her morning tennis match, she shot us a small smile.

"Glad to see you're both studying," she said with a wink. I watched as she bustled around the gleaming kitchen, humming to herself without a care in the world. She helped herself to a glass of filtered water, began slicing plump red strawberries for a smoothie. The kitchen was warm and draped with sprawling green plants. The calendar on the wall was bursting with upcoming appointments and dinner parties. The ring lights were ready to capture another #MamaMaricar moment. I pictured my own mom across town, probably just now falling asleep after her night shift. I envisioned Dad in a shabby hotel room in Des Moines, watching ESPN before his flight. And a fierce certainty settled in my stomach.

I wanted all of this. This life. I was going to be a Serena woman. I wasn't going to fuck this up. If I was going to be miserable no matter what I did, then at least I wanted my life to look like this.

I grabbed a stack of index cards and told Ella to quiz me again.

The streetlights were flickering on by the time Ella and I made our way to the club for the final night. Ella steered carefully, making sure to not smudge her freshly painted nails. I was struggling to breathe in the tight black leather dress she let me borrow. I was also wearing her shoes—sky-high stilettos—because, according to Ella, none of my heels were enough of a "statement." They were pinching my toes, but Ella said I looked amazing, so I didn't complain.

We bypassed the club gates, and Ella slowed the Range Rover down. "Serena's motto?"

"By love and by light," I replied easily. "How many Oscars have been won by Serena women?"

"Two. Eleven founding members?"

I rattled off the list of names in alphabetical order. She nodded in approval when I added Serena Wake, the twelfth girl.

"I think we're ready," she said. I could only hope she was right as we pulled up to the valet booth and handed off the keys.

Ella led the way to the ballroom. We passed the library and the gym, and my cheeks flushed when I remembered the time Ella and I discovered each other on the musty exercise benches all those years ago.

The twelve other pledges were waiting outside of the ballroom's closed doors. I saw Annetta first, wearing a sharp black suit and shiny Oxfords. Her eyes flicked to me and Ella as we drew closer, but she quickly dipped her head when she caught my gaze. Ella and I joined Keiko near the end of the line, and she shot us a weak smile.

"How are you feeling?" Ella whispered.

"Scared shitless," Keiko replied.

We froze when the ballroom doors cracked open. Peals of laughter and soft music trickled out, followed by Roxanne and Alice. They were draped in silver and sapphire, and as they strode over to examine us, Alice's gaze raked over Ella, then me. Any hope that she'd look out for me since she was dating my brother vanished when I met her hard stare. I looked down at my hands and tried to ignore my screaming feet.

"Welcome to the last night," Roxanne said. "We have a roomful of women *very* excited to meet you." Her heels clicked on the floor as she slowly took us all in. When she reached Ella, she nodded in approval. "Nice dress." She continued down the line.

"Tonight will be a test of what you've learned over the course of this summer. Becoming a Serena Society woman is not about memorizing facts. It's about what's in here." She placed her hand over her heart. "And here." Tapped her temple. She stopped near me and Keiko. "If you're meant to be here, you have no reason to worry. Are you ready?"

No one said anything. We just nodded.

Roxanne looked at Alice and lifted her shoulder. "They say they're ready."

"Follow me," Alice said.

My entire body pulsed with nerves.

When Alice opened the ballroom doors, we were greeted with a sea of sapphire blue. It was a packed house. My knees trembled as Alice led us to the center of the dance floor.

"Straight line," Alice instructed. My shoulders brushed Keiko and Ella as I squeezed between them. We faced forward and winced when a large spotlight shone on our faces. I had to blink several times before my eyes adjusted. When they did, a tremor ran to the pit of my soul as a room full of Serena Society women stared back at me.

CHAPTER 19

"HELLO, MY NAME IS Roxanne Garcia, and I'm the undergraduate president of the Serena Society. My vice president, Alice Bui, and I are proud to present this summer's top recruits."

Applause filled the ballroom. My knees were on the verge of buckling. I picked a spot on the wall and focused on it with all my might.

Then a hush fell as someone made their way to the dance floor. I almost cried in relief when I realized it was Mrs. Spencer.

"Thank you, Roxanne," Mrs. Spencer said. Her familiar voice felt like a hug. She walked to the center of the dance floor, studying us. Her gaze slipped past me and Ella without acknowledgment. Tonight, it didn't matter how we knew her. All that mattered was the society.

"For those of you who don't know," Mrs. Spencer said, "I'm Maricar Spencer, the society's undergraduate advisor." She raised her microphone, and her bracelet glittered in the light. "It's an honor to be surrounded by the sisterhood tonight."

While Mrs. Spencer continued on about the society's long legacy of service and scholarship, I subtly scanned the room. The ballroom was filled with tables draped in navy and silver cloths. Bartenders topped off wine and cocktails at a makeshift bar in the corner. I spotted Sophie and Ariana, smirking at their little sister. My eyes snapped back to the wall.

"Surely by now you're all aware of the immense privilege it is to call yourself a member of the Serena Society," Mrs. Spencer said. "We all remember how nerve-racking this night was for us. We remember the endless studying. We remember the parties." A chorus of laughter arose. I swallowed hard, and Mrs. Spencer stopped in front of Corinne. I could feel her quaking two people away.

"And as much fun as you might've been having this summer, Serena isn't solely about that," Mrs. Spencer went on. "Being a woman of Serena is about honor. It's about loyalty. It's about picking up the phone at two a.m. and calling any woman in this room and knowing they'll answer. It's about looking at yourself in the mirror every morning and asking if you can be gentle with yourself in a world that says women of color don't deserve tenderness. And when you can't, can you count on your sisters to do it for you?"

Next to me, Keiko sniffled. I could see a tear sliding down her cheek, and without thinking, my fingers fumbled for hers and squeezed. She squeezed back. Mrs. Spencer continued her slow walk down the line.

"You might look at the faces of women who came before you and think this society is all about power. You might think this is why we do it. After all, what could be better than being in the company of so many awe-inspiring women? I'll tell you what's better."

Every person in the room seemed to lean in, waiting for Mrs. Spencer's next words, even though they must've heard some version of this speech dozens of times before. I tried to stand straighter, but my feet were dying in Ella's heels.

"What's better is having those same people in your corner when things *aren't* going so well," Mrs. Spencer said. "For you incoming freshmen, it's about who can sit with you in moments of overwhelming pressure. Jameswell's academics are notoriously rigorous. Can you depend on every girl standing in this line? Do you know what true friendship is?"

My heart ached for Annetta. How could I have ruined our friendship so spectacularly?

"Outgoing seniors—this world is vicious. The workplace can be brutal. Serena women use our connections to match you with internships. We provide insider knowledge about job opportunities. We help with grad school applications and more. With the Serena sisterhood, you never have to go through anything alone." Mrs. Spencer's heels clicked down the line again. As she passed, I caught a faint whiff of her lilac perfume. She stopped in front of me, and my heart skipped a beat.

"Blake Brenner." My name echoed through her microphone. "How are you tonight?"

"F-fine," I stammered.

She glanced down at my feet. "What size shoe do you wear?"

What? Out of all the questions I'd been prepping for, *that* wasn't one of them. I looked down to see my toes were scrunched and turning red.

"Eleven?" I said cautiously.

Mrs. Spencer hummed. "Those shoes don't look so comfortable."

My face burned. "They're okay."

She turned to the crowd. "Does anyone have a pair of black size eleven flats they'd be willing to loan Blake for the rest of the night?"

Three women stood and began walking in our direction. I wanted to sink into the floor. Of course, the night hadn't even started and I'd put a halt on the events because I wasn't strong enough to tough it out.

But as the women drew closer, I realized that none of them were looking at me condescendingly. They looked like they just wanted to help.

A tall girl with microbraids reached us first. She slipped off her flats and handed them to me with a smile. Shamefully, I kicked the heels off and exchanged them. I had to admit, the flats were much more comfortable.

"That's better," Mrs. Spencer said. "Now, where was I . . . oh yes. The beauty of sisterhood." She winked at me and continued down the line.

After Mrs. Spencer's speech, the true test of the night began. While the Serena women sat around and socialized, the pledges had to stay in line and answer any questions from the women who approached us. It was interrogation on another level. Some of the women—usually the older ones—were friendly and wanted to know more about our majors and dreams.

But the current members and recent graduates were ruthless.

"Why is Lake Drummond significant to the society?" (It was where Serena Wake—the Lost Girl—was found.)

"What is the opening stanza for the official Serena Society poem?" (Easy. *A star shining bright / in silver and sapphire light / Sisterhood, integrity, and wisdom forever entwined.*)

"What Serena woman was responsible for the society's emblem and shield?" (Denise Wilkins, '56.)

Ariana and Sophie took it light on me and Ella when it was their turn. But afterward, a short girl with tattoos covering both arms took their place and smirked at me like she knew a secret.

"So this is who you've been telling me about," she said to Roxanne. "The party animal?"

"Sure is," Roxanne said. "This is Blake. Blake, this is Maya. Graduated two years ago. Probably the only person who could drink you under a table." My cheeks flushed as my reputation slowly snowballed. It wasn't even midnight, and I was officially the flat-wearing lush who couldn't walk in heels.

"I'll see you at the after-party," Maya told me. She and Roxanne exchanged a sly look, and I curled my hands into fists to stop the shaking.

After two hours of putting us on the spot, Roxanne and Alice finally gave the pledges a break. We breathed a collective sigh of relief and made a beeline for the restroom.

"Holy shit, I gotta pee!" Khadija moaned. "I thought that was never going to end."

"But we all did so great!" Corinne squealed. They locked themselves in stalls, and the rest of the girls primped in the mirror.

"Hi, Bee," Ella said. She kissed my cheek. "How are you feeling?"

I nodded and mumbled some kind of answer. After the shoe embarrassment, I was careful to be on my best behavior. But I couldn't get Mrs. Spencer's words about friendship out of my mind. I needed to talk to Annetta before the night was over. The three of us had been waiting on the Serena Society forever, and it felt wrong our trio was so splintered on the final night.

I found my chance when Ella went into the stall Annetta was leaving. I joined her at the sink and hovered as she washed her hands.

"Good job out there," I said quietly.

She scrubbed her hands vigorously. "You too."

"Can we talk for a second?"

She turned the faucet off and nodded. Everyone else was too

wrapped up in their excitement to notice as we stepped out into the dark hallway. Annetta leaned against a shiny credenza. Music thumped from the ballroom.

"I'm sorry," I said. "About everything."

She crossed her arms over her chest. "Go on."

"I was in this hole. A bad one. But . . . I think I'm okay now."

"Blake . . ."

I held up my hands. "Hear me out. Please?"

She sighed. "Fine."

"I shouldn't have lashed out at you. It was wrong. I was lost."

"Oh, and now you're found, Amazing Grace?"

Any other time, I would've laughed. But now my eyes screwed up with tears. "Nettie, I've fucked up so much. With you, with my parents, my brother. But I'm trying to be better."

"Are you? Really?"

"Yes," I pleaded, but my heart was pounding. Remembering my confrontation with Leon and the frozen chasm between me and Mom. The doubtful voice in the back of my mind that still wondered if I was good enough for Ella, for the Spencers, for Serena. "I just want us to be friends again. I want everything to be good again. No one's got us like we got us, remember?"

Corinne, Keiko, and Khadija burst out of the restroom, laughter tinkling, and headed back to the party. Annetta looked at me, hurt.

"It's not that simple, Blake."

"What can I do?" I whispered. "I have to make this right. I feel like I've ruined everything, what can I do?" I looked up, and there were tears in Annetta's eyes, too.

"What's going on?"

Ella. She was so gorgeous, but there was a spark in her eyes that frightened me.

"What's going on?" she repeated.

I managed to choke out, "Nothing."

Ella narrowed her eyes. "Clearly it's something. Are you finally going to explain why you've been such a bitch to us lately, Nettie?"

"I'm not listening to this," Annetta said, and she started walking away.

Ella's jaw dropped. "Seriously? Is this still about your gender problem?"

Her words were a shock to my heart. *No.* I thought I'd dreamed spilling Annetta's secret. Half hoped that Big Bad Bee could only be that callous in a nightmare. But this betrayal was *real* and so deeply wrong. Annetta spun around with a fury in her eyes.

"You told her?" she snarled.

"I'm—"

"Oh, let me guess, you're sorry? You know what, Blake? You *are* fucking sorry. I should've known you couldn't keep *one* secret from Ella, considering you're her little lapdog."

"Nettie, you need to calm the fuck down," Ella snapped.

"And *you.*" Annetta turned her rage toward Ella. "I'm sick of you. I've *been* sick of you. You are such a raggedy, social-climbing bitch, and I never want to see you ever again."

Ella looked like a wild animal trapped, just like the night Alice had her cornered. "Who the hell are you talking to?"

"You." Annetta lifted her chin, and the gold shimmer on her brown cheekbones sparkled in the dark. "You, the girl who slapped me. You, the girl who forces her girlfriend to get blackout drunk all the time but conveniently leaves *me* to clean up the messes. I'm talking to the girl who doesn't care about anything besides appearances. You're a toxic, enabling—"

"Oh, fuck you," Ella interrupted with a tired sigh. "Blake is a big girl. I don't force her to do anything."

"Girls?"

The commanding voice belonged to Mrs. Spencer. She stood a few yards away, propping the ballroom door open with her foot, light from the party spilling over her royal-blue pantsuit. She shot us a quizzical smile. "Everything okay?"

"It's fine, Mom," Ella said. She gave Annetta a look of death and stalked down the hall.

As I stared after her, countless memories emerged. Me, Ella, Annetta at the diner, sides hurting from laughter over yet another ridiculous round of Fuck, Marry, Kill. The three of us at the pool last summer, pruned fingers and chlorine hair. Sprawled on the beach, staring at the stars as we drank in the night. It felt like another lifetime.

"I can't believe you told her," Annetta said.

"I'm sorry," I said again, *again, again*. "I wasn't thinking. I was drunk."

"When aren't you?" she asked with a glare that could carve ice.

By the time midnight rolled around, most of the older society members had called it a night. Without supervision, the younger ones got louder, brasher. Everyone wanted to fawn over the new pledges. They were picking their favorites, declaring us their little sisters. Roxanne had Ella on her arm all night, proudly telling anyone who would listen that she'd met the mini version of her. I lingered on the sidelines, gripping a soda and listening to Corinne fret over who would be the last two girls cut.

"I just feel like it could be anyone. One wrong question and bam! You're done. You know I've been trying to get in for two years?" Corinne groaned and nibbled on her lower lip. "God, I could use a drink right now."

"Go get one," I said, motioning to the corner where a bartender was still pouring wine and mixing drinks. "It's not like anyone is going to card you."

"Can you come with me? Please? I don't want to go alone."

I glanced back to the center of the room, where Ella and Roxanne were singing some ballad off-key, making everyone laugh.

"Let's go," I told Corinne.

As we drew closer to the bar, a panic rose in my throat. I didn't *have* to order anything. I didn't have to drink. I didn't have to go down that road tonight. But when we arrived at the bar, my mouth watered. All these glittering bottles. Delicious deep red wines, bubbly sparkling and crisp white. Vodka, gin, tequila, whiskey, rum. I wanted it all.

And the realization hit me like a fastball to the gut.

I have a problem.

"What are you drinking, ladies!" the bartender asked cheerfully.

Corinne ordered a red wine. My mouth opened, but I couldn't say anything.

I have a problem.

"Make that two," Corinne said with a giggle. The bartender twisted the cap off. The heavy *glug-glug-glug* of wine waterfalling into glasses.

"Blake? You okay?" Corinne asked.

"I have a problem," I said quietly.

"Hopefully this fixes it," she joked. She handed me a glass and held hers up. "To hopefully becoming women of Serena Society!"

I gripped the wineglass so hard I'm surprised it didn't shatter. I didn't drink, and Corinne didn't notice, she was too busy singing along to the music. She shimmied her way back to the dance floor, and I followed with a sick, sour feeling deep in my chest.

"I have a problem," I whispered. The words sounded wrong and right all at once. I had a problem. I had a problem. I was the problem.

I stayed on the fringes of the dance floor as music pulsed. I wanted to get drunk out of my mind to alleviate the weight of this night, but I couldn't because I had a problem. I saw Annetta, and she was looking at me, *judging* me, what was I supposed to do? I wanted us to be friends again, but she hated me and I deserved it, right? I had ruined our friendship, and for nothing because *I* was nothing. I had a problem. This was supposed to be one of the best nights of my life, but all I was doing was pining for my best friend and feeling sorry for myself.

But then Annetta was there. In front of me. Beautiful and blurry. I didn't realize I was crying until she wiped my cheeks with her thumbs and hugged me. Nettie, who had never liked physical touch, was hugging me, comforting me, and it made me sob, and I felt so pathetic I couldn't stand it. Tears seeped between the cracks of all my broken pieces. Everything poured out all at once. There weren't enough apologies in the world for my mistakes.

"I'm here," she kept saying. She had to shout over the music, but I could hear her.

She was here. Even though I didn't deserve her. I deserved to be alone, rotting in a cave, but she was here.

"I'm sorry," I cried. "I don't—I don't—I—"

There was a tap on my shoulder. It was the girl who loaned me her flats. Ella's heels dangled from her index finger. She looked at me and Annetta like we were newborn kittens.

"Awwww!" she squealed. "Babies! I remember I cried on final night, too. Enjoy it!"

"Now is not—" Annetta started, but the girl thrust the heels in my face and nodded at my feet.

"You can cry in these heels, but I need my flats back. I'm going home."

I slipped them off. The dance floor was cold on my bare feet as we exchanged shoes. "Thank you," I said, but I doubt she could hear me between the music and my stuffy nose.

Annetta sat me at a table and helped me with my heels. The music was slowing and the lights were coming up too quick.

When the song ended, Roxanne cupped her hands over her mouth and yelled all pledges needed to be onboard the *Bewitched* in ten minutes for a mandatory after-party.

"Here." Annetta handed me a glass of water. "Drink this."

I took slow gulps until half the glass was finished.

"Why are you being so nice to me?" I asked.

"Maybe because I don't know how to stop caring about people, even when they don't deserve it," Annetta said with a faint smile.

Then she looked over my shoulder and her face hardened. "Or maybe I'm just naïve," she said before standing and leaving. I was about to call after her when I was engulfed in a cloud of perfume.

Ella.

"Hey, Bee," she said, trailing a finger along my jaw, my neck, down my arm. She plopped in Annetta's seat and grinned like a wicked witch. Her eyes were low, lipstick slightly smudged. The wineglass she was holding was empty.

She was drunk. Really drunk.

"Hi," I said.

She leaned in, and her lips grazed my cheeks. "You wanna tell me what the hell is going on?"

"I was apologizing."

Ella's nose wrinkled. "Apologizing. To *Nettie*? For what?"

"She's our best friend." I said it like it was obvious. Like I didn't understand why she didn't share the deep, burning desire to make things right with Annetta like I did. We were supposed to be friends forever.

Ella kissed me, long and hard. My stomach clenched as I tasted the tangy mix of whiskey and wine on her tongue. When she pulled away, she rested her forehead on mine. The glitter from her eyelids had run down to her lashes. "But she called me toxic," she said with a smile.

I swallowed. "She didn't mean it."

"She said she was sick of me."

"I think we all need to talk."

"Whose side are you on?" Then she bit my bottom lip, hard enough to draw blood. When I jerked away in shock, she leaned back in the chair and laughed and laughed and laughed.

CHAPTER 20

THE SMILES THE SERENA girls had been sporting so sweetly in the ballroom vanished the moment we boarded the *Bewitched*.

"Get in line, pledges," Roxanne snarled. Next to her, Maya and Ariana and other Serena girls smirked. When we didn't move fast enough, Roxanne stood on a leather love seat and cupped her hands over her mouth. "*Now*, pledges! Do you think we have all fucking night?"

"Jeez," Ella mumbled. "Is all that necessary?"

"Did anyone ask you to speak?" Alice snapped. "Get in line. Now."

Ella glanced around the lounge. Her own sisters were nodding for her to follow Alice's orders. Even Roxanne didn't say anything to save her.

We lined up, same order from the ballroom. Keiko radiated tenseness on one side of me, Ella swayed slightly on my other. Roxanne glowered down from her perch.

"So y'all wanna be Serena women, huh?" When no one responded, she repeated the question in a shrill shriek; she was drunker than Ella. "*Answer me, pledges!*"

"Yes!" we shouted. I would've laughed if Roxanne didn't look so murderous. And if a bunch of upperclassmen weren't *also* glaring at us.

"And what makes you think you're worthy?" Roxanne snapped. She flipped her long brown hair. The strap of her sapphire-blue dress slipped off her shoulder. "You think we just let anyone join? You know how many girls want to be in your place? Annetta Jones—" She crooked her finger. "Step out of line."

Annetta stepped forward. Roxanne cocked her head, an evil smile playing on her lips. My stomach dipped, and I suddenly remembered I hadn't eaten all night.

"Well, well. Daughter of Lorraine Jones?" Roxanne asked.

"Yeah?" Annetta replied.

"Do you believe you deserve to follow in her footsteps?"

Annetta was silent. The room pulsed.

"We're *waiting*, Annetta."

"I . . ." Annetta looked around, like the answer would be lurking in one of the dark corners of the *Bewitched*. "I don't know."

Someone gasped. Maybe it was Ella. Roxanne, however, was delighted.

"Say that louder," Roxanne said.

"Say what?"

Roxanne got in her face, close enough to kiss. "You want to tell me that after all these weeks, after a *lifetime* of being your mother's *daughter*, you don't know if you deserve to be here?"

"Perhaps I should've clarified," Annetta said. "Maybe I don't know if I *want* to be here. Maybe I don't know if this place deserves *me*."

"Well, now we're getting somewhere," Roxanne said. "Do you know how many *girls* are dying to be in your place, Miss Jones?"

Annetta was quiet.

"Well? Answer me!"

Annetta lifted her chin. "This isn't worth dying for."

Roxanne grabbed her wineglass and sipped. My throat tickled.

"I've had it with you." Roxanne's words fell into her glass, but it was clear their biting sting was directed at Annetta. "I'm so tired of your holier-than-thou attitude. I'm tired of you looking like a sad little puppy at all the parties." She scoffed. "I should've known."

"You should've known what?" Annetta snapped.

"Showing up to events with no makeup. Like, what is this?" she sniped, motioning to Annetta's suit and Oxfords. "You couldn't even wear a *dress* for the final night?"

"Easy now," Alice said. The rest of the Serena girls murmured and laughed and refilled their drinks, watching everything go down like beautiful vultures. I trembled with anger.

"I should've known you weren't meant to be one of *us*," Roxanne said, and everyone fell silent again. She took an angry sip of wine, finishing the glass. She set it on the coffee table and returned her chilly gaze to Annetta.

"The Serena Society is for women of excellence," Roxanne said. "*Wo-men.*" She clapped over the syllables, and my breath caught in my throat. No. How did *she* find out? I only told Ella. That meant . . .

No. Ella wouldn't do that.

"And I heard," Roxanne went on slowly, "that you aren't even sure you want to *be* a woman."

"You don't know shit about me," Annetta snarled.

"No? Ella!" Roxanne's gaze found my girlfriend and Ella stiffened next to me.

"Didn't you tell me the other night that Annetta was . . . hmmm, how did you put it? 'Having another one of her mood swings because she doesn't know if she wants to be a boy or girl'?" Roxanne asked.

"Roxanne, stop." Alice's voice sliced through the room. "This is bullshit. You know this isn't what Serena is about."

Roxanne laughed. "Oh my, someone is up on her moral high horse all of a sudden. Should I remind you that *I* am the president?"

"And I'm your vice president." Alice crossed her arms. "And I'm telling you this is ridiculous."

"This is tradition," Roxanne snapped. "Now mind your fucking place."

"Sit down, Alice," Maya, the girl with the tattoos, said. "We all had to go through final night interrogations." From the nods of the rest of the sisters, it was clear Alice was outnumbered.

Roxanne looked back at Ella. "Ella? Isn't that what you said?"

"I didn't . . ." Ella sputtered, and her hesitation said everything she couldn't. My stomach plummeted, knowing this was all my fault.

"Does your mother know about this?" Roxanne asked Annetta. "Because I'm sure she'd be mighty disappointed to find out you're not worthy enough to follow in her footsteps." She clucked her tongue. "All these opportunities she's handing to you on a silver platter that you don't even want. Her beautiful legacy. Ruined."

"You don't know anything about my mom," Annetta said, but the fire in her voice was ash now. My hands started shaking as I glared at Roxanne. How could I have ever thought she was beautiful?

"Let's find out," Roxanne said. She pulled out her cell phone and, after a couple of taps, recited a string of numbers. She looked up with a smirk. "That's your mom's number, right?"

Annetta was frozen.

"Why so quiet? You don't have shit to say now?" Roxanne put the call on speakerphone. It rang. Taunting, loud.

"Stop," Annetta said. Pleaded. "Hang up."

Two rings. Roxanne held the phone up and waved it in the air like a lighter at a concert. She giggled.

"Please," Annetta said, and the fear in her voice made me tremble in rage.

"Beg for it," Roxanne said. Three rings. "Really *beg* for it. Make me feel it." Four rings. "Don't we wanna feel it, y'all?" Roxanne asked, looking over her shoulder.

"Roxanne, stop this," Alice said, but she didn't move. She was frozen like the rest of us.

"Yeah, I don't think she *really* wants it," another girl chimed in. Five rings.

Time slowed. I was suddenly outside of my body, watching as I crossed the room in long strides. Watching as I yanked the phone out of Roxanne's hand, just as Mrs. Jones's voice mail kicked on. I hung up and scowled at Roxanne, and I was back in my body. I was Big Bad Bee and ready to take her down.

"Serena Wake is turning over in her grave," I said, voice like a dagger, "knowing the society let a power-hungry bitch like you be in charge."

"Oop," Maya said, and the Serena girls laughed. Annetta was silent, staring at Roxanne's phone in my hand as if her mom was going to call back any moment.

Roxanne's amused grin finally fell as she stared me down. A chill ran up my spine and down again, and Big Bad Bee whimpered.

"Blake Brenner," Roxanne said. "How fitting for *you* to have a little outburst like this." She regarded Annetta like a soiled bag of trash. "Get back in line. It looks like Blake is going to take your place."

Now look what you did.

Good luck talking your way out of this one.

You are so fucked.

"Blake." Roxanne's gaze was frigid. "Would you like to repeat that?"

"Repeat what?"

"Oh, don't be shy," Roxanne sighed. "Come on, Blake. Repeat yourself. Since you wanna be all big and bad."

An image of Cody Fisher flashed through my mind. His greasy smirk behind Das Festhaus. Whiskey whispers.

Big Bad Bee.

"Cat got your tongue?" Roxanne stepped closer. "What did you say?"

I swallowed. *Here we go.* "I said Serena Wake is turning over in her grave knowing a power-hungry . . . girl like you is in charge."

"Hmm, I think the word you actually used was 'bitch,'" Roxanne said. "Did you think that was a good idea?" She glanced over her shoulder. "Ladies, wouldn't you say that was mighty disrespectful?"

The Serena girls clucked like judgmental chickens.

"So disrespectful," Maya added as her finger circled the rim of her beer bottle.

"No respect," Roxanne said. "What's got you so riled up?"

"Nothing," I muttered. But *everything* came flooding into my mind at once, clouding my vision and nearly sending me sideways. I closed my eyes and saw Leon's concerned face, his tears. My fight with Ella. How could she tell Roxanne this secret? Annetta's dark eyes in the woods, wondering if any of this was worth it. Annetta pleading with me to stop drinking, *please, please, please.* Losing my job. That searing, *desperate* desire to become a part of Ella's world, *please, please, please.* The descent of a roller coaster, vomit pouring out in a loop. I felt that stinging in my throat, and I wished for everything in the universe to *please, please, please* just let me keep it together.

"I just think you need to leave Annetta alone," I said quietly.

"And *I* think you need to loosen up," Roxanne said. "Khadija, please pour a shot."

Khadija, uncertainly: "A shot of what?"

Roxanne laughed. "I'll let you pick. Anything to get our friend Blake here a little more comfortable."

We waited as Khadija searched through the bottles at the bar. I still couldn't open my eyes, but I felt Roxanne's heavy gaze. Felt her looming presence as she stepped closer and her hot, wine-soaked breath was in my ear.

"You're such a fucking hot mess," Roxanne hissed. "You don't belong here, either."

My eyes snapped open and I came to face-to-face with every pore on Roxanne's nose.

"The only reason you're here," she said, "is because Ella has vouched for you at every turn. She had to *beg* me to let you pledge in the first place. Pathetic."

With every word, I slipped deeper and deeper into the memory of Ella and me fighting in her bedroom, when she was telling me the exact same thing. The storm inside me brewed and brewed and—

"Here you go."

We broke eye contact as Khadija arrived, looking terrified. A shot glass filled to the brim with clear liquid quaked in her hand.

"Thank you, Khadija," Roxanne said sweetly. She grabbed the shot and held it between us. It smelled woodsy. Like pine trees.

Fucking gin.

"Why don't you loosen up?" she cooed. "Take the shot."

My eyes flicked to the gin. I wanted to smack it out of her hand, knowing she just wanted me to drink it so I could lose control. So I could prove her point about not belonging here.

"No, thank you," I said. "I'm good."

"Damn, what is with these pledges tonight!" Maya said from the armchair. "Do y'all even wanna be here?"

"Just take the shot, Blake," Ariana said gently. "It's okay."

"You heard them, Blake," Roxanne pressed. "Just take the shot." She pushed the glass into my hand and some of the gin spilled onto my fingers. My cheeks burned.

"I said I'm good." I tried to hand the shot back, but she refused to take it. Her eyes lit up in amusement as I looked for a place to set it.

"Are you kidding me?" she asked. "If you don't take this shot, I'm going to tell Mr. Peterson *exactly* who it was who threw that paint on his yacht."

Fuck. No. The paint can. My sliced palm. She couldn't. How—

"I got you on video," Roxanne said with a sneer. "And I'm sure the cops would *love* to see."

"Roxanne, stop!" Alice shouted. "You're on a power trip. She said no. Leave her alone."

"I didn't ask you!" Roxanne shot back. "You really want girls like *this* to carry on our legacies?" She pointed at Annetta. "This girl who doesn't know if she even *wants to be a girl*?" Pointed at me. "And this broke loser? Who doesn't even deserve her girlfriend, much less a place in Serena."

"Roxanne," Ella said quietly. "Please don't . . ."

Their words felt so far away. I was underwater, staring at the shot glass with a lump wedged in my throat. I considered taking it. Just to end all of this.

I shook my head, unglued the thought. No. I didn't want this. I didn't know what the hell I wanted anymore, but I knew it wasn't to feel this room-temperature liquor warm my throat. I stared at the four-ounce shot.

I saw *everything*.

I felt the pulse of the strobe light on the first Serena task, when I was curled up in bed, room spinning around me. Envisioned Annetta confronting me, Alice confronting me, Leon confronting me. The anger kept building, and I felt the tremble in my gut as I balanced on a toilet, hiding from Mom, wishing I could flush myself to another world. I felt the torment of ages nine to thirteen, when kids were cruel and made me wish I wasn't alive at all. I felt a fault line trembling, splitting the earth, Mom on one side, me on the other. *Only half. I don't care if you're Black, white, purple.* I saw Dad's disappointment when I came out as a lesbian, another tally marking the ways he couldn't relate to me. I heard Ella's giggle when we were fourteen, and I drank and drank and drank. I felt That Feeling when I became Big Bad Bee, this persona I'd sewn together with desperation and liquor.

I could so easily become her. Land in my soft happy place between oblivion and crushing self-awareness.

All I had to do was take the shot.

"Bee."

I turned toward the honey-sweet voice I'd known for years. My beautiful girlfriend who chose me. Ella's eyes were wide. Scared.

"Bee, just take the shot," she said. "Please."

My heart dropped. I gripped the shot glass so tight my knuckles whitened. I was lightheaded. I barely registered Annetta stepping out of formation.

"Just take the shot," Ella repeated.

"Better listen to your *girlfriend*," Roxanne said at the same time Alice burst out, "Stop this *now.*"

"Just take the shot and get it over with, Bee," Ella pleaded.

Take the shot.

Do it.

Do it.

DO IT DO IT DO IT DO IT DO IT DO IT—

I launched the shot glass across the living room, toward the kitchen.

It crashed into the microwave and shattered. I was shaking, a fury I'd never felt before in full force. Everyone stared at me. Everyone stared at Roxanne.

"Wow, Blake." Roxanne's tone was a mixture of disbelief and wrath. "You are so done here." She shoved my shoulder, pushing me toward the door.

I snapped.

"Get the fuck off me," I growled. I pushed her back, directly in the chest with all my rage. She stumbled with a screech into a group of Serena girls sitting on the couch. I stood my ground, ready to fight if she came up swinging.

"You are *finished*, bitch!" Roxanne screamed. "I hope you enjoy being arrested for vandalism when I show the Petersons the video!"

Somehow, my limbs moved. Several people screamed after me, but I couldn't make out who was who.

"Wait, Blake!"

"Stay!"

Their voices were drowned out by Roxanne's venomous roar.

"And by the way . . . I fucked your girlfriend!"

I stumbled onto the docks. My anger felt like a new version of drunkenness. Roxanne. Ella. Ella & Roxanne . . . *Everything* was drenched in red, I was so pissed my teeth were chattering.

"*Bee!* Wait!"

A hand grabbed my elbow, and I whirled around to see Ella and Annetta. Ella dropped her arm, face full of fear. Her dress was riding up the soft flesh of her thighs, and I fought the instinct to yank it down.

"I'm so sorry," Ella pleaded. "Blake, I can explain—"

"Did you fuck her?" I asked.

There was a Before world. A world where I was Blake and she was Ella and we were Blake & Ella, golden couple. The Couple Most Likely to Still Be Together in Ten Years.

And then Ella started crying and nodding and saying "I'm sorry, I'm so sorry," and we were thrust into the After. I couldn't breathe. Annetta's eyes widened in horror.

"How could you?" I asked, gasping.

"I'll explain everything later, but can we *please* just go back inside?" Ella asked. "We are so close—"

"Then go!" I screamed. "Go!" I pointed at the *Bewitched*. "Go back to Roxanne since she's all you care about!" Annetta tried to pull me away, but I was cemented.

"All I care about?" Ella laughed. "Roxanne is not all I care about. I've been busting my ass all summer to make sure you get into the society because I care about *you*!"

Bitter tears rolled down my cheeks. "If this is your version of caring, then I don't want it."

Ella grabbed my face so hard I cried out in pain.

"How can you say that?" she hissed, tears smudging her mascara. "You know I love you. I wouldn't *be* here if I didn't care."

I pushed out of her grip and stumbled into the dock ropes. The tears made everything blurry, made talking almost impossible. "You *cheated* on me. With Roxanne. How . . . how . . ."

"Please just let me explain," Ella said, crying. "Bee, I didn't mean—"

"Enough of this," Annetta said, pulling my arm again. "We're leaving."

"So you're both just going to leave?" Ella cried. "Blake! You *know* I love you. I slept with her because I thought it'd give me—give *us*—an advantage! This is our dream. Please let's just go back to the party. We're so close. Please, Bumblebee."

I hesitated. I loved her so much. We were Ella and Blake, couldn't we survive anything? Maybe we could work it out. Maybe cheating didn't have to break us.

"Blake," Annetta said quietly. She sounded so *tired*. "If you choose her, I'm done. You know you deserve better than this."

I was suspended between them, teetering on a tightrope. My best friend on one side, my girlfriend on the other. Someone who broke my heart and someone who'd repeatedly been there to pick up the pieces. I stepped away from Ella.

"Don't do this," Ella cried. "Blake, I swear—"

"I'm done," I said, and my world fell away from me.

"Come on," Annetta said. Her voice was a beam of light, guiding me away from Ella. Away from Serena.

The dock creaked as we started for the parking lot. My ankle rolled as my heel got caught between two planks, and in a fury, I ripped Ella's shoes off. I threw them in her direction and one bounced into the water.

"Are you kidding me?" Ella yelled. "Annetta! *Blake!*"

Annetta and I tore off into the darkness. My bare feet were blissfully free. We didn't stop running until we reached the parking lot.

Inside Annetta's car, I buried my head in my hands and screamed. Annetta placed a warm hand on my shoulder and rubbed in slow circles. I bawled until my throat was raw and I was coughing and sputtering.

"I'm sorry," I choked out. "I'm so sorry, Nettie."

"I know," Annetta said. She was crying, too. "I know, Blake. Let's just go home."

Everything was quiet in Winward Commons. Annetta idled in the parking lot outside my building, and we sat there watching blue shadows flicker and dance from my upstairs neighbor's TV.

"You know what's funny?" Annetta asked quietly. I looked at her, but her eyes were still trained ahead.

"What?" I asked.

"A small part of me *wanted* my mom to pick up." Annetta laughed and scrubbed a hand over her face. "Maybe it would've been easier for Roxanne to rip the Band-Aid off instead of me." She finally looked at me, and her eyes were a mixture of fear and . . . delight?

"I'm nonbinary," she whispered, and we smiled at each other, despite everything.

"That's amazing," I said. "I'm happy for you, Nettie. Wait." I cocked my head. "Do you still want me to call you Nettie? Or use different pronouns?"

"I'm still Nettie," she said. "And I'm still okay with *she* pronouns for now." She giggled. "So go ahead and paint *ANNETTA JONES IS NONBINARY* on a billboard since we all know you can't keep a damn secret to yourself."

I surprised myself by laughing. I deserved that. "I know my words probably don't mean anything anymore, but for what it's worth, I really am sorry." I swallowed. "You were right . . . I have a problem . . . with drinking."

Annetta smiled. "God, I really could use my fucking vape now. Gum ain't cutting it." And we laughed until I started crying again.

"I love you, Blake," Annetta said. "What Ella did . . . that's so shitty."

"Did you know?" I asked.

She shook her head. "No. And you know I would've told you if I did. No more secrets between us, okay?"

We hugged awkwardly over the center console. "Okay," I whispered. "No more secrets."

I walked to my building in a delirious daze, thoughts alternating between *I have a problem* and *Ella cheated on me* and *Annetta is nonbinary*.

Inside, the living room was silent. Towers of boxes cast shadows on the walls. I tiptoed to my room and closed the door behind me. All that was left was my old lumpy mattress, a suitcase full of clothes, and a few boxes I was taking to Jameswell. I sank onto the dingy brown carpet and pulled my knees to my chin. My gaze met my reflection in the mirror on my closet door.

I didn't recognize the girl who stared back. She looked like she was afraid of her own shadow. My hair was mussed, makeup soiled. My cheeks and nose were bright red. I curled into a ball and made myself as small as possible. Made myself Little Blake again.

"Blake?"

My door creaked open and I sucked in a breath as Mom saw everything. Saw *me*. There was nothing to hide behind. She was wearing her nightgown and had a book tucked under her arm.

"What's wrong?"

I shook my head, unable to speak.

She lowered herself to the floor and pushed the curls away from my face.

"Oh, baby," she said, "what's wrong? What happened?"

I shook my head again.

The tears welled again.

Everything crumpled *again*.

Mom scooted closer, told me to rest my head in her lap. I hadn't done that in years, but I did it tonight and I was so grateful. She soothed her fingers through my hair, and I cried and cried and cried. She kept asking me what was wrong. What happened?

I didn't know where to start.

CHAPTER 21

ROOT BEER FLOAT

I USED TO BE JEALOUS of families who ate dinner together. As a child, I watched with green-eyed envy as families on television sat at the same table at the same time every night, just to enjoy a meal together. I read books about stay-at-home moms who made spaghetti and kept the noodles on their own separate platter, a big bowl of sauce made from actual tomatoes. Parmesan grated from a block instead of shaken from a bottle. I daydreamed about other families who talked about their days with enough energy to care about everyone else's answers.

The Brenner family wasn't like this. We were takeout on TV trays. We were burritos gulped down while driving to work. For years, this was our standard. And in sixth grade, I got so tired of it that I decided to take matters into my own hands.

One afternoon, I came home from school determined to throw a dinner party. Dad used to post his schedule on the refrigerator, so I knew he was due in from Charlotte at six. Leon was still at wrestling practice, and Mom was sleeping off her night shift. I took to the kitchen, a recipe for spaghetti pulled up on my phone, my backpack bulging with ingredients I'd picked up at Food Lion with money I'd squirreled away from birthday cards. I selected a big pot for the noodles and a cookie sheet for the garlic bread, and got to work.

I set the table while water boiled and the oven preheated. I looked up diagrams of proper place settings. Fork on the left, knife and spoon on the right. We didn't have cloth napkins, so I delicately folded paper towels into triangles, and I was so proud. The Brenners were going to be eating in *style*, just like the families on TV. Just like the families in my books.

Except, somehow, I ruined everything. I got so distracted with trying to make sure the tomato sauce was seasoned perfectly that I didn't remember the garlic bread until I smelled it burning. While I was furiously trying to scrape off the char, I overboiled the noodles and they ended up a soggy mess. Needless to say, by the time Dad and Leon arrived and Mom woke up, I was sitting at our kitchen table in tears.

"What were you thinking?" Dad asked as he picked at a scorched piece of Texas toast.

"We never eat dinner together," I said through tears and snot. "I just want to eat dinner together."

The details became lost to time. I don't remember whose idea it was, but somehow my family ended up on the patio of a Sonic Drive-In, laughing at the whole ordeal over foot-long chili dogs and Tater Tots. That was the first time I'd tasted a root beer float because Dad was aghast when he learned neither Leon nor I had ever had one.

"Outrageous!" Dad said, and he promptly ordered a round for the family. "How have my children never delighted in the sheer pleasure of a good old-fashioned root beer float?" They were delivered on a red plastic tray by a teenage girl on glittery green roller skates.

"To dinner together," Mom said, holding hers up for a toast.

"To dinner together," the rest of us echoed. And we devoured them before they melted, and everything was all right. Saved by soft serve and carbonation.

After that night, the Brenner family dinner became a weekly tradition. When Leon was away at basic training, the three of us jokingly propped his graduation photo on his empty place mat.

We never ended up like the families on television with an aproned mother and organic ingredients. We still kept sitting down in front of fast food and frozen pizzas anyway. Week after week, we still kept coming together, begrudgingly. Exhausted.

We still kept trying.

When I woke up, Mom was still there.

She was curled on my mattress next to me, her mouth hanging open, drool in the corners. All at once, last night's events barreled toward me like an oncoming train.

The Serena Society.

Flash.

Ella cheating on me.

Flash.

Choosing Annetta.

Flash.

My throat was raw from crying all night. I didn't remember falling asleep, and I wasn't wearing Ella's dress anymore. It'd been replaced by one of Mom's long nightgowns covered in cartoon butterflies. Knowing she must've put me in bed filled me with soft gratitude.

The doorbell rang. My heart pounded as I sat up, wondering if it was Ella. Was she here to apologize? Fight some more?

I didn't want to wake Mom, so I moved nimbly. I crawled off the mattress and grabbed my cell from the jeweled clutch I'd borrowed from Ella. It was dead.

The doorbell again. Mom stirred before blinking awake.

"Morning, baby," she said through a yawn. "Who is that?"

I shrugged. Then heard footsteps on the carpet, Dad grumbling. His car wasn't in the parking lot when Annetta dropped me off, so he must've flown in early this morning.

I was halfway down the hall when I heard the low tenor of Mr. Spencer's voice. I stopped, wondering what the hell he was doing at my house.

Then Dad's voice, sprinkled with concern: "Blake? Can you come here?"

My heart was in my throat as I joined Dad at the front door. He was also in his pajamas, a pillow crease stretching across his cheek. He looked at me with a question in his eyes, silently asking, *You want to tell me what's going on?* And I swallowed as I took in Mr. Spencer on the other side of the door, flanked by two white men.

On his right was the Crystal Grove Golf and Yacht Club's owner, Mr. Donohue.

And on his left? Frank Peterson.

"Hi, Blake," Mr. Spencer said with a grim smile. "Mind if we come in?"

"I should have her arrested! I have the video evidence right here!"

"Now, Frank, we've all agreed involving the cops is unnecessary."

"I'll tell you what's unnecessary, Isaac! It's this ... this girl who thinks it's *funny* to deface people's property!"

Back and forth, a furious argument. It was surreal, the six of us sitting in my family's cluttered living room. Me and Mom sitting silently on the couch in our pajamas. Dapper Mr. Spencer casually lounging in Dad's recliner, Dad and Mr. Donohue on kitchen barstools. Mr. Peterson pacing a worn, angry line back and forth in the middle of the room. He shot me another glare and asked me the same question he'd already asked five times in the two minutes since he'd barged into my house.

"You care to explain yourself?"

I *despised* him. So much I couldn't even look at him without seeing the black paint he'd smeared across his face as a pitiful joke.

"Blake, answer the man," Dad said. He'd watched the video with a blank face. The video where I'd stumbled drunkenly toward *La Dolce Vita*, paint can in hand. Screaming, *Who wants to see me fuck up this white man's boat?!* Everyone in attendance cheering, save for one. Annetta's voice, panicked, in the background: *This isn't a good idea!* Me launching the paint can, cackling like a wild woman, a yellow tornado, the satisfying *thunk* as it made contact with steel. Me turning back to the crowd with a proud smile. Laughing, bowing.

Roxanne secretly recording it all.

"I don't know," I finally said. "I'm sorry. I was drunk. I didn't mean—"

"Horse shit," Mr. Peterson interrupted. "You didn't mean? 'Who wants to see me fuck up this white man's boat'? That sure as hell sounds premeditated."

"Let's all calm down," Mr. Donohue said. I was used to seeing him wandering around the Grove in tailored suits, schmoozing with members. Now he was in my living room in a polo and chino shorts, looking Very Much Over this whole situation. He leveled his gaze at me. "We came here directly because Mr. Spencer insisted you're a good kid. You worked for us for two years—"

"Before she got fired for attacking *my son*," Mr. Peterson interrupted again. "This young lady has a personal vendetta against my family! And now I'm supposed to 'calm down'?"

I didn't realize I was shaking until Mom placed her hand on my knee. She'd been quiet this entire time, but I could feel disappointment radiating off her in waves.

"Blake is going to Jameswell this fall," Mr. Spencer said, somehow still sounding proud of me. "Do we really want to ruin her future over a drunken mistake?"

"It cost me thousands in detailing fees to get rid of the mess she made," Mr. Peterson spat, but everyone in the room knew it wasn't about the money. Mr. Peterson had more money than he knew what to do with, and he would be the first one to tell you that.

This was about respect and my lack of it.

"I'm sorry. I'll pay you back," I said, even though the concept of *thousands* of dollars made me lightheaded.

"There." Mr. Donohue slapped his knees. "It's solved. Ms. Brenner will work out a payment plan with you, Frank. All is well."

"I don't care about the money!" Mr. Peterson stopped pacing, and I felt his glare heavy on my temple. "I just want an actual apology! I don't think she's *actually* sorry."

Because I'm not. He was right. I wasn't sorry for throwing the paint. He was a piece of shit human who donned blackface and cheated on his wife and had no manners, and I wasn't sorry. I was sorry Roxanne got it on camera. I was sorry to be sitting here now, wilting under my parents' disappointment. I was sorry for causing trouble when they were already so stressed with their impending move.

"See?" Mr. Peterson chided. "The girl can't even *pretend* to be sorry. I should—"

"I'm sorry," I interrupted. I met his pissed-off gaze with my own. "I'm *so sorry* for throwing that paint. I'm *so sorry* I got worked up after someone shared a photo of you in blackface. I'm *so sorry* that I became so upset imagining the future mayor of Virginia Beach condoning such a racist, heinous act that my hands simply could not control themselves."

Mr. Peterson's face paled to its rightful color.

"Well, just a minute," Mr. Peterson sputtered. "That's not—"

"Frank, is it?"

I looked up to find Dad rising from the barstool, his no-nonsense pilot face on. His *I can handle this* face. He slowly made his way to Mr. Peterson, his eyebrows drawn together.

"My daughter has apologized," he said. "You've gotten what you came for. Now please, get out of my house."

Mr. Peterson sized Dad up, like he was debating whether he wanted to keep going. Then his shoulders slumped and he muttered, "Fine."

Mr. Donohue stood. "Thank you for your time," he said, clapping Mr. Peterson on the shoulder and steering him toward the front door. Before they left, Mr. Donohue looked at me, almost sadly. "In lieu of pressing charges, you will be banned from Crystal Grove indefinitely. If you're found on company property, we *will* contact the authorities."

It was a gut punch. Four years I'd spent as Ella's plus-one in the club's nooks and crannies. So many parties, so many memories, up in smoke. I'd practically grown up there.

Mr. Donohue and Mr. Peterson left, the latter still mumbling under his breath. Mr. Spencer lingered in the foyer.

"I'm sorry for bringing them here," he finally said, more to Dad than to me. "I was golfing with Jeff when Frank contacted him about the video and he wanted to go to the police." He looked at me with a twinkle in his eye and it killed me, knowing there was no way he was aware Ella and I might be over for good. "Nice move," he said quietly. "I haven't seen Frank speechless in a really long time."

Dad eyed Mr. Peterson and Mr. Donohue out in the parking lot, climbing into Mr. Spencer's Mercedes. "You have a lot more patience than I do to put up with men like that."

"It's all business," Mr. Spencer said with a weary shrug. "You know how it is, right?"

Dad hesitated, and I wondered if he was thinking about the racist bullshit he must've heard when trapped in a flight deck with a white superior. "Yeah. I do," he said finally. He and Mr. Spencer shook hands, and then Dad closed the front door.

I should've been grateful that it was just me and my parents now. But their confusion shrouded the room in a mist, and I knew there was no running away this time. This was not a situation that could be fixed with a trip to Sonic and a root beer float.

"What the hell, Blake?" Dad finally asked, dropping into an exhausted seat in his recliner. "Is that what you've been doing all summer with those girls?"

I shook my head, eyes screwing up with tears. "It was just that one night. I don't know what got into me."

"Was this another task?" Mom asked. "Like the pennies? Did they make you do this?"

"No," I cried. "No one made me do anything."

"Then I don't understand what could've possessed you to do something like this," Dad went on. "This isn't how we raised you. Hell, I don't even recognize you right now."

I laughed through my tears. "Come on, Dad."

"What's that supposed to mean?"

"Recognize me? When was the last time you *looked* at me? You haven't recognized me since I was fourteen." My heart was twisting, my throat tightening. But everything was coming out, so why not this, too?

Dad shifted uncomfortably. In his silence, I found strength. "You want to know why I'm always at the Spencers'? Because they *see* me. I never feel small there." But as the words left my mouth, I realized that wasn't necessarily true. Maybe it was the daylight bringing my fight with Ella into sharp focus. But I was suddenly outside my relationship, watching Ella grab my arm in her bedroom. I heard her say, 'Awww, Bumblebee, you're *jealous*,' when I shared my concerns about the Truth or Dare kiss. I imagined how she felt having sex with Roxanne. If she liked it more than sex with me.

"I don't understand," Mom said. "How do your father and I make you feel small?"

My eyes burned with tears. "I've always felt like I'm a disappointment to you, Dad," I said. "It's like you were sad when you found out I was afraid of flying so you just . . . stopped trying. Then you completely checked out when I told you I was a lesbian."

"That's not true," Dad protested, but Mom shot him a look and he sat back in his recliner.

"Let her talk, Will," Mom said quietly. "Blake, you were saying?"

"It *is* true," I said. "You never ask about Ella. You never ask how we're doing. You'd rather talk to Leon about fuel leaks!"

I looked up through my tears, and his blurry face was contemplative. And ashamed.

"I'm sorry," he said finally. "I never knew you felt that way."

I pressed my fingers to my eyes, trying to stop crying because the next part would hurt even more and I didn't know if I was ready.

But I had to. Everything needed to be laid out on the table. I couldn't hide from this anymore.

"And, *God*, Mom," I said, and she stiffened next to me on the couch. "I don't know how many times I've tried to tell you this."

"Tell me what?"

"How . . . upset I am with you! How much you've hurt me without realizing it." I turned to her, and her face was whiter than usual, her wispy brown ponytail flat and limp from sleep.

"Do you remember that night before my sixteenth birthday? When we were talking about music and Mariah Carey?"

Confusion clouded her face. The moment that'd lived in my head rent-free for years, she didn't even remember.

"No, I don't," she said.

"You said, 'Even when I tried telling them that Mariah was only half Black, they still wouldn't budge.' You said that to me, your biracial daughter. Like Blackness is only acceptable in light-enough doses."

Mom looked shocked. "Blake, honey, you know that's not what I meant."

"It's not just that," I said, full-body crying now. Years of unsaid words unspooled from my throat like thread. "Why did you *never* make an effort to surround me with Black role models growing up? Why didn't you know how to do my hair? Why have you never *talked* to me about race? I just feel like . . ." Mom was crying now, but I pushed myself to keep going. "I never had to deal with that around Mrs. Spencer. And I guess . . . somewhere down the line I started seeing you as just another white lady instead of my mom. But I *want* you to be my mom."

And there it was. Saying the words felt like ripping off a tattoo. But it also felt like taking the deepest breath I'd taken in years.

"And, Dad," I continued, "I never went to you, either, because it felt like . . . after I came out, you only cared about Leon. Because he's a boy, and he's straight. Dad, I want you to care about me, too. I *need* you to care about me, too."

Dad stared at the floor.

"Why didn't you ever say anything?" Mom asked, her hands kneading anxious circles into her thighs. "Sweetheart, how long have you been holding all of this in?"

"For years," I answered. "Years."

"I'm sorry," she said through her own tears. "I'm so sorry, baby. We—*I* never meant for you to feel that way."

Dad joined us on the couch, and we somehow managed an awkward group hug, me caught in the middle. I felt like Little Blake between them, but in a good way. Like I was finally in a safe harbor after the longest journey on choppy waters.

"I'm sorry, too, baby girl," Dad said into my hair. "We didn't realize."

After The Talk, the energy in the Brenner house was tender.

There were less than two weeks before the big move, and the kitchen still hadn't been packed. So Mom and I slowly tackled it together, tension aching between us. I wrapped chipped plates and worn silverware in newspaper. Mom went through the freezer, tossing out frostbitten leftovers and cracked ice trays. Every once in a while, she'd look at me with a sadness in her eyes but say nothing. Every once in a while, I found myself doing the same.

Dad spent the afternoon making runs to the local thrift store to drop off donations. By the time evening rolled around, my family had run out of distractions and found ourselves together in the living room again.

"Since we're all airing our grievances today," Dad started with a teasing glint in his eyes, "your mother and I had something we wanted to say."

I plopped on the couch, exhaustion pulling at my bones. Mom perched on the arm of the recliner, unable to meet my eyes.

"The stunt you pulled at Busch Gardens? Not cool, kid," Dad said. I inhaled. "I know."

"Your brother came to us concerned and after . . ." He trailed off and looked to Mom for support.

"After seeing that video of you today, we're concerned, too," Mom finished. "Blake, I know things haven't been easy . . . but you can talk to us if you're having a problem."

Guilt made it hard to look at them, so I focused on the carpet. The same nondescript brown carpet of my childhood. Eighteen years in this apartment and only today had I ever found it so fascinating.

"I know," I said. "I'm—" *Fine*, I started to say, but stopped myself. I wasn't fine. As many grievances as I had stacked up against my parents, I couldn't forget my own mistakes. More than anything, I wanted to be back at Busch Gardens with my family in the lively Festhaus. I wanted to say no when Cody offered me the whiskey. And I wished more than anything I had climbed down from the toilet when my mom called my name and let myself be found.

I didn't want to run anymore.

Dad cleared his throat. "After the move, you'll only have Leon here. Dallas is a couple of hours away. You have the flight benefits . . . if you want to use them. But we won't be here."

I smiled softly. "I know, Dad. I'll come visit."

Mom studied me, concerned. "And the Spencers . . . ?" She let the question dangle. Sure, Mr. Spencer had come to my rescue earlier. But that didn't mean Ella and I were good. I hadn't charged my phone all day because I was afraid of what I'd find when I did.

"I think . . . Ella and I . . ." No, I couldn't say it. But my parents understood.

"I'm sorry," Mom said, and *she* sounded so resolute that I wanted to cry again. "I know how much you care about her."

"Yeah," I said, eyes sweeping to the floor again. "I really care about her."

And then my parents were by my side again, and I allowed myself to be held. Dad hugged me when I couldn't hold the tears back anymore, and Mom cooed, "I know it hurts, baby, I know you care." She kissed my temple. "Sometimes you just need to care about yourself more."

I sobbed. Harder than I'd ever cried in my entire life. Everything was changing and life was an express train and I just wanted to get off. I wanted to go back in time, to an age where these arms and this house were my safe space. Before I'd started looking at these walls and these people as an embarrassing pit stop on the way to Better. When did that happen? Was it solely because of Ella? Did it happen before her glitter, before the Spencers' house on the bay?

These linoleum floors, the humming refrigerator, the scratched kitchen table. Was Little Blake still here?

Was she there? Age twelve, at the stove, tearfully trying to save burnt garlic bread?

Was she there? Age fourteen, by the refrigerator with a rotten bottle of wine?

Or maybe she was here, with me now. Sandwiched between my parents, their shirts in my balled fists like a desperate toddler. Age eighteen and afraid of all the versions of myself that I'd yet to see.

Midnight found me alone in my bedroom. I'd been staring at my phone for ten minutes, anxiously imagining what I'd find when I turned it on.

A breakup text from Ella? A rambling, incoherent voice mail?

I was cried out. I had nothing left, so I decided to bite the bullet. Surely, whatever Ella was going to throw at me couldn't hurt more than what today had already brought.

As my phone came to life, dozens of texts poured in. A stream of names. Annetta, Alice, Leon, Eden, Khadija, Keiko, Corinne.

But from Ella? Nothing.

I ignored everyone's messages and went straight to her social media. Her latest upload was only an hour ago, and when I saw what she posted, my heart shattered.

A video of Roxanne on the beach in golden hour, splashing through the surf. Gorgeous in a white bikini. Blowing a kiss at the camera.

There was no caption. Just a single red heart.

I had made my choice.

And, apparently, so had Ella.

HOW TO PIECE YOURSELF TOGETHER AGAIN

YOU'RE GONNA FEEL LIKE shit for a while.

First, burrow under a blanket. Create a fort with your pillows (the more, the better). Close the blinds and hide from the sunlight. Listen to a breakup playlist on repeat (it helps when the songs are *really* sad). Treat yourself to ice cream. When you finish the chocolate, move on to the cookie dough. Scroll through old photos. Delete some. Keep some.

Sleep. As much as you need. Dream of happier times, when she was all you needed to feel whole. Wake up broken in this nightmare world, dizzy and disoriented, still reaching for her across your empty bed.

For the next step, you'll need some ingredients:

- Yourself
- An old friend
- Her new boo
- One bottle of sparkling lemonade
- Three BLT sandwiches
- A family-sized bag of BBQ chips
- Six chocolate chip cookies baked in the heart of a queer kitchen
- One oversized blanket that smells like the trunk of your best friend's car

The sunnier the day, the better. Scope out a suitable spot at your neighborhood beach and take up space. Let the waves be the soundtrack to your lunch.

Play cards. In between rounds, cry when you talk about Her. Stir up the emotions. Let yourself be held by your oldest friend. Believe it when the new friend says you deserve better. Gradually trust them both when they say things will be okay.

Dip your toes in the ocean. Inch toward the blue-soaked horizon. Baptize yourself and emerge gasping. Laugh when your friends drag a pink boogie board into the water.

Grab hold. Tight.

Fold into one another when the waves get rough.

Stay afloat.

Read. Curse. Cry. Cling to the voice in your head that says you will survive this. Trust yourself for the first time in years. Dig your heels into the earth. Grit your teeth. Feel your boundaries harden like a rock in your stomach.

Somehow survive. Somehow keep waking up. Somehow buy the dorm room supplies and overpriced textbooks. Somehow go through these necessary motions even though when you look back, you'll have no idea how you did it.

Cover the cinderblocks in an effort to make your new dorm room feel like home. You put up the *Wicked* Broadway poster because it's your favorite musical. Your nerdy roommate chooses the periodic table because sometimes you need a little order amidst the chaos. You've recently realized you like sparkling apple juice because it makes you feel bubbly, so stock your mini-fridge with little cans. Laugh when your dad complains about the view of a brick wall from your second-story window. Hold back tears when your mom neatly hangs your winter coat. She used to button your jackets when you were little and now she's leaving and you're not so little anymore.

Humor your brother when he lectures you on campus safety. Promise you'll always travel with the small whistle he presses into your palm. Suggest that the two of you establish a weekly lunch date to replace family dinner nights. Smile when he says that's a great idea.

When everyone is gone, crawl into bed with your new roommate (who is also an old friend). Simmer. Watch movies together. Crack up when she says, *Remember that time we almost got into the Serena Society?*

Mourn the loss. Remove from heat. Move on and begin again.

And begin again.

Begin again.

SEPTEMBER

CHAPTER 22

"I GET TO HAVE tacos for dinner every night. Maybe there *is* a God."

My eyes trailed over Annetta's tray as she doused her chicken tacos with salsa and sour cream. It was the fourth time this week we'd eaten in the dining hall, and the fourth time Annetta had had this same meal.

"How am I supposed to choose between pizza and tacos?" I asked as we moved down the buffet line. Annetta placed a greasy slice of pepperoni on my tray.

"I'll choose for you," she said. "Better?"

"Yes, thank you."

"We're going to eat like queens every night," she said as we queued to swipe our IDs.

"Good," I said. "We deserve it." My mouth watered as she added slices of chocolate cake to our trays. Happily indulging in comfort food was apparently our new routine.

We'd been at Jameswell a little over a week. I'd already gotten lost three times, once walking into an anthropology lecture I thought was my bio class. Annetta had already accidently brushed against the bronze statue of one of Jameswell's founders in the middle of the quad, even though it was supposedly bad luck to touch it before graduation. When an upperclassman broke the bad news to her, Annetta rolled her eyes and told him she made her own luck.

We settled into our favorite table in the back of the dining commons, near a wall of windows that faced a cluster of oak trees. It was like eating in a tree house.

"Have you seen her?" Annetta asked.

"Not yet," I replied, teeth sinking into cheese. It'd been radio silence since the final task. Ella had worked magic to get out of the triple dorm room we'd planned to share with Annetta. We'd started using her empty bed as storage until they assigned us a new roommate.

It was still hard to believe four years could end in just one night.

After dinner, Annetta and I wandered around campus as twilight emerged. I remembered how we'd darted between the trees the night we got our acceptance letters, so nervous security would kick us out. How strange it was to take our time now, knowing we belonged.

"Have I mentioned how sorry I am?" I asked.

"Blake, please. I said I've forgiven you a *million* times. Besides." She thrust her nose in the air. "We're in college now! To new beginnings."

"To new beginnings," I said, my heart warming.

"Hey, pledges!"

The rumble of skateboard wheels on concrete drew near.

It was Alice.

She hopped off her board and tucked it under her arm. On move-in day, Leon told me they were still dating, but I hadn't seen her until now. There was a pinch in my gut when my gaze landed on the tiny calla lily charm on her necklace.

"Where y'all been hiding?" Alice asked.

"Around," Annetta said.

"These past few weeks have been . . . a lot," I added.

"I'll say." Alice leaned against the low concrete wall outside the education building. "I've been wanting to talk to both of you. The last night was completely out of control. Neither of you deserved that. I should've stopped Roxanne in her tracks a long time ago."

I shrugged. What was there to do now? Annetta started popping the bright bubble key chain toy she recently bought to help her anxiety. Chewing all that gum had started to give her jaw aches.

"I'm headed to a physics lab," Alice went on. "But let's talk on Sunday morning. Come by the house at eleven."

"Alice, honestly. It's fine," I said.

"My mom has made peace with the fact that I will not be following in her footsteps," Annetta added wryly.

"La la la, can't hear you." Alice set her skateboard back on the ground. "Didn't you hear the news? I'm the president now. I guess that means you should listen to me." She took off. "Sunday! Eleven! Be there!"

Over the next few days, Annetta and I considered Alice's invitation. On one hand, I didn't want to go somewhere that reminded me of Ella. But that was proving to be hard, considering I started seeing her everywhere. Hanging in the student union with a new group of friends she'd seemingly made overnight. Stretching out like a satisfied cat under one of Jameswell's many weeping willow trees that dripped Spanish moss. I dodged her every time, still not ready to deal with the ache of our breakup.

Annetta was on Team Fuck the Society before considering the possibility that we might actually be invited *inside* the Serena house. And that appealed to her inner nosy child.

So on Sunday morning, we walked over a mile across campus. On the way, our phones buzzed with a message from Xan. It was a video of CeeCee winding her hips in the Sugar Mama kitchen while she meticulously piped frosting on a rack of freshly baked sugar cookies. Xan announced, "Here at Sugar Mama, all our cookies come with a nice side of twerk."

"Oh my God, I love CeeCee," I said, laughing. "Can we just live at Sugar Mama?" The dining hall's desserts were good, but they had nothing on CeeCee's and Xan's creations.

Annetta didn't even try to hide her happiness about Xan anymore. Right before we started school, she and Xan made it official. Virginia Beach was only half an hour away, so they spent practically every weekend together.

I didn't register Mrs. Spencer's silver Audi in the Serena Society house's driveway until Annetta was ringing the doorbell. I looked around frantically, afraid Ella was near. But the front door opened and only Mrs. Spencer and Alice greeted us.

"So glad you could make it," Mrs. Spencer said, holding the door open. "Please, come in."

Annetta's eyes widened with excitement. "In . . . inside?" she clarified. *Like, inside the house? Where no one but official Serena women were technically allowed?*

Mrs. Spencer nodded, so Annetta and I took timid steps forward.

"Don't worry," Alice said. "The floor isn't going to open up and swallow you."

"Alice, hush," Mrs. Spencer said. She gestured to a small sitting room off the foyer. "This way, ladies."

Annetta and I sat on a cozy love seat. A small fireplace was nestled in the corner, and the mantel was filled with potted plants and pictures of Serena women past. So many women of color that I still yearned to know.

Mrs. Spencer and Alice sat in cream-colored armchairs across from us. Behind them was a dash of bold floral sapphire-blue wallpaper. A tea set, a plate of scones, and a vase of fresh-cut calla lilies rested on the coffee table.

"Tea, girls?" Mrs. Spencer asked as she poured herself a cup. I nodded, and Alice poured some for me and Annetta. Mrs. Spencer carefully dropped a sugar cube in and stirred with a tiny spoon. The gentle, muted *ting* inside the cup was the only sound in the room.

"Thank you for coming," Mrs. Spencer said after a slow sip. "I've heard the past few weeks have been rather unfortunate."

Alice nibbled on a scone. Annetta shifted uncomfortably. The teacup was hot in my hands, but I was afraid to move. Mrs. Spencer wasn't looking at me. She knew about the breakup; she was the one who helped Ella get out of our dorm room.

"The foundation of Serena was not built on what happened that night on Roxanne Garcia's yacht," Mrs. Spencer continued. "I've spoken to everyone who was there that night. That never should have happened, and I'm sorry."

Annetta and I exchanged glances. She looked just as confused as I felt.

"I'm not going to pretend like hazing doesn't occur," Mrs. Spencer said. "I'm not ancient. I went through it. We've all been through it. But I can see the process is changing in several ways in which I have no choice but to intervene." She set the mug on the coffee table. "You should not have been punished for choosing not to drink, Blake." She looked at Annetta. "And you should not have been harassed about your gender identity. Or for *any* reason."

Mrs. Spencer pursed her perfect red lips. "I think it was a wise choice you both left when you did. But please do not think that your experience this summer is the sum of the Serena Society. I meant what I said in the ballroom. Serena women are there for one another. And the best ones step up when things go awry. Annetta, as a legacy, you know this." She stared at her sparkling sapphire bracelet grimly. "And we also apologize when we are wrong. As the advisor, I should've known that things were getting out of hand. And for that, I extend my sincerest apologies."

"Um," Annetta said. "Thank you?"

Mrs. Spencer nodded. "As with any organization, Serena has our fair share of women who have strayed from the society's founding purpose. Sisterhood, integrity, wisdom." She ticked off each one with a pale pink manicured finger. "I have spoken to Roxanne extensively about what happened that night . . . and what happened with my daughter. The senior counsel and I have decided to expel her membership status."

My heart stopped. As much as I disliked Roxanne, I never thought I'd see the day when *she* was on the outside of the society, and Annetta and I were—possibly—still in the running. I sipped my tea. It was Earl Grey, still too hot. It burned my tongue. I set the teacup on the coffee table.

"And we will be cracking down on hazing going forward. Forced drinking, inappropriate relationships between pledges and leadership . . ." Mrs. Spencer shook her head. "That's not who we are."

Alice sat forward. "Look. The induction is next Friday. You both belong there."

"But . . ." I looked at Annetta, whose eyes were narrowed.

"You only accept twelve girls," Annetta said. "And we got cut."

"I'm aware," Alice said simply. "What's your point?"

"What about tradition?" I asked.

Mrs. Spencer smiled. "Some traditions are meant to change. Some things don't last forever." I didn't imagine her lifted eyebrow; she was *definitely* talking about me and Ella.

"I understand if y'all don't want to come back," Alice said. "But I've talked it over with the other girls, and everyone is in agreement you're more than welcome here. I'll be in charge this year, and I'm not going to let any bullshit go down."

"Alice," Mrs. Spencer scolded.

"Sorry. No bull*stuff*." Alice leaned back in her armchair and shrugged. "Not gonna lie, you two were my favorites, anyway."

Mrs. Spencer sighed. "Alice . . ."

"What! It's true. And I'm not just saying that because I'm dating Blake's brother!"

"But . . ." I glanced between everyone in the room. I figured my relationship status was no longer a secret. "What about Ella?"

"What about her?" Alice asked. "You think you're the first person to have drama with someone in the society? You'll form other connections." She wrinkled her nose. "Okay, maybe not *romantic* connections. Maybe chill on that."

Mrs. Spencer set her tea down and waved for Alice to be quiet.

"I'm aware that you and my daughter are no longer dating," Mrs. Spencer said. "That still doesn't change the nature of this conversation. I've known you for many years, Blake. You deserve to be here just as much as she does. Just like you, Annetta. Just like everyone who has walked through those front doors. I believe you're all worthy."

"Do we have time to think about this?" Annetta asked.

"Of course," Mrs. Spencer said. "Do you have any other questions for me?"

A few weeks ago, I would've thrown my arms around her and thanked her for a second chance. But now Serena was being offered to me on a sapphire platter, and all I felt was hesitation. For so many years, it was Ella's dream that I'd wanted by association. But now that Ella was gone . . . what did I want?

Alice escorted me and Annetta outside.

"Look," Alice said. "I'm really sorry about how everything went down. That night was fucked up. As the new president, you have my word things are going to change."

Annetta and I looked at each other again. I saw the doubt in her eyes; I wondered if she saw it in mine.

We needed way more caffeine to make this decision. So Annetta and I headed to Sugar Mama.

When we walked inside the warm, bustling café, Xan's eyes lit up behind the counter. They came around to give us hugs and kissed Annetta on the cheek. By this point, they knew our orders by heart.

"Iced hazelnut coffee and a flat white coming right up," they said.

"And two slices of the lemon cake," Annetta replied. "We have big decisions to make."

Xan's eyebrows shot up. "This *is* serious, then. Right away, right away."

We settled on the worn sofa in the back. We'd unofficially claimed it as our spot. I brought my knees to my chest. "That was not how I was expecting that conversation to go," I said.

"Seriously. After all that shit this summer, now they're asking us for *their* time?" She bit back a grin. "It feels pretty great, doesn't it?"

I thought it'd feel great. I felt empty.

"What are you thinking?" Annetta asked, playing with her mini pop key chain.

"Incoming!" Xan set down a plate of lemon cake slices, handed over our drinks, and wiped their hands on their apron. "All right, I'm on break for ten minutes. What's going on?"

I munched on cake while Annetta filled Xan in. Afterward, they blew out a breath.

"Okay, so what's the problem? You've been wanting this for years, and now that snake Roxanne is gone. Seems easy enough."

Annetta's eyes slid over to me. I swallowed a lump of cake.

"It might be . . . weird for Blake to be in close proximity with Ella," Annetta explained. "Annnd, I still don't know how I feel joining an organization where I was harassed like that."

"So don't do it," Xan said. "Screw them and their little blue sweaters."

Four years ago, on that snowy night Ella and I first learned about the society, I wanted it more than anything. Throughout high school, I believed that becoming a Serena woman would change my life. But that life always included Ella and now that we might be done for good, I didn't know what to do. I stared at my empty wrist and wondered what it would feel like to have a dream not crafted by someone else's hands.

CHAPTER 23

THE DAYS WENT BY and I couldn't make up my mind. To join the society, to not join the society. Plucking the possibilities out like petals.

On Wednesday afternoon, I was so deep in thought that I wasn't paying attention after leaving my stats class, and Ella and I collided.

Literally.

"Oh, I'm so sorry—"

"I didn't—"

We froze when we realized who we were talking to. And I got my first good look at her in weeks.

The red was fading from her hair. She was wearing more eyeliner than usual. She had a new pair of earrings, tiny gold lightning bolts. She was so gorgeous, my beautiful, beautiful girlfriend—

No. Not anymore?

"Hey, Bee," she said softly.

"Hey," I said.

"You just get out of class?"

"Um, yeah. Stats."

"Oh, cool. I was meeting my advisor." She hitched her tote bag up her shoulder. "So . . . how have you been?"

"Okay . . . you?" I wanted to die. What was this flimsy conversation? Four years. In love. And we were doling out small talk. Regret whittled away my anger. Maybe I'd made a mistake when I told her I was done. We had so many plans. Two-mom household, Serena golden couple. Was it too late to get it all back?

"Um, do you want to grab some coffee or something?" she asked.

More than anything, I thought. But when I looked in her eyes, I saw Roxanne. Betrayal.

"Never mind," she said, sensing my hesitation. "I get it."

She started to walk away, and my heart picked up speed. I couldn't let her go. Even after everything.

"Wait."

She paused, and I inhaled.

"Um. Yeah. Coffee sounds great."

There was a small coffee lounge on the top floor of the Visual Arts building that had a bird's-eye view of campus. Most students didn't know about it because of its tucked-away location and simple menu. But, of course, Ella had insider info from Sophie and Ariana about Jameswell's best hiding spots.

"I've been studying here lately," Ella said when we emerged from the elevator. We ordered two hot coffees—iced wasn't an option, let alone flavors—from the sleepy-looking barista. Even though it was the middle of the day, we were the only customers. Ella paid for hers in cash. I swiped my student ID. We settled at a table near the windows. Gentle classical music drifted from an office down the hall.

"I never would've known this was up here," I said, peering out the window. Nine stories below, students trickled in and out of the building.

Ella ripped open two sugar packets and swirled them around with a wooden stir stick. She took a sip, and her nose wrinkled. It was too bitter. She was going to add another packet, maybe a couple of creams. Seconds later, she did just that. All these random Ella facts I had stored away . . . where was I supposed to put them now?

"It's pretty great," she said. "It's really quiet. I like the library, but don't you think it's so distracting?"

I shrugged sheepishly. I'd been doing my assignments in my dorm room, partly from fear of running into her. I sipped my coffee. It tasted like shit. No wonder no one ever came up here.

"I'm sorry," she finally said. "I've been wanting to talk to you."

"So why didn't you?"

"I didn't know what to say."

"'I'm sorry for cheating on you' would've been a good start. Are you dating her now?" It'd been weeks, and I still had the image of Roxanne frolicking on the beach with that fucking little heart seared into my brain.

Ella's eyes widened. "What? No! No, we're . . . not dating. It happened one time, Bee, I swear."

"When?" I asked. As if the details would make me feel any better.

Ella sighed. "That night . . . she kissed me during Truth or Dare."

I palmed my coffee cup, tried not to cry. My chest hurt, *everything* hurt. I thought about the argument I witnessed the night in the Great Dismal Swamp. Roxanne trying to convince Ella to sleep together again when I was fifty feet away. I felt so pathetic.

"Why?" I managed to ask.

"I don't know," Ella said. "It happened so fast. We were both drunk. It was after the party. I couldn't drive. We ended up in one of the cabins . . ."

She started crying, and that pissed me off. How dare she cry when *I* was the one hurting so badly.

"You didn't believe I could get in myself," I said in disbelief. "So you fucked her."

"I looked *up* to her!" Ella said, and I softened, slightly.

"Did she . . . force you?" I asked.

She ran a hand through her hair. "No, no, it wasn't like that. I just thought . . . maybe she'd owe me one. But afterward, she wanted to keep going . . . keep sleeping together. I told her no because I'm with you." She sniffled. "I love you, Bee. You have to believe me."

"I love you, too, Ella, but . . ."

"But what?"

"Not being around you these past few weeks made me realize a lot." I sipped my coffee again, nearly spilling it because my hand was shaking. I couldn't look at her anymore; her doe eyes would do me in.

"What did you realize?" she asked.

"I don't like who I am when I'm around you." I stared across the campus, trying not to cry. I could see the domed roof of the planetarium from here. "I realized how much time I spent worrying about being good enough for you. How hard I tried."

"You *are* good enough," she said. "I get that you're mad at me. But you have to believe I did it for you."

"Ella, please."

"Please *what*?"

"I don't know! I don't . . ." I bit my lip in frustration. "I'm just—"

"Use your big-girl words, widdle Blake," Ella interrupted.

Something inside me snapped. How quick we could both go from weepy to pissed. I looked at her, this gorgeous girl with a bruise of a face, and suddenly *hated* her. I hated her like I hated the people who used to bully me. I hated her like I hated Roxanne. I hated her like I hated Todd's pleated fucking shorts. Four years. Four years of memories and so. many. firsts and now I hated her.

The elevator pinged and a woman wearing a sleek suit stepped out, chatting on her cell phone. She glanced our way and kept walking, barely a pause in her step. To her, we were just another couple breaking up.

"You," I said quietly, "are such a bitch. God. I never realized just how mean you are, but wow. Bravo."

"How am *I* a bitch?"

"You must get off on being mean to me, huh? Does it make you feel good to boss me around like your little puppet? Be your little prop in all your videos?"

"My prop? Please," she said, seething. "If I wanted a prop, I would've picked someone I don't have to train so much."

"Train," I echoed. "You train me."

"God, you're so dramatic. Just apologize!"

The barista looked over at us, mildly interested. I leaned forward, lowering my voice. "*You* apologize."

"For what?" she asked.

"Um, how about for cheating on me?"

"I already said sorry!" she hissed. "Now what?"

"You always encourage me to keep drinking even though you know it's not good for me," I said. "Even *Alice* talked to you about it, and you still ignored it."

"Oh my God, the drinking dilemma. Again, really?"

"Yes, again! Ella, do you know where my head goes when I'm drunk? Do you know how much I hate myself?"

"How am I supposed to know that?" She fiddled with empty sugar packets. Her hands were shaking, too. "How am I supposed to know you're having an existential crisis if you don't open your mouth and say something? You never say no when we're partying the night away on my friends' yachts."

"Because I don't tell you no," I said. "Because I don't want to disappoint you."

Ella was silent. She blinked and looked away, eyes welling again.

"Ella," I said slowly. "I don't think we're good for each other anymore."

She barked an empty laugh. "Oh yeah? So now *you're* breaking up with *me*. Are you serious?"

"You don't see the signs?"

"We can't throw away four years, Bee. You're pissed about the Roxanne thing, I get it." She pushed our coffee cups to the side and held out her hands, palm up. I looked at them, knowing exactly where my fingers would fit.

I pulled my hands into my lap.

She laughed in disbelief. "After everything I've done for you. You want to break up with me." She swallowed. "If this is about the drinking thing, then fine! Don't drink. I don't care!"

"But you *do* care. You told me I was being dramatic when I was worried."

She threw her hands up. "I'm sorry, okay? I'm sorry. I made a mistake. You're breaking up with me for one mistake? Think about all the things we had planned. Golden couple dreams?"

"It's not just one thing."

"Then explain it to me! Explain it to me, Bee, 'cause it's not making any sense from where I'm sitting."

The realization was hard in my core.

I don't want to be Ella Spencer's girlfriend anymore.

"Do you know why I fell for you?" I asked.

Tears trailed down her cheeks. It made me want to forgive and forget everything, so I settled for staring at the table.

"I fell for you because you made me feel seen," I said. "I spent so long waiting to be noticed. You noticed me. You made me feel wanted. You made me feel like I finally belonged somewhere. But now I don't even know who I am without you. We're *toxic*, Ella. I'm not happy."

"And you think you'll be happier without me?" she asked.

Her question hung in the air. I stared across campus, at all the people enjoying the sunshine. Having a regular afternoon. Not going through their first breakup.

"Blake?" Ella asked. "Do you think you'll be happier without me?"

"I'm willing to try."

I felt like my stomach was going to drop out of my body, down all nine floors. Ella fiddled with the coffee cup. When her eyes met mine, they were resigned.

"So that's it?" When I didn't say anything, she nodded. "Okay, then."

My throat tightened. "I'm sorry."

"You . . . don't have to apologize. For anything." She stood, slinging her tote over her shoulder. "I guess I'll see you. Maybe . . . Um. I'll see you around."

I nodded numbly. "Yeah. See you around."

She headed for the elevator. Pressed the down button twice. When it dinged, she looked at me and raised her hand in a small wave.

"Bye, Bee," she said quietly.

"Bye, Ella," I said. And I finally started crying.

She stepped into the elevator and the doors shut. I stared at her empty chair, wondering if she would come back. Wondering if I should wait for her. But I knew she was gone.

I *knew*.

This wasn't a kiss-and-make-up fight. We weren't starting over. Everything inside me knew with certainty that we were done. It was as if the old Blake and Ella were now ghosts, floating through some alternate timeline where there was no bitterness, no resentment, no cheating or uncertainties.

Maybe that Blake and Ella were just two girls in love who knew how to get it right.

JUICE BOX

We don't fall in love with the worst versions of people. Their tired or worn down or *I can't take this anymore* versions. We fall in love with people in their glitter and their shine. Their polished firsts.

When I was fourteen, I fell in love with a girl named Ella Spencer. It was easy. Happened almost immediately, the first day I saw her. You might've, too, if you'd been in my shoes. If you'd spent years as a loner whose voice had been snatched away. If you'd just wanted to fit in, wanted friends. If you'd been convinced that the Drama Club was the only way to shed the old you, the boring you. The loser you. If you'd gotten up onstage as an eager freshman in front of a drama teacher and whispering upperclassmen and choked because the lights were too bright and you couldn't remember your lines and everyone started laughing at you. If you'd returned to your plush auditorium seat, choking back sobs, so sure your middle school torment was about to repeat itself for four more years, and then someone whispered, "Hey. That was rough. Are you okay?"

You would've fallen in love with Ella Spencer, too.

I'd read about girls like Ella. Cool, smart, rich girls that sashayed down red carpets in LA or attended swanky boarding schools in New England. I never thought I'd stumble across a girl like her in suburban Virginia Beach, Virginia. Despite the picturesque postcards of the oceanfront, the Virginia Beach I knew was dull. It was the only home I'd ever known, and there was nothing interesting about its long, humid summers or my apartment complex filled with identical boxy buildings under the fighter jet flight paths from the nearby military base.

Quite simply, my life was a gray sky until Ella Spencer ripped through it like lightning.

After she aced *her* Drama Club audition, Ella grabbed my hand and led me out of the auditorium. When Mr. Abrams asked if she wanted to stick around for callbacks, Ella laughed and said she had no interest in theater. She was simply trying to kill time before the Queer Pride Club meeting down the hall.

"I like doing things just to prove I can," she told me as we left behind a bewildered audience. "Plus, Mr. Abrams was being a dick. It was obvious you were nervous. He deserved to be rejected, too."

She was my knight in shining Air Forces. I loved her without question.

I used to think it was fate that Ella and I met in the first place. Kids in her rich Crystal Grove neighborhood usually attended a private Christian academy that boasted a class size of twelve and a 100 percent college acceptance rate. But to Ella, the academy kids were boring, too familiar after spending kindergarten through eighth grade with them. Ella wanted something new. A challenge. She didn't want to be known as Sophie and Ariana's little sister. She was tired of being a big fish in a small pond—she wanted to be a big fish in a big pond.

She persuaded me to accompany her to the Queer Pride Club. At the time, I hadn't come out to anyone, hadn't even come out to myself. But after the way she stood up for me, I would've followed her anywhere.

At the meeting, they had cheese pizza and an assortment of juice boxes. Ella picked the raspberry flavor, so I did, too. She sipped until the straw squeaked, twisted the cardboard until there was nothing left but air. So I did, too.

"I like you, Blake Brenner," she told me that day after the meeting. We were wandering around school, wasting time before the late bus. I would've stayed there all night, pitched a tent between the rows of blue lockers. Anything to get just one more minute with her.

"I like you, too," I said. We stopped in an empty hallway. When I finally met her gaze, I started trembling.

She giggled, grabbed my hands. "Whoa, you're like *buzzing*. Why are you so nervous?"

"Because I like you!" I repeated, and she laughed and laughed and laughed. Her tongue was bright artificial red.

"Little nervous Blake," Ella said, her fingers braiding with mine. Her nails were painted glittery black. "Buzzing like a little bee," she whispered. Then she pressed me against a locker and kissed me, and everything tasted saccharine.

CHAPTER 24

and I received a text.

> The house. 5pm.
> Dress Code: All white.
> SS

After our last classes, Annetta and I met on the grassy slope that overlooked Greek Row. We couldn't see the Serena Society house from here, but I swore I could feel it beating like a heart, could feel the weight of a sapphire bracelet on my wrist.

Annetta's decision was easy—she wasn't going. At the end of everything, she'd decided it wasn't worth it.

"I talked to my mom last night," she told me over dining hall hash browns. "I told her I wasn't going to do it, and she understands. She's upset, but she understands."

Now we sat silently on the lawn, and I debated walking down the hill. Waited for some type of sign.

We saw Corinne first. She looked like a brown goddess, braids hanging to her waist, ivory dress falling in ethereal layers over her curves. Annetta and I watched as she floated down Greek Row like a cloud.

Then Khadija in a beaded white gown, curls bursting around her face like a sun, walking with a purpose.

Eden and Bianca, arm in arm.

Keiko. I smiled when she appeared, anxiously smoothing her hair. I remembered her tear-streaked face in the Dismal Swamp, when she was so convinced she was about to lose everything.

The girls drifted down the street like dandelion seeds in the wind. But I was looking for one girl. Thinking maybe if I saw her, an answer would root in my stomach, bloom in my mind.

And then she appeared, the last of them. Two minutes before five p.m., as fashionably late as the Serena Society would allow.

Ella Spencer strutted down Greek Row in stilettos and a high-neck dress made of white lace. Something was woven in her auburn waves. Flowers or pearls, she was too far away to tell. But she looked beautiful, and I wanted to cry.

"You okay?" Annetta asked.

I nodded. I took a deep breath and looked up at the sky. It was impossibly blue today, not one cloud. If you'd told me autumn was coming, I would've called you a liar.

"Hey," Annetta said, and when I looked down, I was staring at Ella again. Except this time, she was staring back.

We were too far away to speak. But, really, what else was there to say? She was over there in a white dress, and I was over here in black jeans and a T-shirt emblazoned with Dad's new airline logo. We stared for what felt like hours, but then I blinked and she was gone.

Five o'clock came and went, and somewhere down the hill, twelve girls became Serena women. Annetta checked the time on her phone.

"You ready?" she asked. "Meeting starts in twenty."

I nodded, and we helped each other up from the grass.

We walked away from Greek Row.

We didn't look back.

The Jameswell student center was buzzing with activity. Annetta and I made our way past the tantalizing scent of waffle fries and chicken nuggets, between crowds of people singing and laughing and studying and living. We walked until we reached a long stretch of conference rooms and the bustle of the food court faded away.

At the end of the hallway, a dark-skinned girl was taping a sign on a door. She didn't hear us approaching, too preoccupied with the laughter spilling from the conference room next to her.

"Shut up, Quinn! I can *hear* you!" the girl shouted. Then she stood back to made sure the sign wasn't crooked. A burst of purple glitter spelled out THAT'S THE TEA! Below it was an illustrated mug overflowing with hearts.

"Blake! You made it!"

The girl crushed me in a hug. Her name was Rachelle. She was a sophomore, and I met her in my Intro to Theater class.

When she released me, she was beaming. She had bright red glasses and so many moles. "And you brought a friend!" she said.

"This is Annetta," I said, and they waved.

"You're just in time," Rachelle said. "And you picked the best day. Tonight's mocktail is a mint julep."

"Sounds good," I said. My heart pounded, but I wasn't afraid. I could do this.

We were greeted by an array of faces when we walked into the room. Sitting around a large table there was someone with a colorful mohawk, nibbling on a cookie; a chubby white girl with long blond hair and a slash of black lipstick; a short brown guy with a pair of headphones around his neck and a fitted T-shirt that read SOBER IS SEXY!

Rachelle and I had been sitting next to each other for two classes before she'd extended the invitation to The Tea. I was the one who actually brought it up when I noticed a sticker on her water bottle that had the words SOBER AND PUNK twisting around a skull.

"You don't drink?" I'd asked carefully. Our lecture on the origins of storytelling had just wrapped up, but neither of us were in a rush to go anywhere.

"Nope," she'd said. "You?"

I shrugged. I didn't know yet. I'd been Some Drunk Girl all summer. But it was almost autumn and I was surrounded by new faces and I guessed I could be anyone I wanted.

"Well, you should come to The Tea," Rachelle had suggested. "It's super chill. We make mocktails and talk about our traumas around drinking." I must've looked like I was going to faint because she burst out laughing and said, "Just kidding! Kinda? It's really just nice to have a club on campus that isn't super focused on partying. You know how Jameswell loves their frat-boy ragers." She made a face as she zipped up her backpack. Before she left, she told me they met every Friday at five thirty.

Now Annetta and I sat. My knees were bouncing, nerves shooting off in my stomach. Annetta held my hand under the table.

"All right, all right, all right," Rachelle said. "I call this meeting to order!"

"'Bout time," a Black guy with a shaved head said with a sigh.

"Porter, don't start with me today. I *will* body-slam you," Rachelle replied.

Porter sipped his mint julep with his pinkie in the air. "I'd love to see you try."

The room erupted into giggles. Someone poured me and Annetta a mocktail. Pretzels and sour-cream-and-onion chips were passed around. Someone put on lo-fi music.

Then Rachelle called the meeting to order.

"So tonight is gonna be super chill and low-key," she said. "We're gonna do some check-ins, bask in each other's radiance. But we do have some new faces, so let's go around the circle and say names and pronouns, okay?"

My heart pounded as my turn neared, but Annetta's hand remained firm in mine. A spark in my stomach flickered, then burned. So steady and sure.

Then all eyes were on me.

I cleared my throat. "Um, hi. My name is Blake. *She/her* pronouns. And . . . I'm here because Rachelle invited me."

"Us theater kids gotta stick together!" Rachelle said, singsong. "Thanks for coming."

I loosened my grip on Annetta's hand. I relaxed. For the first time in forever.

"Thank you," I said. "I'm glad to be here."

DECEMBER

CHAPTER 25

THE FOOD AT THE Rocky Stop Drive-In isn't that great. The service lacks enthusiasm, and their milkshakes are overpriced. But its location is perfect, situated close enough to campus that Leon can meet me whenever his chaotic work schedule allows. Once a week, we sit in his Toyota and listen to the radio and munch on garlic fries. It's a new tradition. Something we created together.

"I don't know why I keep getting this," Leon mutters, extracting a limp lettuce leaf from his burger. "I just want this burger to do better."

"It's trying its best." I pop another fry into my mouth. After three months, I'm convinced it's the only consistently good thing on the menu.

"Yeah, well, for eight ninety-nine, it needs to try a little harder." He sets the burger on the dashboard and sips his root beer float. "How was your last final?"

"Killer," I admit. It was stats, and I shudder thinking about how many answers I left blank. Even after weeks of Annetta tutoring me, the numbers still managed to trip me up. "But I'm pretty sure I passed the class, so whatever."

Leon swirls a straw around his float. It's an unseasonably frigid day, but his ice cream has already melted. "You want some?"

I shake my head. "I'm going to Sugar Mama later." And knowing CeeCee, she's going to make me try a little bit of everything she's whipped up.

Leon takes a few more bites of his burger before giving up, mumbling under his breath about how he's going to try the chicken sandwich next time. I laugh because this is just another part of the ritual. Weeks ago, when I jokingly told him that he'd never be happy unless he was a *little* disappointed in something, his cheeks flushed red. We're still maneuvering around our relationship, trying to patch up the holes. Slowly building something new.

On the drive back to Jameswell, we bypass a minivan with a faded FRANKLY? I'M WITH PETERSON! sticker peeling off its bumper. It makes me laugh, remembering his sorry-ass concession speech after losing last month.

"Be quiet," Leon says, turning the radio up. "They're talking about the storm." A rare December snowstorm is crossing Virginia and is expected to hit the area this evening. The announcer warns of an accumulation of up to four inches and dangerous road conditions. Leon's gaze flicks to me.

"I really don't want you and Annetta out in this weather," he says.

I pinch his cheek, cooing. "But it's perfect weather for a cozy snowed-in movie night for you and Aliiiice."

He blushes. "I just don't want to have to explain to Mom and Dad why you're not at Christmas," he says. "Because you and your friends care more about baked goods than your safety."

I snort. "You know it's about more than baked goods."

He smiles faintly. "I know."

Although the dorms don't close for five more days, campus is quiet. Bundled-up students trudge between buildings, air puffing out of their mouths like cigarette smoke. Leon circles around my dorm, Riggins Hall.

"So I'm picking you up when?"

"Next Friday," I recite. "Seven a.m."

"Thank you. You know Dad will kill us if we miss this flight." He hugs me, and I lean into the scratchy stiffness of his uniform. "Tell Annetta's dad thanks again for letting you stay with them for a couple of days."

"I will."

I watch his car disappear, shivering in my parka. Students slowly trickle out of my dorm with suitcases and duffel bags, heading to warm cars that will take them home for winter break. A gust of wind rattles my teeth, and I hurry inside.

The scent of pine needles swirls in the lobby. Haifa and Brianna, the resident assistants on my floor, are lounging near a Christmas tree.

"Have a good vacation, Blake!" Haifa says.

"Your piece in the playwright festival was so good!" Brianna says, and I blush because she tells me that *every* time I see her. She's a junior in the theater program, and when she found out I was considering it as a potential major, she took me under her wing.

"Thaaaanks," I say, swooping them into hugs. "See you both next year."

When I make it upstairs to my room, Annetta looks over the side of their loft bed. We jokingly call it their crow's nest.

"How was lunch?"

I shrug my jacket off. "Subpar. As usual."

"And your brother?"

I grin. "He's Leon."

"As usual," we say at the same time.

I kick my boots off and toss them on my side of the closet. We never got assigned a new roommate, so we've been enjoying the extra storage space.

"I think I'm going to take a nap before tonight," I say. "That stats final whooped my ass."

"Sounds good." They swing a leg over the side of their bed and make their way down the ladder. "I'm gonna grab a late lunch with Zariah and Kira," she says, referencing new friends she met in one of her bio classes. "You need anything?"

"Your undying love and affection?" I collapse in bed and wrap my favorite knitted blanket around my shoulders. The one Mom made me.

"You should know you already have that," they say, and I do. Annetta pulls a red beanie over their shaved scalp. They cut their hair off the same day they started trying on new pronouns. Right now she's loving *they* and *she*, but they're less sure about the haircut, especially on cold days like this.

As I'm falling asleep, my phone buzzes with a message. It's a photo of my parents, lounging by the pool at their new apartment complex in Dallas. Mom has a book in her lap—*White Woman / Mixed World*. I smile and roll my eyes. Maybe a little late, but hey. She's trying.

See you in a few days! I love you so much.

Love u 2.

When I wake up, it's dark and snowing. I race to the window outlined in multicolored string lights to find a pristine layer of snow coating the world like a wedding cake. I blow on the glass and trace a heart in the condensation.

Annetta barges through the door moments later, shaking snow off their beanie.

"You sure the meeting is still on?" they ask. "It's really coming down."

I nod. Rachelle would insist on meetings even during the apocalypse; it's one of the things I like about her.

"Well then, hurry up," Annetta says, stomping over to the restroom. The faucet turns on, followed by the rhythmical swish of a toothbrush. I go to the closet and pick through my options.

"I saw Ella," Annetta calls. "In the student center."

"Oh." I pause sorting through my sweaters. My heart sinks. And it hurts. But not as much as it used to. "Was she with Renée?" Ella's new girlfriend is as beautiful and tall as she is. Point guard on the women's basketball team. Nothing like me.

Annetta emerges from the bathroom and rolls her eyes. "Of course. Attached at the hip, like always."

I pull a black sweater over my head. Once, I googled how long it takes to get over someone, and the answers varied. *Two to three months. One month for every year of the relationship.* Or worse: *Double the amount of time the relationship lasted.* I don't believe that last one, though. It's been three months since our breakup, and even though some nights hurt like hell, it's getting better.

"You ready?" Annetta asks.

I push a curl behind my ear and nod. "Yeah. I'm ready."

The snow is coming down in heavy drifts by the time Annetta and I pull into the parking lot of Sugar Mama. The windows of the café are perfectly framed in tinsel and Pride flags. I can already hear the crackling fire, feel its warmth. Annetta and I emerge into the blustery night, snow crunching under our boots. I smile at the sign on the front door as we draw closer.

CAFÉ CLOSED FOR "THE TEA" HOLIDAY PARTY!!!!!

I thaw the moment I step inside, greeted by cheerful holiday music and the tantalizing aroma of nutmeg and cinnamon. At the couches in the corner, Rachelle shows off her new forearm tattoo to Quinn and Diego. Porter is sipping a cup of tea as he scrolls on his phone, oblivious to the shrieks and laughter around him. It feels like home.

"Y'all made it!" Krishna cheers as Annetta and I join the cacophony.

"They better have!" a loud voice booms. CeeCee bursts out of the kitchen with a tray of hot gingerbread cookies. "Since it was Blake's idea to have this little party here in the first place. Hey! Boy, if you don't get your damn feet off my couch!"

Porter scowls and slowly lowers his feet to the floor.

Rachelle wraps me in a huge hug, somehow still managing to keep her conversation with Quinn and Diego going. Annetta plops down next to Gigi, and they immediately start commiserating over their chemistry final. The energy of the room is heightened, but familiar.

This is The Tea.

At first, it was hard to sit in a room and expose every side of myself—the beautiful, the haunted, the hurting—to strangers. I thought it would feel humiliating saying the words *I think I might drink too much* aloud. But I said it, and I was held. Seen and understood. The Tea is a no judgment zone. These are my people.

Some members describe themselves as sober or in recovery. Some people still drink occasionally. Some people drift in and out of meetings. Some are there every Friday, five thirty on the dot. I'm somewhere in between. I haven't had a drink since August. Yes, there are times when I see someone with a drink in their hand, and I get a lump in my throat, remembering Big Bad Bee and That Feeling. I'm making good use of the free on-campus counseling, and I'm learning how to open up with my therapist. But when it's late and I'm lonely and full of doubts, I lean on Annetta. I text Alice. I call Rachelle. And they remind me why I decided to stop drinking when remembering on my own is too hard.

We don't have to think about forever, Rachelle told me the first time I called her crying one night, shortly after my first meeting. I was coughing, sputtering, saying, *I can't do this forever.*

We take it one day at a time, Rachelle said. *We wake up. We ask if drinking is a good idea today. And hopefully we get to a place where we don't have to ask anymore.*

What if I keep asking? I cried. *What if I say yes? What if I black out again? What if—*

We begin again, Rachelle replied simply, voice like a warm latte. Then she asked if I wanted to come over to her dorm room and order Insomnia Cookies.

It's a lot easier to let something go when you have good people keeping you grounded.

Annetta comes to The Tea every now and then, when they're not consumed with their heavy course load. One time, Alice even showed up. Of course, it was the meeting where I completely broke down and shared the story of what happened at Busch Gardens. Through gulps and tears, I laid it all out on the table. Afterward, Alice and I took a long walk around campus and she told me she'd never been prouder of me.

"You've come a long way from Winward Commons," she told me.

I shrugged. "Not that long." I think a piece of me will always be there. At least that's what I hope.

"I made an assortment of mocktails for y'all," CeeCee announces. "We got Bellinis, mistletoe tea, cider. Help yourselves, but remember y'all are cleaning all this shit up!"

"Thank you for letting us use the space, CeeCee," I sing, giving her a quick hug as she breezes by. "You're the best."

Rachelle claps to get everyone's attention. "Thank y'all so much for coming to The Tea's holiday party! Special thanks to Blake for securing the dopest space!"

I give a little bow as everyone claps. Annetta pulls one of my curls teasingly.

"So tonight we are gonna talk about tips for surviving family time over the break," Rachelle says. "But mostly we're just here to relax and blow off some steam after finals. We're gonna get started in a couple of minutes!"

Conversation breaks out like little fires, and Xan emerges from the kitchen, looking cute in a red apron and Santa hat. Annetta kisses them. I smile and feel so full.

The meeting starts. Rachelle kicks it off by sharing a personal story before opening up the conversation. No one is required to speak, but most meetings run long because we all want to. And as I settle in next to Annetta and Xan, I know this one will be no different. Once someone stirs the tea, it's hard to stop.

I am here, where I belong. Ready to drink.

HOW TO BE THE LIFE OF THE PARTY

ARRIVE LOOKING HOWEVER THE hell you want. Maybe it's a dress that hugs your skin like a glove, maybe it's sweatpants and a hoodie. Either way, you look amazing.

Sip hot chocolate with all the whipped cream and marshmallows your mug can hold. Relish the decadence. You deserve it.

Witness other people when they show you their scars. These people are your people, so you listen and uplift them. In turn, they do the same for you. You still love the sound of your own name, but you no longer need to hear it screamed in parties or covered in glitter to know that you are witnessed.

Dance with your best friend. Dance with that cute girl. *Dance with yourself!*

(*Doesn't it feel good?*)

Glimpse traces of That Feeling whenever you catch your reflection in the mirror over the fireplace. That Feeling of warm cheeks, vulnerability, sexiness, love—so much damn love. You are loved and witnessed and whole, and you know it. You don't have shit to prove anymore.

Volunteer to go first for karaoke. Sing "Seasons of Love" because the spring musical is *Rent* and you want to audition. Imagine if Little You— wilting in the auditorium after a stage-fright-induced panic attack— could see you now.

(Would she be proud?)

Yes.

Hug her. Tight. Remind her dreams don't have an expiration date.

Eat until you are full. Toss stories around the circle. Cry, maybe. Sip hot cider.

Everything *really* is good again.

Admire everyone in the room. You are in great company. New friends. Old ones.

Every version of yourself that's gotten you to this point.

Honor them. Toast them.

Drink until you are quenched.

AUTHOR'S NOTE

I'm an air sign. Which means—according to my astrology-loving friends—I enjoy doing things on a whim. *Maybe I'll cut my hair off. Maybe I'll run a marathon.* Sometimes I follow through (the haircut) and sometimes I let these ideas gather dust (the marathon). When I made the decision to stop drinking for thirty days in the fall of 2019, I'd expected the latter. In fact, I didn't even tell most people I was doing it just in case I changed my mind. After all, I didn't have a *problem* . . . right?

As the month unfolded, so did *Thirsty*. This novel about a girl who thinks she needs alcohol in order to survive social settings. I couldn't write fast enough, couldn't stop pulling back layers. Blake uses alcohol to quiet her anxiety. Blake drinks because the people she's desperate to impress seem to like her better when she's drunk. At one point, it became clear that Blake's story was my story, and we were figuring things out together.

When I was first exploring sobriety, I picked up a lot of rock-bottom narratives and didn't see myself in them. To anyone on the outside, my drinking probably mirrored a lot of people in their mid-twenties: sometimes excessive, a lot of drunken mistakes, embarrassed mornings. But not necessarily something to scream *HIT THE BRAKES* and cut alcohol out of my life altogether.

But people didn't see the shame that sat heavy in my stomach all the time. They didn't feel the internal urge I felt to push everyone away, didn't hear the voice inside my head that told me I was worthless and unlovable. This wasn't solely alcohol's doing; a lot of it stemmed from my struggles with depression and anxiety. But nevertheless those feelings refused to be ignored and I ended up cutting drinking out of my life altogether. At the time of writing this, I've been sober from alcohol for 1,635 days. Some of those days have been harder than others.

Drinking alcohol isn't inherently wrong, immoral, or immature, and not everyone needs to cut it out of their lives. But if you've ever questioned your drinking habits, I want you to know you're not alone. It can be scary realizing something (or someone) that once brought you comfort is no longer serving you. I didn't write this book to provide any answers. I wrote it to ask questions, such as: *Is alcohol adding or subtracting value to my life? Why do I drink? Do I even like drinking? Are there people in my life who push alcohol on me, even when I say no? Have I been that person?*

If you're curious about cutting alcohol out of your life, there are so many resources, from multistep programs to therapy to online support groups. Whatever path you take, just know there's no "one size fits all" perfect solution. I tried several options before I found my version of The Tea. I hope you find yours.

You deserve that.

Love,
Jas
January 2024

ACKNOWLEDGMENTS

I can't believe I get to do this again. *Thirsty* was a tough book, but I sit here at the end, proud. Blake says it's easier to let something go when you have good people keeping you grounded. As I let this story go and pass it off to readers, I'm so grateful to be surrounded by a community that fills my days with light. Good people.

So much love and gratitude to the following—

Kay Ulanday Barrett: My *heart*! Thank you for always finding me, even when I didn't want to be found. It's you, me, and Biggie till 2040 and beyond, dancing at the Good Big Dinner concert.

Faye Bender: Thank you for adopting me (haha). You are the gentle shark agent of my dreams, and I'm honored to work with you. Let's get fro-yo soon.

Mekisha Telfer and Eleonore Fisher: Thank you both for handling Blake's story with such delicate hands. Your editorial visions challenged me in the best way and made this book so much better.

My fantastic team at Roaring Brook Press and Macmillan: Julia Bianchi, Celeste Cass, Beth Clark, Jackie Dever, Molly B. Ellis, Teresa Ferraiolo, Chantal Gersch, Jennifer Healey, Connie Hsu, Hayley Jozwiak, Kelsey Marrujo, Alexandra Quill, Katie Quinn, Nicole Schaefer, Kristen Stedman, Emily Stone, Mary Van Akin, and Allison Verost.

Thank you to Suzie Townsend, Stephanie Kim, Sophia Ramos, and Kate Sullivan for providing feedback during the early, messy stages of this book.

Thank you so much to Charlie for capturing Blake in such a beautiful, distressing way with this cover art.

To Yasmin Curtis, Lexi Mingo-Smith, and Shatika Dodson. My St. Louis crew, my besties for life. Loving y'all is effortless.

To Jen St. Jude: you're the best friend and critique partner a queer could ask for. It's an honor to swap gossip and messy first drafts with you.

To all the amazing writers, booksellers, friends, teachers, and librarians who inspire me and remind me why I write, especially: Samira Ahmed, Camille Baker, Bethany Baptiste, Terry J. Benton-Walker, Nicole Brinkley, Aislinn Brophy, Gabi Burton, Quierra Chalar, Dujon Curtis, Sami Ellis, Kirt Ethridge, Alison Green Myers, Elnora Gunter, Meghan Horvath, Lisa Krok, AM Kvita, Ebony LaDelle, Sacha Lamb, Britney Lewis, Katherine Locke, Amber McBride, Avery Mead, Miriam Zoila Pérez, Shauna Robinson, Octavia Saenz, JD Scott, Courtney Summers, Lin Thompson, Trisha Tobias, Addie Tsai, Allison Vazquez, Alexandra Villasante, and Jacqueline Woodson. Thank you all for being my cheerleaders, for making me laugh, for uplifting my work, or all of the above. Xoxoxo.

Thank you to the authors who took the time to blurb *Thirsty*. When curating the list of who I wanted to send this deeply personal story to, I sought out authors whose own books have brought me comfort during dark days. To K. Ancrum, Rebecca Barrow, Sara Farizan, Stephanie Kuehn, Ebony LaDelle, Mariama J. Lockington, Cory McCarthy, Mark Oshiro, Jen St. Jude, Courtney Summers, Alexandra Villasante, and Julian Winters—I appreciate you all so much for witnessing me and Blake.

Thank you so much for the 2023 Coretta Scott King Book Awards Jury for awarding my debut novel, *We Deserve Monuments*, the John Steptoe New Talent Award. It was truly one of the highlights of my life.

Whenever I feel doubtful about my writing, I remember that phone call when I got the news.

Thank you to the Highlights Foundation for always supporting me! That little campus tucked away in the Poconos will always have a piece of my heart.

To every librarian, teacher, bookseller, blogger, reader, and reviewer who has shouted about my debut novel, sent me kind messages, and rooted for my writing career: Thank you from the bottom of my heart.

Special shoutout to the Kaptivating ladies of the Kappa Gamma chapter of Alpha Kappa Alpha Sorority, Incorporated, especially my Spring '13 line sisters. I'm very happy our pledging experience was nothing like the Serena Society's.

To my goddaughter, Kira: You're only three, and you're already the coolest person I know. I hope we'll always share a love of stories.

To my parents: Thank you for your patience when I spent hours browsing in the bookstore, meticulously deciding which one (or two . . . or three) to take home. I love you both so much.

To my cat, Nina, who my family lost in October 2023. She gave me over seventeen years of companionship, and I miss her fiercely. She was there throughout every book I've ever written, purring in my lap and plopping onto the keyboard. Ella's tubby cat, always basking in the sunlight, is an ode to her.

Finally, a toast to the drunk girl in the mirror. Sixteen, full of glitter, searching for something. Twenty-six and depressed and full of wanting. I love you. Yes, even then. Even now.